DEVIL'S CRY

SHADE OF DEVIL BOOK 2

SHAYNE SILVERS

ARGENTO
PUBLISHING

COPYRIGHT

This is a work of fiction. Names, characters, businesses, places, events, and incidents are either the products of the author's imagination or used in a fictitious manner. Any resemblance to actual persons, living or dead, or actual events is purely coincidental.

Shayne Silvers

Devil's Cry

Shade of Devil Book 2

ISBN: 978-1-947709-33-1

© 2019, Shayne Silvers / Argento Publishing, LLC

info@shaynesilvers.com

ALL RIGHTS RESERVED. This book contains material protected under International and Federal Copyright Laws and Treaties. Any unauthorized reprint or use of this material is prohibited. No part of this book may be reproduced or transmitted in any form or by any means, electronic or mechanical, including photocopying, recording, or by any information storage and retrieval system without express written permission from the author / publisher.

DEDICATION

*To that person in front of me at the coffee shop who didn't pay for my drink...
this book is dedicated to someone else.*

*And to anyone who thinks I didn't deserve that drink, I once won a race
against a billion other competitors. It was do or die. If you're reading this, you
probably deserve a coffee, too.*
And a laugh.
Enjoy my words. This book is for you, because you're a winner.
I'm not buying you a coffee, though.

-Shayne

EPIGRAPH

"There is no death. Only a change of worlds."

— CHIEF SEATTLE

CONTENTS

The Shade of Devil Series—A warning   1

Chapter 1   3

Chapter 2   9

Chapter 3   15

Chapter 4   21

Chapter 5   26

Chapter 6   32

Chapter 7   36

Chapter 8   42

Chapter 9   47

Chapter 10   52

Chapter 11   58

Chapter 12   64

Chapter 13   69

Chapter 14   75

Chapter 15   81

Chapter 16   89

Chapter 17   96

Chapter 18   102

Chapter 19   108

Chapter 20   111

Chapter 21   118

Chapter 22   125

Chapter 23   130

Chapter 24   137

Chapter 25   145

Chapter 26   154

Chapter 27   159

Chapter 28   164

Chapter 29   171

Chapter 30   177

Chapter 31   184

Chapter 32   194

Chapter 33   201

Chapter 34	207
Chapter 35	212
Chapter 36	217
Chapter 37	223
Chapter 38	230
Chapter 39	237
Chapter 40	242
Chapter 41	248
Chapter 42	254
Chapter 43	260
TRY: OBSIDIAN SON (NATE TEMPLE #1)	265
MAKE A DIFFERENCE	271
ACKNOWLEDGMENTS	273
ABOUT SHAYNE SILVERS	275
BOOKS BY SHAYNE SILVERS	277

THE SHADE OF DEVIL SERIES—A
WARNING

Many vampires were harmed in the making of this story. Like...a lot of them.

If you enjoyed the *Blade* or *Underworld* movies, you will love the *Shade of Devil* series.

The greatest trick the First Vampire ever pulled was convincing the world that he didn't exist.

Before the now-infamous Count Dracula ever tasted his first drop of blood, Sorin Ambrogio owned the night. Humanity fearfully called him the Devil.

Cursed by the gods, Sorin spent centuries bathing Europe in oceans of blood with his best friends, Lucian and Nero, the world's first Werewolf and Warlock—an unholy trinity if there ever was one. Until the three monsters grew weary of the carnage, choosing to leave it all behind and visit the brave New World across the ocean. As they befriended a Native American tribe, they quickly forgot that monsters can never escape their past.

But Dracula—Sorin's spawn—was willing to do anything to erase Sorin's name from the pages of history so that he could claim the title of the world's first vampire all for himself. Dracula hunts him down and slaughters the natives, fatally wounding Sorin in the attack. Except a Shaman manages to secretly cast Sorin into a healing slumber.

For five hundred years.

Until Sorin is awoken by a powerful Shaman in present-day New York City. In a world he doesn't understand, Sorin only wants one thing —to kill Dracula and anyone else who stands in his path.

The streets of New York City will flow with rivers of blood, and the fate of the world rests in the hands of the Devil, Sorin Ambrogio.

Because this town isn't big enough for the both of them.

Now, our story begins in a brave New World...

DON'T FORGET!

VIP readers get early access to all sorts of goodies, including signed books, private giveaways, and advance notice of future projects. AND A FREE NOVELLA! Click the image or join here:
www.shaynesilvers.com/l/219800

FOLLOW AND LIKE:

Shayne's FACEBOOK PAGE:

www.shaynesilvers.com/l/38602

I try my best to respond to all messages, so don't hesitate to drop me a line. Not interacting with readers is the biggest travesty that most authors can make. Let me fix that.

1

In my chambers far below the Museum of Natural History, I sat behind my desk, staring at the crackling flames in the fireplace. The steady hum of activity outside my doors made me smile, recalling the old days at my castle and the constant bustle of vampires going about their business.

Back before I had changed the direction I wanted the vampires to take—the role I had demanded they play without giving them any warning whatsoever.

That decision quickly resulted in my empire crumbling, the pieces secretly collected by Dracula as he amassed his own cabal of vampires who wanted to go back to the old ways. Luckily, I'd managed to escape before they could depose me in a more violent manner, and I'd absconded off to the New World with my best friends Lucian and Nero, the world's first werewolf and warlock, respectively.

My smile slowly faded as the memory brought up thoughts of *why* I had chosen to change my creed—the conquest of carnage and blood-lust that I had originally set my children on, sending them out to rampage across the lands and to take whatever they chose. Me wanting to punish the world for the cruel curses inflicted upon me by the sadistic Greek gods. For many years, the resulting bloodbaths had sustained me, granting me a measure of justice, even though humanity had never been to blame for my curses.

But humanity worshipped those same gods—or gods just like them —and I'd considered it poetic justice to let them suffer the rewards of their gods' actions.

That their blind faith carried a price tag.

I had never told a single person what had made me suddenly alter my course from a lifetime of vengeance. Not one.

And I never would. I would carry that secret to my final resting place. Period.

I realized I was staring at the newspaper on the desk. It was from a few weeks ago, but I'd kept it at hand for some unspoken reason. Nosh Griffin was featured on the front page in an article about his legal battle to reclaim his inheritance after the death of his parents—a task which had prevented us from communicating for multiple obvious reasons. Primarily that I was the prime suspect—or, more accurately, a nameless picture of me was the prime suspect.

Mina Harker had coerced the Griffins to modify their will so that only blood relatives could accept their fortune and business, because she had learned that Nosh had been adopted and was not, in fact, related to them. Then Mina Harker had killed them, framing me for the gruesome crime.

For what purpose, I still had no idea. She hadn't known about my existence, so my involvement had been pure bad luck, and I had yet to come up with an answer as to why she had targeted Nosh or his parents. The only thing I could think of was that she had wanted to obtain the magic tomahawks we had taken from his parents' penthouse —but she'd never mentioned them outright. Even the Necromancer— whom I later learned was actually my old friend Nero—hadn't known Mina's intentions. He'd only been commanded to acquire Deganawida's journal for Dracula, and he hadn't even received an explanation for that.

No one had known about me, and we'd found no direct reason for the attack on Nosh's family. It was an unsolved mystery.

But it was the newspaper article below Nosh's picture that truly intrigued me—a related story about a beast of a man breaking into the evidence lock-up and destroying every shred of evidence the police had accumulated from the murder scene. The unknown culprit had simply bulldozed through the walls—without explosives or any kind of vehicle —and then lit the evidence on fire before leaving the same way he'd entered. Seven cops had opened fire on him, allegedly hitting him a dozen times.

But the man was never found. Not even a drop of blood was found.

Which had made the police look incredibly incompetent, almost drawing more attention than Nosh's legal battle over the past few weeks, since he had appeared on every available talk show in the city to share the sad story.

The destruction of the evidence had benefited Nosh because a test had been run on the DNA found at the crime scene, apparently proving that Nosh and his parents were not blood related, which would have ended his inheritance dispute for their gambling empire and various fortunes. Furthermore, another set of DNA from the murder scene— presumably mine—had shown a genetic match to Nosh. I still wasn't entirely knowledgeable on what any of these scientific analyses meant or how they were determined, but I knew enough to accept the facts and results at face-value, leaving the processes to the scientists.

Although it felt like a new kind of magic to me—the magic of science.

And now all of that evidence was missing. Although everyone had tried to lay the blame for the evidence destruction at Nosh's feet, I knew it had not been him. Unfortunately, that was all I knew. Whoever had done it had not taken credit. To be fair, I had considered sending in a team of vampires to enthrall every policeman and steal the evidence for myself, but this unknown beast of a man had done it all on his own, solving the problem for us.

An added benefit was that it coincidentally destroyed all physical evidence of me at the crime scene. The picture of the prime suspect— me—that had been disseminated was still available, but the physical proof was now missing, and lawyers were making a healthy profit debating the legal merit of whether duplicates of my photo from the news could be considered evidence.

Luckily, no one had learned my name.

With all the evidence destroyed, I'd tasked an associate to run her own blood tests to see if Nosh and I did in fact share the same DNA, because the entire frame-job had been orchestrated by Mina Harker, so there was every possibility that the first blood test had been doctored in some way, claiming a false genetic match, so as to make Nosh look like a blood relative of the alleged murderer.

I stared at Nosh's picture on the front page. He was speaking into a microphone, the very essence of confidence and resolve—not an entitled brat as some of the media outlets had tried to portray him. I couldn't see anything of my features in him, but it had been five hundred years since I last walked the earth. Since my son had been born.

So...was Nosh my son? Immortal, thanks to my vampire curse?

Or was he possibly a descendent?

If either of those claims were true, he *had* to have known before teaming up with Deganawida to wake me up. Coincidences could happen, but never so many all at once, and all of them in perfect harmony with each other. Rather than improbable, it was impossible.

Which would mean he had known about our blood relation, and had *chosen* to lie to me. On one hand, this infuriated me, but on the other, my fiery passion and fury had somewhat faded over the passing weeks. I had even grown somewhat empathetic to his suspected lie. When I had awoken, I had been violent and starving. If he'd told me he was my son or a descendent of mine, I would have likely killed him outright for being a liar.

So, he had known and had lied to me or a series of impossible coincidences had taken place.

Or—most likely—Mina's evidence had been a flat-out lie. Which was why I had requested independent verification.

The truth would come out tonight, one way or another. Evidence or not.

Because Victoria Helsing and I were attending a dinner with Nosh and Isabella—the Sister of Mercy I had met at the auction a few weeks back. It was a calculated risk being seen together, but Victoria had found a restaurant outside of the city's elites, and I had a very important ulterior motive to pursue. Apparently, the pair had been spending considerable time together since we first met. I was entirely certain that I would confront Nosh about our potential blood relation, since it was apparent that he had no desire to do so.

I sighed tiredly, shifting my gaze away from the article. In my peripheral vision, I saw Renfield pause from his work on the couch as he checked to see if I needed anything. I didn't look up. After a few moments of silence, he went back to work on the stack of cards before him.

I stared at the old tattered journal occupying the opposite corner of my desk and pursed my lips. Deganawida's journal—something that Dracula had wanted more than anything else in the city. I hadn't determined exactly why he wanted it, although I had my suspicions. Even the Necromancer—Nero, my old warlock friend—he'd put in charge of New York City, hadn't known the reasons for Dracula's interest in the legendary Medicine Man's journal.

Despite learning that Nero had been working for Dracula against his will, I hadn't entirely forgiven him, and I definitely didn't yet trust him, despite his recent semi-successful efforts to assist me in deciphering the journal's secrets. I'd even acquired a new collar to put around his neck in order to limit his powers—one not tied to Dracula.

The journal was open to the cursed page that had plagued my thoughts for weeks.

It was a list of names of just over one hundred vampires that Deganawida had killed in his unnaturally long life. The journal even had something called GPS coordinates—numbers that showed precise locations on a map that were accurate within fifteen feet—leading to where Deganawida had buried the bodies.

The following pages consisted of a spell to raise those dead vampires—necromancy—followed by notes documenting Deganawida's attempt to perform the dangerous magic. His experiment had been swiftly abandoned, summarized by a chilling footnote.

Subjects neurotic and feral. Uncontrollable. Without a soul, they are mindless killers, only able to follow explicit commands, and only for a limited time before even that ability is absorbed by their animalistic tendencies. I believe it's caused by an internal conflict—they remember dying and can't understand why they are back. This makes them suspicious and paranoid since they cannot think for themselves. The subjects need another vampire master, but even that might not be enough for absolute control.

The next page showed a brief spell that would destroy them from further necromantic experiments—by exploding their hearts within their chests.

Although concerning, it hadn't been what I'd hoped to find. If that had been Dracula's focus, he would have told his sole necromancer—Nero—of his plan, because the spell required a warlock or shaman to perform it.

I had hoped that the journal would have elaborated on the events of that fateful night when my family had been murdered and I'd been put into a magical slumber. Especially now that I had learned of the possibility that Nosh shared my ancestry somehow. But there had been very little mentioned on the topic of that night. Suspiciously little, as a matter of fact. I also hadn't found much about Deganawida's search for my missing—assumed dead—family, even though he'd told me he'd documented it.

Instead, I'd found signs of pages torn from the binding. Someone had removed them prior to giving the journal to Nero, and with Mina Harker dead, I had no one left to question.

I sighed, withdrawing my phone from my pocket. Apparently, there were creatures called hackers who could steal information from electronic devices, so I'd resigned myself to using cheap, disposable 'burner' phones rather than the more sophisticated 'smart' phones.

I used a new burner phone every day or two—and I wasn't happy about it, even though I understood the necessity of secrecy.

I had placed Renfield at the top of my new vampire command structure, tasking him with overseeing the three survivors of Dracula's organization here in New York City—because he'd killed every vampire under his command here after I'd broken his control over Nero. Dracula hadn't wanted to risk me stealing his entire organization, so he chose to simply murder them all in one fell swoop. I'd only managed to bond Hugo, Aristos, and Valentine before Dracula's curse dropped over the city.

But according to Renfield, those had been the three most valuable vampires to acquire, even though he did complain about their general lack of progress any time I asked—which always happened to be within earshot of them. Whether the complaint was warranted or not, productivity always increased afterwards.

The executive team, as Hugo referred to us, consisted of Renfield, myself, Hugo, Aristos and Valentine, and with the growing number of vampires I'd acquired from the homeless underground community, they had their work cut out for them. We were rapidly approaching one hundred vampires, but most of them were fledglings and needed direct supervision until they grew accustomed to their new and powerful bloodlust.

An old war veteran named Gabriel had quickly risen to a position of authority over the underground vampires, organizing them into efficient military sub-units that reported to him, leaving Gabriel to report to Hugo. Gabriel had been the first man I had turned on my exploration of the underground, and I vehemently approved of having him in charge because he had managed and organized the vampires— without needing to be asked—exactly the same way I would have done in his place.

I was very specific in my selection process regarding what type of man or woman I would permit to be turned into a vampire, and I had only just begun delegating the duty of evangelizing the underbelly of New York City to Gabriel.

Benjamin, my werewolf friend, had called it *evampirizing*, switching out the root word *angel* for *vampire*. Apparently, people made up their own words these days, but the phrase had quickly caught on, instilling an inner sense of pride in my new family.

My Kiss, as I had taken to calling them.

I stared down at my phone, frowning impatiently. "What is taking her so long?"

"If you value your life, I would recommend not repeating that question in her presence, Master Ambrogio," Renfield said, not looking up.

I grunted, agreeing with his warning. Some things would never change. Women would take as long as they pleased to get ready, and then they would nitpick every second that their man took to drive them to their planned destination until the man came to truly believe that it might actually be his fault that they were late to their appointment.

"I might as well check in with Dr. Stein," I said, my shoulders instinctively tensing. Renfield grew momentarily still as if a ghost had just tickled his neck. Then he resumed his work at twice the speed, as if fearing to even be within hearing distance of the good doctor. I scrolled through my phone's history and placed a call. "The smart phones let you call people with verbal commands," I complained testily.

"Right, sir," Renfield replied in a sympathetic tone, having heard me say as much at least a dozen times in the past few weeks.

"She works for me, not the other way around," I said, bolstering my courage as the phone rang in my ears. Renfield shot me a panicked look, his eyes briefly darting towards the door as if searching for an escape. "It's about time she showed me the proper respect—"

"What?!" Dr. Stein's sharp voice snapped by way of answer.

I flinched, my body instinctively reacting to the undeniable tone of command that seemed to ooze through the phone. I forced myself to relax, reminding myself that I was the person in charge.

"H-hello, Dr. Stein," I stammered, shifting in my seat. "I was j-just calling to see if you needed anything."

"Of course I don't need anything, you fool! If I did, I would have called you to get it for me!"

Renfield was as still as a statue, eyeing the door again. I narrowed my eyes at the coward. "Right. So...all is going according to plan?"

She sighed impatiently. "Gabriel—now there's a fine young boy who minds his betters," she said, her tone softening to something that was somewhat akin to affection, "unlike *some* men who seem to think with the hair on their chests," she added in an altogether different tone. "He brought your newest shipment over. I've got them all ready for Nero, if Renfield deigns to get off his lazy backside and bring the warlock over here. You probably have him doing some inane task that any dumb and blind idiot could accomplish in half the time." The stack of postcards Renfield had been putting stamps on abruptly fell off the table as he flinched, obviously overhearing Dr. Stein's comment thanks to his enhanced senses as a vampire.

In fact, I realized that she had a point. Putting stamps on cards wasn't difficult. Renfield hurriedly dropped to the floor and began scooping them up, returning them to the table as if the militant Dr. Stein stood over him with her tool of justice.

Her wooden spoon.

Benjamin had semi-jokingly called it *testoster-spoon*, swearing that he had never seen the weapon used on a woman. Dr. Stein had educated me long and hard on testosterone, informing me that it was something men had an overabundance of—the prime reason for our gross incompetence.

In addition to testosterone poisoning our souls, we apparently had hair and biceps for brains. The only things we could be trusted at doing without supervision was showing off our muscles or moving heavy objects—and only in rare circumstances.

The rest of our existence was better relegated to servitude and finding a woman who could properly manage us. I wasn't entirely sure if she was being serious or mocking me. She was a doctor, after all, and I was not. And I hadn't heard anyone object to her claim.

"You tell that lousy waste of space Renfield to get Nero here in the next twenty minutes or I'll have his skinny little hide," she commanded. "I'll paddle him so hard that he will sing!"

Renfield jumped to his feet, nodding. "Of course, Dr. Stein."

I scowled at him, holding up a finger to silently counter Dr. Stein's command. He winced but remained in place, shifting awkwardly from foot-to-foot, dry-washing his hands. "Have you had time to run the blood tests?" I asked, my eyes catching the picture of Nosh on the newspaper.

She scoffed. "Time to run the blood tests!" she snapped, mocking my tone. "Not there, you ten-thumbed cretin!" she suddenly shouted at someone in the background, and I heard her wooden spoon strike something fleshy, immediately followed by a manly squeal and an effusive apology. "No, *Master Ambrogio*," she said dryly, focusing back on my question, "because I am not your minion to be sent running around making coffee and cleaning up your messes. I already cleaned up the one at the police station for you. You're welcome for that, by the way," she added, sounding as if she was clenching her teeth.

I stared at the newspaper, blinking rapidly. "That was *you*? The fire at the evidence lock-up?" I hissed incredulously. "Why didn't you tell me?"

"Of course it was me. Who else keeps everything running smoothly around here so you can maintain the delusion that you're in charge? If I wasted my time explaining to the men all the subtle ways I had saved their hides or fixed their asinine mistakes, I'd never get anything else done."

Renfield stared at me with his jaw hanging open, obviously not having known about her involvement in the evidence lock-up either.

"They say you tore through the side of the building..." I said, under my breath, wondering how the tiny woman had done such a thing.

"I used my spoon, you idiot," she muttered sarcastically. "I sent another muscle-brained brute to do it since it involved destruction—about the only thing you lot are good at." She swore under her breath and then shouted into the background again. "Not there either! Do I need to paint directions on the floor or are you truly that incompetent? It boggles the imagination to watch you work, as if you're purposely trying to find the most inefficient way to move a godsdamned box! Here's a grand idea—place it beside the other godsdamned boxes!" She was panting heavily into the phone, and I realized my palm was sweating, wondering which one of my vampires was about to die for incompetence. "If there was nothing else, Master Ambrogio..."

"Um. Y-yes. The blood tests. I need them. I planned on bringing it up at dinner tonight with Nosh. We're going on a double-date."

She was utterly silent for a few seconds, but I could hear deep, measured breaths over the phone, letting me know she was attempting to force herself to calm down. "Sorin, that is the stupidest, most idiotic thing I have *ever* heard you say—and that's a high standard to exceed."

I swallowed, wincing in shame. "Why?" I asked hesitantly.

"Maybe because I haven't independently verified the results yet! If Mina Harker was involved in the first analysis, you can bet your fuzzy little peaches she outsmarted everyone and manipulated the results. I won't trust anything until I oversee every step of the process. Since you are determined to make a fool of yourself, I'll run my own tests now. But Renfield and Nero better already be halfway here, or so help me God..."

Renfield made a strange panicked sound and I nodded hurriedly into the phone. "Yes. Yes. He left a few minutes ago—"

"Don't you *dare* lie to me, boy," she snarled, interrupting me. "Renfield just earned one spoon."

I winced guiltily and Renfield wiped his sleeve across his forehead, licking his lips. He was slowly sliding his feet towards the door without lifting them, as if hoping he could slip away before I noticed. "Sorry, Dr. Stein. I'll send him right over. Please let me know the moment you get the results."

She sniffed primly. "I should have them within the hour. Now, if I hear you say one more word before Renfield arrives, I will march over there myself and rip his ear off with my bare hands," she promised darkly.

I nodded, seeing that Renfield was only a pace away from the door now, his hand already reaching for the handle. "Thanks—" Too late, I remembered her warning about saying one more word and, in a frantic thumb spasm, I promptly pushed the *end call* button. Then I realized I had just hung up on her and I froze still, unable to lower the phone from my ear as I shot Renfield a terrified look. His eyes were bulging out of their sockets.

We shared that silent horror together for an eternal second.

Then he lunged for the door. It opened up before he touched it, and he recoiled with a squeak, covering his ear and crouching in submission. "Not the ear! I'm sorry!"

3

Victoria Helsing frowned in confusion, staring down at him with a concerned look. "Your ear?" she asked, puzzled. "And what are you sorry for?"

I realized that I still had the phone pressed to my ear and that Dr. Stein hadn't actually somehow made good on her promise to rip off Renfield's ear. I began speaking into the phone on reflex, hunting for a last sliver of my dignity, even if it was fraudulent. "Listen closely, Dr. Stein. You will get me those reports now." Then I clicked the phone shut, setting it down on the desk.

Renfield bolted out the door without answering her, leaving a very confused Victoria to look at me with a suspicious frown. Her pale blue eyes drifted to the phone. "Bullshit."

I arched an eyebrow. "Pardon?"

She folded her arms, a smile stretching across her face. "I saw the screen before you closed it," she explained, struggling to bite down an obvious laugh. "Your burners stay illuminated when you're on a call."

I narrowed my eyes. "Has anyone told you that you look particularly ravishing in that dress, and that it's not kind to kick a man when he's down?" I asked, letting out a sigh as a smile of my own crept into place.

I couldn't help it—Victoria's entire face seemed to light up when she smiled. It was contagious.

She blushed at my compliment. "I haven't been ravished yet, unfortunately. Someone has been too busy," she said, casting me a smoldering look that made my pants tighten. She was right. But we both knew that my being busy wasn't the entire reason. We were both concerned about the effects that her blood might have on me—our shared ties to Artemis. Allowing passion to run rampant between us could be profoundly pleasurable or catastrophically fatal.

It was one of the other blood tests I had requested from Dr. Stein— to analyze our blood and look for unique markers when compared to blood samples from normal humans and various monsters, or supernaturals as they called them these days—to see what made us unique or similar to other beings. Dr. Stein already had extensive collections of human and supernatural blood, having made her own study of such matters. But she hadn't ever tested my blood.

Or Victoria. Or Nosh.

"And for the record, I think it's cute how you let Dr. Stein feel important. Very gentlemanly."

I realized that my mouth was hanging open and I let it shut with a click. "Yes," I said stiffly. "It is how a gentleman is supposed to treat—"

She burst out laughing, cutting me off. "You are such a *liar*!"

I tried to scowl defensively, but I finally let out a sigh. "I wonder what a blood test would show about *her*?" I muttered. "She has to be something supernatural or godly."

Victoria nodded her agreement. "She absolutely terrifies me, too, but I think she really is just a human."

She sauntered closer, and with my pride in a shattered but honest ruin, I allowed myself to feast on her beauty with my eyes. Aristos and Valentine had taken me shopping—a torture I'd somehow managed to endure only due to my incredible fortitude as the world's first vampire —so I was somewhat up-to-date on modern attire.

Aristos and Valentine had also been adamant about showing me how much female undergarments had changed since my time, warning me that most of the upper tier lingerie styles and brands required informational manuals so one knew how the various clasps, zippers, and buckles fastened.

So, I was now an aficionado of high-class lingerie that I would never wear—but might have reason to hastily remove. I was a particular fan of *Agent Provocateur*. Aristos had even proudly taken to calling me a lingerie snob.

Victoria wore a black cocktail dress with white polka dots. A broad, ruby-red belt hugged her waist, matching the color of her high-heeled shoes. She carried a very small black purse, and a simple bracelet made of round, wooden beads. A golden chain as thin as a strand of spider's silk somehow held a ruby pendant the size of my thumbnail against her chest, low enough to draw attention to her breasts yet maintain decency. She wore a white silk jacket that hugged her waist and flared out at her knees, a contrast to the black dress beneath. Her brown hair was done up in a complex bun with her signature silver chop-stakes— vampire killers disguised as jewelry.

I wouldn't have been surprised to learn that she had other blades hidden about her person in easy to reach places. She wore bright red lipstick, but that seemed to be the extent of her make-up, which I much preferred to the layering of muds and powders and paints that most women in this time used to cover up every tiny blemish or mark they might have.

She paused at my sudden attention, sensing the stark shift from polite words to something more primal and natural—a predator scoping his prey.

To be fair, there were times when I wasn't sure which of us was which.

And that was a remarkably euphoric sensation.

She glanced down at the cards on the table where Renfield had been working, and her eyes widened in disbelief as she scooped up a handful, rapidly flipping through them. "Really?" she giggled, looking both amused and mildly alarmed.

I grinned. "It was Renfield's idea," I said honestly.

She held up one of the cards, waving it at me. It was a light-painting printed on paper of me posing in front of the Museum of Natural

History, beckoning towards the camera with my finger as I flashed a roguish grin. It had been taken during the day, timed so that I ran out from a nearby shadow to quickly pose while Natalie snapped the picture—before the sunlight gave me discomforting burns.

Renfield had used a computer to add words in bright red letters to the bottom of the image, calling it a homemade postcard. "Wish you were here?" Victoria laughed, reading the card. She flipped it over and laughed even harder. "To the best deuce I ever took, love, Sorin."

I frowned. "I don't really understand why Renfield thinks that one is so funny. He said *deuce* means *two*, and that it was making fun of Dracula having been my second-in-command since I took New York City from him. But the others laugh harder at that one than some of the others," I mused, shrugging. "Is Renfield being petty since he's my new deuce?"

She pursed her lips, suspiciously averting her eyes back to the cards. "That must be it," she murmured in an amused tone—just like everyone else had been doing. She flipped over another card, one of me standing in a fountain in the same pose. "Class of '42 Reunion?" she read aloud, shaking her head.

"It doesn't state which *century*," I said, enunciating the last word.

She rolled her eyes, flipping through a few more. "Happy Last Birthday." She finally lowered the cards, tossing them back on the table with a grin. "And they're all taken during the day—another jab at Dracula. I'm guessing he doesn't share your tolerance for sunlight?" I shook my head, smirking. "Why do you have so many of them?"

"Renfield has been building a stockpile of them. He thought it would save time preparing them in advance so he can get one of the fledglings to mail them out every day. He's sent out twenty so far," I said, grinning proudly.

Victoria gasped. "You're kidding me. Has Dracula responded?"

I sighed, shaking my head. "Not yet."

"Renfield is surprisingly malicious," she said in a complimentary tone. "It's almost easy to forget that when you're talking to him."

I nodded proudly. "It's why I put him in charge of everyone. And why I didn't kill him in the first place. He's got a personal vendetta that is more important than anything else in the world—a vested interest in making sure I succeed."

At times, I found myself wondering if Renfield wanted to kill Dracula even more than I did, which would be saying something. He also wasn't a fan of Nero, since my old friend had betrayed me—at least in Renfield's eyes. Renfield was not a forgiving person, which was ironic, since he was only alive because I had forgiven him.

Victoria lifted her small purse, shaking her head in amusement. "You ready?" she asked. "Natalie is waiting for us outside with the car."

I smiled at her, steepling my fingers as I studied her up and down in silence. I lifted a finger and gestured for her to twirl. She beamed from ear-to-ear and did so, showing off her dress. "Slower," I said in a firm tone. Her eyes smoldered again as she nodded, and then she twirled much slower for me.

Because I hadn't cared about her dress, although it truly was beautiful. She could have been wearing sack cloth and I would have stared in admiration. I wanted to see what lay beneath the wrapping paper. Her body was like a master carving of feminine potential—showing off both the gentle grace and vicious lethality, the natural beauty and the iron spine of confidence that held it all together.

There was no question that Victoria was gorgeous in the physical sense, but like a stained-glass window, her elegance truly shone when illuminated from within by the fiery light of her soul.

Beautiful enough to destroy a man without ever lifting a finger.

She whipped out a sleek compact gun from her purse and kissed the barrel. "For the times when lipstick just won't do." She puckered her bright red lips, showing off her lipstick, before shoving the gun back into her purse.

Deadly enough to destroy a man with a slight squeeze of a finger, too.

"If I have any say in the matter, I choose the lipstick," I said, smiling.

She walked over to my side of the desk and assessed my own light gray suit with an approving hum. Then she bent down and lightly kissed my cheek. "Play your cards right," she whispered in a smoky tone, "and who knows what might happen?"

I reached out to grab her, but even with my enhanced speed she managed to slip away, laughing as she fled to the door despite her dress and high heels.

The Devil followed, licking his lips hungrily.

For his hunger was great enough to consume the world.

4

Natalie had offered to chauffeur us since I had been banned from operating automobiles of any sort; I'd wrecked the car during my first driving lesson with Aristos. Plus, I didn't have a driver's license in the event that I got pulled over.

Natalie and Benjamin were commanding lieutenants in the Crescent, the local pack of werewolves in Manhattan. The Crescent consisted of five sub-groups—one for each of the five boroughs in New York City—and all of those were run by Stevie, the alpha werewolf. He seemed to spend the majority of his time in Manhattan, but he left most of the day-to-day work to Natalie and Benjamin.

Natalie had been adamant about needing to remain close to me, ultimately choosing to run the pack with Benjamin from the Museum of Natural History. It worked better than their old warehouse, and it put them in constant contact with my executive management team since they were renegotiating various business interests with each other in the new power vacuum that had appeared since I had taken over Dracula's operations.

It also let Natalie remain close to me, and she made no secret of wanting to be available in the event that I ever needed to drink some of her blood. The last time I had bitten Natalie, she'd practically collapsed in orgasmic ecstasy—which was not a typical response from a vampire's bite. Sure, it happened often with werewolves, and sometimes with willing blood donors, but I had never seen such a *strong* physical reaction. Especially when I hadn't tried to give her such a sensation, which was usually a requirement.

The same thing had happened when I had bitten Victoria, but she and I shared ties to Artemis, and there was definite attraction between us, so it made more sense. The only excuse for Natalie's reaction was that it had been a very long time since I'd last bitten a beautiful woman's neck, and I might not have been as careful as I'd intended. I might not have shielded her at all.

Victoria and Natalie got along quite well, but Victoria rarely let Natalie or me out of her sight. It made me feel like I was a raw steak hanging between two ravenous lionesses. And I couldn't deny that an insistent part of me often gave serious thought to letting both of those lionesses have a go at me, consequences be damned.

We pulled onto a quiet street of modest two-story homes, far removed from the constant flow of humanity that plagued the rest of the city. For the first time since waking, I felt a slight sense of tranquility in the air. But my mind was having none of it.

I'd been unable to speak to Nosh without drawing unwanted attention that might connect him to the alleged murderer, so I'd asked Victoria to reach out and request a double date with Nosh and Isabella.

The entire ride here, I had been chewing over what I wanted to say to him—debating whether to confront him about the DNA results from the police investigation. Even though the evidence had now been destroyed by Dr. Stein's mysterious associate, it had been all over the news that someone—allegedly the killer—who shared DNA with Nosh had been in the penthouse. Nosh had answered the stream of ensuing questions, demanding to uncover the identity of this supposed relative, but he also brought up the point that there had been no evidence stating exactly how old that DNA had been. For all anyone knew, the mystery relative could have left that DNA behind weeks or months prior. And he'd pulled no punches upon hearing about the evidence being destroyed by a lunatic starting a fire—pointing it out as yet another fault of the police department in this whole fiasco.

Natalie parked the car on the side of the street and turned around to look at us with a bright smile and a playful gleam in her bright green eyes. Her short bob of blonde hair hugged her jaw line, flaring out in sharp points like wings. "Call me when you're finished. I know a great little dessert place," she said as Victoria opened her door and began to climb out.

Victoria hesitated at the door, smiling interestedly. "Oh? Where?"

Natalie shifted her attention to give me a smoky look as she lifted two fingers to tap her neck, smiling wickedly. Victoria stared at Natalie for the longest three seconds I'd ever experienced. I couldn't tell if she was considering partaking in Natalie's offer or how best to kill the werewolf without getting blood on her white coat. Instead of answering, Victoria simply pulled me from the car and shoved me towards the restaurant, ignoring the sound of Natalie's laughter as she slammed the door closed.

We entered the Italian restaurant Victoria had picked to find a young mousy hostess speaking to an older woman—who was draped in a heavy fur coat with golden earrings laden with precious stones hanging from her earlobes as if they were testing how much weight the thin skin could hold. A meek older man stood beside her with slumped shoulders and a submissive, fatalistic aura oozing from every pore of his body. He even smelled cowardly. "What do you mean you don't have a table available? Do you know who I am?" the woman demanded.

"My apologies, ma'am. We should have a table available in ten minutes."

"In ten minutes, you will no longer have the benefit of my patronage!" she snapped back.

Victoria rolled her eyes at me and sidled up to the podium. "Excuse me. We have a reservation. I believe the rest of our party are already—"

"Excuse *me*, trollop!" the older woman interrupted. "You will wait until I am finished!"

Victoria slowly turned to face her and openly eyed her up and down with a glare cold enough to cause frostbite. Then she sniffed disdainfully and turned back to the hostess. "I wasn't aware you allowed service animals in your establishment. How very considerate of you. Unfortunately, I am allergic to the beasts."

The hostess blanched and I grinned. The old man glanced up at me with a panicked expression as if begging me to rein her in.

"Service animal!" the older woman hissed, her shoulders visibly trembling as she returned the up and down maneuver with a disgusted sneer. "This is a mink coat. A harlot like you would have to live on her back indefinitely to ever earn something so fine." My humor evaporated, and I grew completely still. I was about two seconds from doing something reckless when Victoria shot me a stern look. I relented, pursing my lips as the old woman stormed away, flicking her mink coat behind her dramatically. "Come along, Harold," she snapped at the old man.

He flinched, startled to be addressed by name.

"What do you say, Harold?" Victoria asked, turning to the old man with a dark grin. "I have it on good authority that you have ten minutes to spare and that I need to do some dirty work in order to afford a nicer coat. Do you know how to be dirty, Harold?" she asked, licking her lips.

His eyes widened, instinctively assessing Victoria as if entertaining her proposition, and then he immediately flushed a dark purple color as he realized what he'd done.

"Harold!" the woman snapped, her face flushing a matching purple. He scrambled after her like a whipped dog.

I burst out laughing, especially at the look on the hostess' face. Victoria slipped her arm through mine and pulled me up to the podium. "Our table?" she asked sweetly.

The hostess couldn't comply fast enough. Luckily, the dining area was through another door, so our confrontation had gone unnoticed by everyone but the hostess. I shot a long look at the old bat's back, wanting to yank off her coat and flush it down a toilet. Victoria squeezed my arm, shaking her head. "Not worth it," she murmured. "She'll get what's coming to her someday." I nodded stiffly clenching my jaw as the old woman turned to look at us and noticed the cold look on my face.

"Oh, isn't that precious. The pimp was going to defend his whore's honor," the woman cackled in a cruel, bitter, carrion crow.

"And, we're going to our table," Nosh said, suddenly appearing at my side and firmly shoving me ahead of him, guiding me through the swinging door that led into the dining area and away from the potential crime scene. I wasn't sure when he had slipped in or if he had overheard us through the door, but I complied, following him stiffly. "You're already suspected of two murders, Sorin," he said softly. "Let's not draw any further attention to your face."

I took a measured breath, nodding. Not because of his words, but because I suddenly visualized the possibility that Nosh might be my son—that he was touching my shoulder and guiding me to our table where we were going to spend a nice peaceful evening together.

That a son was trying to keep his father out of trouble.

And I felt a strange, powerful emotion that I didn't quite know how to process. Victoria seemed to understand and squeezed my arm reassuringly. Although she hadn't brought it up—knowing how uncomfortable it made me—she was acutely aware of what was on my mind and what I wanted to ask Nosh. She also wanted to let me handle it in a manner of my own choosing rather than prodding me in any specific direction. She knew me well enough, even after only a few weeks, to know that unless Dr. Stein was in the room, no one was going to make me do anything that I didn't want to do.

But I could sense the excited anticipation in her touch, as well as the gentle resolve to stand beside me whatever I chose to do. I smiled gratefully at her, nodding. "For the record, I'm buying you a mink coat."

Her eyes twinkled devilishly. "Then it looks like I have some dirty work ahead of me."

I chuckled, shaking my head. "That was not what I meant."

"But I want a *really* nice coat, not a consolation prize."

Nosh gave us a puzzled look before guiding us to a table in a somewhat secluded alcove, granting us a measure of relative privacy from the general hum of conversation and the clinking of glasses and silverware. The restaurant was indeed full, the patrons primarily wearing suits and gowns, and waiters in black suits with white shirts drifted from table to table like graceful swans in a lake, barely causing a ripple as they poured glasses or balanced trays of steaming pasta to set before their guests with subdued murmurs and easy smiles.

5

Isabella, the Sister of Mercy I had met at the auction my first night back in the land of the living, was seated at our table, smiling self-consciously. She wore a modest white dress with a high neckline, and she had simple silver rings on each ring finger. Her fiery red hair drew the eye like a moth to a flame.

I wasn't entirely sure of the current relationship status between her and Nosh, but I was assuming that he was courting her—or dating her, as unromantic as that sounded to my ears. It was rather strange to see a woman of God interested in courting a shaman, but I had given up on my old-world view having any relevance in current times. My preconceived notions and beliefs resulted in laughter more often than not. I pulled out an empty chair for Victoria and smiled at her. She grinned, and sat down so that I could slide her chair in.

Isabella watched with an approving smile of her own. I reached out a hand, holding it up before her in a polite unspoken request. She blushed faintly before lifting her hand. I accepted it, gently gripping the first two fingers—careful not to touch the silver ring—and lowered my mouth to kiss the back of my thumb, not wanting to kiss her actual flesh and alarm her. Then I released it and stepped back. "Pleasure to see you again, Isabella."

She beamed, nodding back. "Pleasure to see you as well, Sorin."

I glanced back at Victoria. "Did I do it right?"

She was biting back a laugh, but she nodded. "Yes." She glanced over at Isabella. "We've been watching period shows and movies to catch him up on the history he missed."

Nosh smiled, shaking his head as he looked up at me. "Although incredibly polite and formal—and perfect for this dinner—that type of greeting isn't typical for other social occasions. I'm sure Victoria neglected to tell you that part," he said, chuckling.

Isabella smacked his shoulder playfully. "You could learn a thing or two from Sorin about how to properly treat a lady."

I smiled crookedly, dipping my head as I made my way to my own seat. Her comment had brought to mind the idea of a son needing to learn lessons from his father, sending another icy chill down my spine.

Victoria and Isabella began speaking in low tones, leaning closer to each other, obviously preferring a bit of privacy. I felt Nosh glancing at me, and I forced myself to remain calm as I tried to figure out how I wanted to bring up the topic of our DNA—or if I should at all.

I still hadn't received a call back from Dr. Stein, after all.

"How is the legal case progressing?" I asked stiffly, not really needing an answer since it was all over the recent news.

He shrugged. "Slow and painful. To be honest, I don't really care how it pans out, as long as I am not associated with the crime," he said, speaking low enough so as not to be accidentally overheard by anyone listening in. "I've saved up enough money to live comfortably, but it would look very strange if I didn't fight it."

I nodded, licking my lips. "I was surprised to hear about the evidence being destroyed. Convenient for your case."

He nodded slowly, studying me like a hawk. "Yes. I thought so as well. An unexpected gift from an unknown friend, perhaps..." he said, trailing off curiously, as if hoping for me to admit my part in it.

I shook my head faintly. "It was not me. I would have just enthralled everyone in the building and stolen it with none the wiser." Part of me wanted to tell him about Dr. Stein taking the initiative to resolve the situation, but I also didn't want Nosh knowing too much about her recent activities with Nero and Gabriel—not even considering the blood tests she was running.

He harrumphed softly, nodding. "I hadn't thought of that," he said, leaning back with a thoughtful frown.

I felt my pulse accelerating, and finally made the decision to just get it over with. No matter what Dr. Stein discovered, the topic raised many other questions that needed to be answered—like if he had any idea what Mina Harker's true intentions had been with his parents, the missing pages from the journal, and why he hadn't seemed even remotely interested in retrieving the journal from me since I'd taken it back from Nero. That had been his entire goal, yet it may as well have not even existed for all he seemed to care. So much depended on Nosh's responses to my various questions—whether he had known about our possible blood relation or not, and why he was holding so many secrets from me and others. Because if he felt the need to not fully trust me, should I not fully trust him with my own actions? What greater game was he playing and why? He'd woken me up after all, so whatever his motivations were, they included me to some extent, and I wanted to make sure he wasn't using me as an unwitting pawn.

If I was wrong, at least it would be out in the open and we could talk about it like two grown men. Possibly like father and son.

"Nosh, I've been meaning to ask you—"

I cut off, my phone suddenly ringing loudly inside my pocket. I hissed, shoving a hand inside to grab it and check the screen. It was Dr. Stein. I hit the button on the side to silence it, ignoring the glares from other patrons a few tables away. I had forgotten—and didn't remember how, anyway—to silence the damned thing before coming into the restaurant.

Nosh was watching me curiously, his eyes flicking from the phone to me. "You were saying?"

I nodded, taking a calming breath. I opened my mouth and my phone chimed loudly, letting me know I had a text message. I ignored it and it chimed again. Then again. And again.

Victoria was grimacing, silently urging me to take the call or at least shut off the phone.

I held up a finger to Nosh, clenching my jaw as I flipped open the phone to read the texts.

Emergency. Answer me, boy! Then there was a tiny image of a wooden spoon and a yellow sad face that made me wince. Victoria had called the strange hieroglyphs *emojis*, but I didn't understand why anyone used them rather than words.

I climbed to my feet and sighed irritably. "My apologies. Excuse me for just a moment." I noticed a bar nestled up against the back wall and made my way past several tables of wine-guzzling guests bedecked in gems and furs. No one sat at the bar, leaving the lone bartender—a thin man with a curled, bushy mustache wearing suspenders over his white dress-shirt—with nothing to do but polish glasses with a white towel. I called Dr. Stein, lifting the phone to my ear as I sat down at the bar. "I'll take a chianti," I told the bartender, recalling Hugo's favorite wine.

He nodded, plucking out a fresh bottle and a clean glass, understanding that I was not in the mood for conversation.

"About time!" Dr. Stein snapped. "You told me to rush the blood tests and then you don't answer!"

"I didn't think you'd get results so fast," I muttered. "What did you find?"

Nosh suddenly appeared beside me, almost making me fall out of my chair as I hurriedly switched ears in an effort to get the phone as far away from him as possible. He shot me a curious look before turning to the bartender and clearing his throat as he sat down.

The bartender was still uncorking the wine bottle, so he flashed Nosh a polite look. "Just a moment, sir. I'll be right with you."

Nosh nodded, waving a hand to let him know he wasn't in a rush. Another waitress slipped into the bar area, glancing briefly at the bartender who was still fighting with the cork, having partially turned his back to me to mask his struggle. "Don't worry, Matthew. I'll get it." Then she turned to Nosh, smiling brightly. "What can I get for you?"

The bartender paused to glance over his shoulder with a frown. "My name isn't Matthew. It's Oliver," he muttered grumpily before resuming his fight for my simple glass of wine.

She smiled at Nosh, completely ignoring Oliver's wounded pride as she flicked her head of thick, wavy brown hair over her shoulder. "First day. It's hard to remember all the names. Speaking of names, mine is Winnie," she said, leaning closer with an inviting grin, her pale skin was almost translucent.

"I'll take a dirty martini," Nosh said absently, not seeming to care one way or another—about her, her name, or the drink. I had no idea what a dirty martini was, but my solitary bar had just turned into a social gathering—exactly what I had wanted to avoid. Especially with the subject of my conversation sitting right next to me. Winnie was unperturbed by Nosh's disinterest as she began mixing up a brew from various bottles she found below the bar, pouring them into a metal cup which she promptly began to shake loudly as she smiled coyly at Nosh, obviously determined to catch his attention. She was cute, but it was blatantly obvious that the stoic shaman had no interest in her or anyone else other than Isabella. In fact, he was glancing back at our table, smiling privately at our women—

"Are you listening to me?" Dr. Stein demanded.

I flinched involuntarily. "Sorry. It's loud here. I'm listening," I told her.

Winnie began to pour Nosh's drink into a strange glass, spilling some onto the mahogany bar since she was too focused on trying to bat her eyelashes at the obtuse shaman. My own glass of wine was set before me at almost the same time.

"Thanks, Oliver," I said, reaching for my glass.

"I assume he's sitting nearby since you haven't said his name," Dr. Stein said, sounding as if she was speaking quietly—although it was hard to tell as Winnie resumed her attempts to entangle Nosh into a conversation as she slid the sloppy drink closer to him.

"You're Nosh Griffin, right? I've seen you on the news," the bartender said, smiling at him.

"Yes," he replied politely.

"Yes," I said into the phone, at almost the same time. "Victoria and I are having dinner with Nosh and *Isabella*," I said, heavily enunciating the name in an effort to get Winnie to shut the hell up.

Winnie shot me a brief, irritated look before turning back to Nosh, leaning forward to prop her elbow onto the bar and rest her narrow chin in her palm. "Go ahead. Try it, Nosh," she said, letting his name slide across her tongue in a way that seemed highly inappropriate.

I rolled my eyes and saw Oliver doing the same, frowning disapprovingly at Winnie's blatant attempts to snag Nosh with her feminine wiles. Nosh turned back to the bar, finally peeling his eyes away from Isabella to glance down at his drink.

"Okay," Dr. Stein said. "I took some magical liberties with my tests, not bothering with the scientific method since this is a rush. Nero has been exceedingly helpful in teaching me to color outside of the lines." That sounded ominous, but I couldn't speak openly, so I continued listening without interruption. "I had plenty of Nosh's blood to use since I tended him after his injuries a few weeks ago," Dr. Stein said, choosing her words carefully.

I nodded, listening closely as I stared at the mahogany bar. What seemed to be faint tendrils of mist drifted up from where Winnie had spilled Nosh's drink, and I idly wondered again what the hell a dirty martini was.

He said something to Winnie, but I didn't catch it over Dr. Stein's voice in my ear. "I haven't run your blood yet, but I ran his against samples from both of his parents, and they were matches."

I blinked in confusion, watching the strange tendrils on the bar as they shifted harmlessly back and forth. I wasn't sure where she had acquired blood samples from his parents, and I couldn't very well ask with Nosh sitting right beside me. "That's impossible."

"My thoughts as well, but this test doesn't lie," Dr. Stein said. "Even though I haven't finished running yours yet, this indirectly gives you your answer. Unless you're related to his parents as well, he is not your son."

I stared at the bar counter, blinking slowly as I tried to process her simple statement. All I could hear was a dull roar in my ears as part of my heart that had recently been rekindled was instantly extinguished.

6

The strange vapor on the bar shifted back and forth as Nosh swirled his glass in slow, lazy circles, an idle gesture, as Winnie laughed loudly at something he'd said.

"I don't think that's possible, but I don't know," I admitted. Deganawida had said that Nosh was a descendant of my original tribe, but I couldn't recall if Deganawida had known that Nosh had been adopted. Perhaps the Medicine Man had really meant that the Griffins were descendants of the tribe, which might also explain Mina Harker's interest in them. She worked for Dracula, and Dracula hated the tribe.

But how could his blood match theirs if he'd been adopted?

"I'll have to call you back. Thank you," I said numbly, realizing that our dinner was at an end—even though we hadn't eaten a thing.

"Don't do anything foolish, boy," Dr. Stein warned. For the first time, I sensed a matronly concern hidden in her tone, but my mind was too distracted to acknowledge it. "I need to see you in person about the Phoenix project anyway. I should have the rest of the blood tests in an hour or so. Stevie and Renfield are working with Nero on them as we speak. You should come by. Stevie has a dozen wolves patrolling the marina so it's safe for you to come without anyone noticing."

I nodded. "Okay." Then I hung up, lifting my wine to my lips in an attempt to fill up the sudden hollow sensation in my chest. I wasn't sure why it hurt to learn that he wasn't my son, but...

It did.

A lot.

As frustrated as I had been about the lies it would imply, I had obviously been hoping for it. To learn that my son had not only survived, but that I was having dinner with him and a woman he cared about, would have been wonderful.

Winnie's laughter raked across my ears like nails on a chalkboard.

"Cease that incessant screeching, girl. You'll attract feral cats if you keep it up," I growled, settling a glare on Winnie.

Her laughter cut off abruptly and I sensed Nosh turning to me with a startled look, lowering the drink he had been about to taste. Her face blushed bright red and her shoulders wilted.

Oliver had a panicked look on his face, shooting his attention from me to Winnie, uncertain whether he should defend his coworker or agree with his customer. Nosh slowly shook his head. "That was unkind," he said gently.

I gritted my teeth, unable to meet Nosh's eyes.

"I didn't mean to offend you, sir," Winnie apologized. "I was just trying to be friendly. It's my first day and I'm nervous, is all."

I didn't care about her hollow apology. There was professional courtesy and there was desperate, pitiful flirting. Winnie hadn't acted even remotely professional or genuine, especially after I'd spoken Isabella's name. That single name should have instantly ended her ruse. Whatever game she was playing, I could see right through it.

I'd met thousands of women like her—throwing themselves at the feet of powerful men, hoping that a faux act of adoration would net them a fine catch. She would get no forgiveness from me. Better for her to learn her lesson early.

Powerful men gobbled up girls like Winnie by the dozens, forgetting their names the moment they got what they wanted, leaving them tarnished and jaded like discarded, broken dolls to litter the streets of the forgotten pages of history.

And I was having a hard-enough time trying to calm my own turbulent emotions. Because I wanted to kill something. To destroy something priceless. To drink an ocean of blood. I settled for my wine, careful not to break the stem of the glass in my grip as I guzzled it down in one swift pull.

I carefully set down the glass, locking my attention onto the wooden surface so that I didn't spout any further cruelty to the desperate bartender. My eyes settled on the shifting tendrils of fog—which no one else seemed to have noticed. Or maybe they didn't care because they all knew what a dirty martini was. I was the only ignorant one at the bar, after all.

I belted out a harsh laugh, shaking my head at the humorless, unspoken joke.

"Are you alright?" Nosh asked warily.

I peeled my gaze away from the strange tendril of vapor on the bar to look over at him as he lifted his drink to his lips. "We're leaving," I said abruptly, standing to my feet.

Nosh froze, his eyes widening as he lowered the glass without drinking. "What?" he asked, sounding baffled. "We haven't even eaten yet." He glanced at the phone in my fist and frowned. "Who—"

"We're leaving," I repeated, cutting him off as I shoved the phone into my pocket.

"Oh, don't leave," Winnie said sadly. "Finish your drink at least. You haven't even *tried* it yet," she complained sadly, sniffling in fake tears to garner his sympathy.

I turned to glare at her and her inane comment just as she was wiping her forearm across her nose, but she wasn't looking at me, proving my point about her ridiculous, suicidal game.

"Good idea, Winnie," Nosh said, lifting his glass in my peripheral vision. "I have a feeling I might need a drink to understand what the hell he's talking about," Nosh said in a gruff, disapproving tone. "And why he's being unnecessarily cruel."

I hesitated as the familiar scent of hot blood struck my nostrils and I saw a fresh drop of blood roll down Winnie's upper lip. She hardly seemed to notice, staring hungrily at Nosh, gripping the bar with both hands. Another drop of blood rolled down her lips and I saw the strange vapor shifting across the surface of the bar.

I suddenly hissed, backhanding the drink away from Nosh's mouth just before it touched his lips. The dirty martini splashed all over Winnie and she let out a sudden gasp. Then she simply disappeared, leaving her clothes and a pair of shoes behind the bar.

Nosh's instinctive anger transformed to disbelief, and I noticed heads swiveling our way from nearby tables. Oliver stared from me to the pile of empty clothes, his eyes widening in confusion and horror. I sensed him taking a deep breath before opening his mouth to shout out an alarm as his eyes locked onto mine, assuming I had just killed the new bartender, Winnie.

I enthralled him in the blink of an eye and his mouth clicked shut. *Sing*, I told him, using our sudden connection to make him obey my silent command. He instantly began to belt out *Happy Birthday*, of all things, at the top of his lungs, drawing every eye in the restaurant.

I gripped Nosh by the elbow and forced him back towards our table, plastering an embarrassed smile on my face while my eyes darted warily from face-to-face, searching for any other threats. "What the *fuck*, Sorin," Nosh demanded in a breathy whisper, but he let me guide him back to our table, unable to deny that I'd just saved his life.

"Winnie just tried to kill you," I said, gritting my teeth as the other diners began to clap and sing along with Oliver, assuming I was the shy birthday boy trying to flee from Oliver's song. Victoria and Isabella were staring at us in blatant confusion, crooked smiles on their faces as they likely wondered if this was some orchestrated surprise that Nosh and I had cooked up for them as a special treat.

I jolted to see that Isabella's nose was bleeding, and that her crooked smile was actually a delirious expression frozen onto her cheeks. Nosh cursed, lunging for her just as her eyes rolled back into her skull and she passed out.

7

Nosh managed to catch Isabella just before her face struck the table, and Victoria leapt to her feet, spinning to stare at me with wide, startled eyes.

"We're leaving," I commanded. "Now—"

Victoria abruptly reached back into her hair with a snarl, yanking one of the silver chop-stakes out and hurling it over my shoulder. I sensed the threat behind me the moment her projectile left her fingers —too late to save myself. The silver metal missed me by a finger's width, and I heard a sudden gargling sound from over my shoulder.

I spun and saw a vampire crumple to his knees, blood burning away to ash around the silver chop-stake through his eye, radiating outward like cracking ice. Diners instantly leapt to their feet in a collective gasp, and I realized I only had seconds to save their lives.

I pulled deep on my blood reserves, using up a ridiculous amount of energy to enthrall everyone except Nosh, Victoria, and Isabella in a brute-force blast that left twinkling stars at the edges of my vision. *Sleep*, I commanded, not having time for finesse. Oliver's song instantly cut off and the humans all dropped bonelessly where they had been standing or seated, catapulting bowls of soup, drinks, and plates of food up into the air in a messy chain reaction.

Other than my party, only three men remained standing. Two wore the clothing of the wait-staff and one man wore a white apron, walking out from the kitchen to see what the commotion was about. The three of them took one look at the piles of sleeping bodies and narrowed their eyes, baring their fangs at me as they comprehended that their efforts had been foiled.

Vampires had crashed our dinner party.

And I'd just used up a good portion of my blood reserves to enthrall the entire restaurant. In the past few weeks, Dracula must have sent more of his army to New York City, hoping to amass a small force that might be capable of taking me out without a full-blown war.

It's what I would have done in his shoes. Luckily, I'd anticipated the move, which was why I'd been working so tirelessly with Gabriel to increase our own numbers. It was also why I'd spent an exorbitant amount of money on project Phoenix with Dr. Stein and Nero.

But that didn't explain Winnie. She definitely hadn't been a vampire, and I feared that she might have found a way to kill or injure Isabella, judging by the sudden nosebleed she and Winnie both suffered. But what had been in the drink to make her simply disappear? Had she actually died or was she still here? Her final gasp had sounded fatal.

Victoria crouched down beside me and tugged her chop-stake free from the dead vampire—who had also been wearing a wait-staff disguise. How had they known where to find us? Had they simply enthralled their way into the restaurant, posing as employees? And why hadn't I sensed them?

Victoria unceremoniously stabbed him in the heart for good measure—or petty violence for ruining her date night—and then pulled it back out, wiping off the blood on his suit.

Then she stood, grinning savagely at the three remaining vampires as her hand drifted to her purse. "Sorin, this might just turn out to be the best date I've ever had."

The three vampires pulled out gleaming knives from their suits—definitely not from the restaurant's silverware collection—and began throwing them at us. I leapt up onto the nearest table, hoping to block my friends from the projectiles—especially Nosh and the unconscious

Isabella. Three concussive blasts rocked the restaurant as Victoria whipped out her pistol, and two of the vampires went down in an explosion of gore as their heads simply exploded.

She had her gun loaded with the silver bullets that had almost killed me a few weeks ago—the ones that shattered into tiny silver fragments on impact.

The third vampire—the one in the apron—was mine. I batted away one knife as another sliced into my side with a fiery flash of pain. But I didn't stop running, hopping from one table to the next. I stepped onto an old woman's head, shoving her face deeper into her bowl of soup as I used her skull as a steppingstone to tackle the last vampire. My claws ripped through his chest and out his back just as he was preparing to throw another knife.

I held his still beating heart in my palm and I crushed it with a snarl, not daring to try drinking his blood. Dracula would have anticipated that.

I discarded the oozing hunk of meat and yanked my hand clear as I spun back to check on Victoria. She nodded at me before scanning the rest of the room for any other threats. Nosh had Isabella draped over his shoulders, using one hand to hold her in place, and he had a fierce, furious look on his face as he clutched a magic tomahawk in his other fist—a weapon made from pure light and energy like I had seen him use at the auction. He could make it change shapes and even throw it, much like warlocks could make blades of magic fire out of thin air, bending the elements to their wills.

I could sense Isabella's heartbeat, so I dismissed her for the moment. No one else moved, and I let out a faint sigh. "I didn't sense any of them," I said out loud, letting my friends know that they needed to remain alert for more enemies.

They nodded, scanning the eerily silent restaurant and the dozens of bodies. At a sudden realization, I walked back to the woman I had used as a steppingstone and grabbed a fistful of her hair to lift her head from the bowl of soup.

I belted out a laugh when I confirmed that it was the horrible woman from earlier—the one with the mink coat who had been so rude to Victoria. They had finally been given a table. Her lapdog husband, Harold, was sprawled out on the floor, but his face was buried deep into the buxom cleavage of a young woman who had been sitting at a neighboring table. She had been wearing a dress that did not allow a bra, and it also did not allow proper protection from sudden falls, leaving her breasts fully exposed. But Harold was doing his part to protect her modesty—by shielding her nudity with his face and hands. She had to be a third of his age, and I was already considering waking his wicked wife up prematurely just to behold the look on her face when she saw Harold's good fortune.

Not wanting to embarrass the young woman, I abandoned my idea and turned to Victoria instead. "Heh," I said, pointing the old hag's face towards Victoria like it was a lantern.

My vampire hunter smirked, nodding with an approving sniff. Her smile turned into outright laughter as she noticed Harold sleeping like a babe at the teat—quite literally. "Dirty old man," she cheered. "Get her a mink coat!"

I chuckled as I let go of the hag's hair, letting her face splash back into the remainder of her soup. Then I wiped off the vampire's blood from my hand into her fancy mink coat. I stared down at her for another moment before swiftly picking her up by the shoulders and setting her down beside the heartless vampire, making sure to get the victim's blood on her hand.

"There. Now she's a suspected murderer."

Victoria was smiling, but also shaking her head in disapproval as she motioned for me to join her in leading the way out of the restaurant. "I take care of my whores," I told her, leaning close.

She snorted, elbowing me in the spot where the knife had cut me. I bit back a hiss so as not to alarm her. Nosh carried Isabella behind us. "Less petty vengeance, more getaway vehicle, you twisted lovebirds," he growled, his magical tomahawk winking out of existence with a crackling pop as I led us back into the area with the hostess' podium. The hostess was slumped over the podium, snoring loudly.

"There might be more vampires outside waiting for us. Where did you park?" I asked Nosh, hesitating at the doors leading outside.

"One block down. To the left."

"Call Natalie," I told Victoria as I glanced out the window, checking the street. The area was quiet, and I didn't sense any vampires, but I hadn't sensed any of our enemies inside the restaurant either. "We need to get Isabella somewhere safe. Make sure she's okay." Victoria had her phone pressed to her ear, but she gave me a meaningful glance. I sighed, understanding her silent suggestion.

I pulled out my phone and called Dr. Stein. She answered, but I immediately interrupted her. "We were attacked at the restaurant," I said, trying to block off Victoria's conversation with Natalie.

Dr. Stein cursed, but the connection was poor, sounding as if I was only hearing every other word or so. "Phoenix too far—" Her voice cut off and I growled, noticing Victoria's frustrated frown. She must have a bad connection as well—meaning that it wasn't on Dr. Stein's end.

"Dr. Stein!" I snapped angrily, but all I heard was random snippets of partial words. "Where else can we go quickly?"

I wasn't sure how much of my question she'd heard. My phone had worked perfectly fine when I'd been speaking to Dr. Stein at the bar. Victoria had tried to explain it to me once before, telling me that it was a common problem with our cheap burner phones since they borrowed towers or something.

I hadn't paid much attention since each question only led to more questions. I walked closer to the door, wondering if it would work better outside. Victoria was doing the same, pacing back and forth to find a spot where the connection was stronger, but she didn't look to be having any more success than me. If Dr. Stein had no suggestions, we would just have to head to the museum, but that was not very close, and I didn't have anyone there who could check on Isabella to make sure she was okay. Because she still hadn't woken up. And there was a good chance that Dracula's vampires were trying to lead us into a trap, forcing us to head back to the museum for an ambush.

Nosh was staring at me impatiently, so I placed my hand on the door, drawing Victoria's attention. "Maybe they will work better outside." She nodded, joining us. "Ready?" I asked.

They nodded. I shoved open the door, ushering everyone outside as Victoria continued shouting into her phone for Natalie to come get us.

Dr. Stein's voice suddenly came through my phone, but it was still choppy. "You...need—" I kept my eyes out for enemies, cringing at the

sound of distant sirens, wondering if they were headed our way. "Off...
streets—" I took another step towards the street, hoping for Dr. Stein to
give me something useful. "Danger...*hide!*"

"Where?" I shouted, taking another step.

A bottle of glass flew through the air, shattering on the ground in a
roar of sudden green flames at least ten-feet-tall, separating me from
the others. I fumbled my phone into the fire and watched it instantly
vaporize. Two women stepped out from behind a lone car parked on
the street, cackling creepily as they stared at me.

Witches.

8

They had to be witches, judging by the glass vial of flame. But they must have been masking their powers for me not to sense their magic. Had they been working with Dracula's vampires? Was that why I hadn't sensed either?

I watched my foes from a wary crouch, assessing their level of threat. I hadn't squared off against witches since I'd awoken from my long slumber, and I wasn't entirely sure what they were capable of—other than the green fire, obviously. I frowned as their noses suddenly began to bleed. What the hell was that all about? They cocked their heads, jerking their attention towards my friends on the other side of the roaring flames. Through the flickering inferno, I saw Nosh racing away from the restaurant in the direction of his car, carrying Isabella over his shoulder. Victoria was staring at me, torn between who to protect.

"GO!" I shouted at her. "He can't defend himself carrying her! Phoenix!" I snapped, hoping she understood that I wanted her to take Isabella to Dr. Stein's new secret laboratory. The museum was too far and there wasn't any help there. Also, no one knew about Stein's lab.

I hoped.

Victoria nodded stiffly, and I saw her sprint after Nosh—because a third woman was racing after him now, raising her hand as she hurled another glass vial at him with a malevolent laugh. Victoria began firing at her with her pistol, but the woman moved as fast as a snake, zigzagging back and forth as she darted around the corner, already wielding another potion in her hand. Victoria disappeared after her, no longer shooting as she sprinted for all she was worth, a chop-stake in each fist. She had run out of bullets and the witch was still pursuing Nosh and Isabella.

I spun to the other two witches, snarling as I bared my fangs. They were both brunettes and looked no different than any other middle-aged woman I'd seen—nothing to signify that they were more than human. "What the hell is this?" I demanded, drawing their attention from my fleeing friends. "You're working with Dracula's vampires?"

They narrowed their eyes, but the taller one answered in a scratchy voice. "Never! Had we known they were here, we would have brought more of our sisters! We thought you had killed them all when you took over. We came for the vile shaman."

I stared at them in confusion. What were the odds that both groups wanted to murder Nosh on the same night at the same place? And sending four witches after Nosh seemed rather excessive. What had he done to offend them?

"Tell us where the tomahawks are and we will let you live," one of them said.

"No. You won't," I said dryly, not swayed by their obvious lie. I kept the surprise from my face upon hearing them mention the tomahawks. They had to be referring to the ones Nosh and I had hidden with Redford, but hadn't Nosh already retrieved them? At least I now knew why they wanted him dead. But how had they even known about them?

The lead witch licked the blood dripping down from her nose. "You're right. We won't. But if you don't have them, your friends must, because we sensed the cursed blades inside," she said pointing in the direction of Nosh and Victoria.

Wait a minute...

Were they talking about the magic tomahawk Nosh had called up a few moments ago? Did the witches think that was one of the tomahawks we'd taken from his parents' penthouse the night of their murder?

A chilling idea suddenly came to mind. Were Nosh's elemental tomahawks not actually shaman magic like I'd thought? What if they were the very weapons we'd taken from the penthouse? The ones we had entrusted to Redford, to keep safe. I'd seen Nosh use them at the auction shortly after we'd turned over the box, and I had assumed the glowing blades were formed from his shaman magic, not that they were the actual tomahawks we had given to Redford for safekeeping. Had we given him an empty box?

Had Nosh lied to me? Again? And if so, *why*? It had been my idea to grab them in the first place after I'd seen them on the wall and sensed their inner power.

The witch grunted, reading the look on my face. "Aww, the poor dearie didn't know!" she cackled, glancing at her fellow witch as she pointed a wicked dagger at me. "No worries. Our sister will pry them from their cold, dead, fingers. Unfortunately, you won't be around long enough to—"

I closed the distance between us, swinging wildly with my claws, but it was like attacking silk ribbons, their bodies bending unnaturally to evade my strikes. And the moment I focused on one, the other was attacking me from behind, harrowing me. I instantly changed tactics, knowing that I didn't have a lot of blood left in my system for a prolonged fight. Because using my speed and strength also burned away my blood reserves.

I feigned lunging at one, only to pivot at the last second. They both dove forward with their daggers aimed at the spot they had anticipated me to land, almost killing each other and solving my problem for me. It was a near miss, but they did manage to trip each other up. I reared back and kicked one in the spine, laughing as I heard her bones splinter at the overpowered blow, sending her flying out into the street where she landed on all fours like a cat, her body bent strangely where I had broken her spine.

But she didn't seem to register the pain or injury, straightening awkwardly to glare at me.

Her compatriot spun to check on her friend with the shattered spine. She was just in time to see a luxury car slam into the wounded witch at full speed, casting up a spray of gore before the car ran over her with a pair of sickening *thumps*. Natalie was behind the wheel, grinning like a maniac. She slammed on the brakes and the car began to spin wildly before slamming into a light pole, shattering the light and casting the street into darkness as a white balloon exploded out from the steering wheel and struck Natalie in the face, seeming to swallow her.

I winced, using the distraction to decapitate the distracted witch as the sound of many, many approaching sirens filled the streets, much louder than before. They were alarmingly close, and coming from both directions, preventing me from chasing down Nosh, Victoria, and Isabella.

Not with me covered in blood and with a dazed werewolf in tow—because Natalie had destroyed our car. I ran over to her, pouring on the speed as the crumpled hood caught fire. Natalie was struggling with the white balloon, tearing into it with her claws, and her forehead was bleeding steadily. But she was awake and angry, at least. I yanked the entire door from the frame, hurling it behind me. Then I scooped Natalie up from under the shoulders and dragged her away, not wanting to stand beside the car a moment longer than necessary in case it exploded.

Natalie stumbled, regaining her feet in a clumsy shuffle as she shoved me away from the street, pointing to a narrow drive leading back behind the restaurant. Other than the restaurant, the rest of the street consisted of homes, and it looked like Natalie's plan was our only chance to get out of sight. We began jogging down the darkened drive, aiming for the backyards of the houses on the next street. We could hop a few fences to get out of the immediate area, putting some distance between us and the police.

The car exploded behind us and I grunted, increasing my speed. That would draw the police here faster. I wasn't entirely sure that I had the energy to enthrall more than a pair or two of police officers after the fiasco I'd just survived. "Nice driving, Natalie," I said, urging her onward. "You okay?" I asked, concerned by the amount of blood painting her face. I knew werewolves healed fast, but head wounds were dangerous.

Despite my obvious concern, a very strong part of me wanted to grab Natalie by the shoulders and taste some of that hot blood. I was feeling weak after the recent fighting, and she was walking around covered with the one thing that would make me stronger and happier. I gritted my teeth, fighting down my impulses with a shiver of shame.

She nodded, waving off my concern. "Airbag was a bitch, but I'm fine. Please tell me I didn't just kill an innocent old grandmother," she said, glancing over her shoulder.

9

I grinned, shaking my head. "Witch. I think."

"A witch?" Natalie grunted, sounding surprised. "Victoria said vampires—which already didn't make any sense because all Dracula's vampires died."

I grunted. "Looks like he's been sneaking in reinforcements."

Natalie pursed her lips with a growl. "Since when are witches trying to assassinate you?"

I shrugged, hopping over a rickety fence and landing in an ankle-deep inflatable pool. I cursed angrily, especially when Natalie hopped over it as nimble as a deer, despite her injuries from the crash. "Apparently, they coincidentally both tried to assassinate me on the same night," I muttered. "The witches seemed just as surprised about it as me. Or maybe it's more accurate to say the witches tried to kill Nosh the same night that the vampires tried to kill me. Luckily for them, we decided to hang out together tonight."

Natalie frowned, wiping some of the blood out of her eyes. "I didn't smell any witches," she said warily, "but I've definitely never heard of them working with vampires. They hate your kind. They hate everyone but fellow witches," she added. "Where is Victoria?" she asked as we hopped over another fence and into a yard with a vicious guard dog.

I didn't want to kill the creature, not when he was just protecting his family's yard, but he instantly began barking at me in a furious snarl, snapping his teeth at my ankles.

Natalie snarled back at him and the dog yelped, cowering down onto his back and lifting his paws in the air with a submissive whine. "Who's the bitch now?" Natalie snapped, grinning at me. The scarlet blood on her cheeks made my mouth water, but I managed to force down my desires once again to return a smile.

I hopped over the fence and slowed down as we came upon the next street. It was peacefully quiet, but it looked like we had left the residential area for a more commercial one. At least it seemed that way, judging by the metal shutters barring the doors and windows, and the signs hanging overhead.

"What happened, and where are we going?" Natalie asked, scanning the street for threats.

"Isabella's nose started to bleed, and she passed out right after the first witch tried to kill us inside," I told her, slowing to a less conspicuous pace down the sidewalk. "Then the vampires attacked us. Nosh was carrying Isabella to their car and I told Victoria to watch his back since he had his hands full. I was pinned down by a bunch of green fire from one of their glass vials," I muttered.

Detailing the events of the night helped to curb my hunger, and I scanned her face again to make sure her injuries weren't too serious. She was a werewolf, so her healing factor would take care of anything that wasn't immediately life-threatening. That didn't mean she would be up for a fight any time soon, but it did mean I wouldn't have to carry her.

She was staring at me, her face pale. "Isabella's nose started bleeding?" she asked uneasily.

I nodded, frowning. "Yeah. The witches had sudden nosebleeds too," I said slowly, only just now connecting the dots. Natalie grimaced. "What does that mean?"

She stared at me for a few moments, as if debating whether to answer. "I can't say for certain, but I've heard witches get nosebleeds when they encounter witches from other groups or clans or whatever they call themselves."

I skidded to a halt, snatching her wrist. "Other covens? Are you saying Isabella is a witch?" I demanded. "She's a Sister of Mercy. The Nuns with Guns."

Natalie stared back at me. "Maybe she's both, or..."

"Or she isn't really a Sister of Mercy," I said, finishing her thought. I glanced back towards the restaurant and the chorus of sirens, hoping they'd made it out okay. I growled. "Fuck. I lost my phone in the fire."

Natalie checked her own pockets and grunted. "I must have dropped mine in the crash."

I scanned our surroundings, not familiar enough with the city to know exactly where we were or which way to go. But I did have some cash in my pocket. "We need to find one of those yellow coaches. Dr. Stein said the streets aren't safe."

Natalie smirked. "A cab, not a yellow coach. Did Dr. Stein say anything else?"

I shrugged. "She kept cutting out on me, but I think she said her lab is too far away, or maybe she was trying to tell me the lab was in danger," I growled, running a hand through my hair. "All I heard before I lost my phone was *danger...go hide!*"

Natalie skidded to a sudden stop. "Hide?" she asked, sounding suddenly uneasy.

I frowned at her. "Yes. Why?"

She studied me thoughtfully. "I didn't even think about it, but we are very close to him," she said, as if talking to herself. She noticed the confused look on my face and sighed. "Hyde, not hide. I think she was telling you where to go. It's a name."

I shrugged. "Maybe. It has to be better than here," I said, indicating the sound of sirens.

She nodded, glancing up at a nearby sign. "We're only a few blocks away from Tequila Mockingbird. That's his bar. He's a...well, I'm not really sure what he is. He's kind of a jack of all trades. Need a job done and he can probably do it for you, no matter how difficult."

I arched an eyebrow. "Okay. Maybe he'll have a phone so we can check on the others at least." Natalie nodded, using her sleeves to wipe away more blood. She'd stopped bleeding, which was a good sign. It would also be less distracting for me. "Which way?"

"Follow me. I hope you heard her right," she said in resignation, tugging me down the sidewalk.

"Why?" I asked as Natalie turned at the next street, leading us down an even darker, emptier section of the city. It looked practically abandoned, as if the businesses had closed long ago. For sale signs lined the street, sending a foreboding chill down my neck.

"Mr. Hyde has somewhat of a temper, and doesn't like strangers," Natalie said.

Two old women rounded the corner up ahead, making their way towards us, using four-legged canes to shuffle down the sidewalk at a turtle's pace. They were probably residents of the neighboring residential areas we had left behind. Natalie used her sleeve to wipe off the rest of the blood on her face, not wanting to startle the old women who were chatting back and forth as they shuffled their walking aides ahead of them with a repetitive scuffing sound followed by a thud.

It had to be harder to lug those things around than it was to just walk with a cane. Metal wasn't light. I nudged Natalie, discreetly pointing. "What are those?"

"Walkers. Helps them move around easier," she said.

"Made of metal? Aren't they heavy?" I asked.

She shook her head. "Lighter than wood, probably. It's made of aluminum."

I frowned suspiciously. Metal that was lighter than wood? It had to be hollow. That was the only explanation. They were drawing close enough for me to overhear them bickering with each other. We came upon a dark alley, and Natalie hesitated, sniffing at the air.

The two old women continued ambling down the sidewalk, bickering back and forth.

Just as I was about to ask Natalie what she was doing, a chilling laugh suddenly bubbled out from deep within the alley. The two old women paused, glancing nervously towards the darkness as if reconsidering the direction of their walk.

"Witch," Natalie whispered. "I can smell her skanky ass."

I stared deep into the alley, wondering why she would give away her presence.

Then I heard matching laughs from behind us, but lower, throatier, like bubbles rising up from a swamp. I spun to see the two old women shuffling our way, cackling gleefully.

Shit. A trap.

10

The witches had to be in their eighties and wore scarves wound around their heads like hoods with thick, tattered, woolen cloaks trailing down their backs. They stared at us with merciless, violent eyes. They were both still hunched over their walkers, but their eyes glinted like polished obsidian. They looked to be twins; the only differentiation was the color of their shawls. One wore a stained red shawl and the other a swampy green.

"He looks as if he's seen a ghost, Lucille," the one in the red shawl said.

Lucille chuckled, tugging absently at her green shawl. "We are far worse, Camille."

I shook my head, turning from the green shawled Lucille to the red shawled Camille with a grimace. "I'm just trying to process how terrible your father must feel for not putting your mother out of her misery during childbirth. To have one beast for a daughter is a curse, but to have twins..." I shuddered. "It would have been kinder to leave you to the wolves." I glanced at Natalie. "A point we can rectify. Immediately."

Natalie growled hungrily, her eyes twinkling.

The witches hissed simultaneously, their hunched backs trembling as they clutched their walkers.

Lucille tapped her ear, speaking into an earbud as she stared at the alley behind us. "Don't dawdle, Agatha. Dinner has been served," she clucked with a cruel laugh that sounded like gravel dribbling out of a bag.

I cast the elderly witches a wary look, wondering why I couldn't sense any power from them.

A young, beautiful woman—Agatha, I assumed—sauntered out from the shadows about thirty yards down the alley, smirking at us and licking her lips. She had a ridged scar on her cheek, but other than that, I couldn't find a single blemish to mar her perfection.

And she was powerful. Alarmingly powerful. Although she seemed to be the only one with magic—according to my senses, anyway, which I knew were not as reliable as I hoped—she seemed submissive to the twin matrons with the walkers.

"So, you're the new blood-sucker in town. Pleased to eat you," Camille said.

"Meet?" I asked, hoping to clarify.

She simply shook her head, grinning toothily. "Eat."

"You've caused quite enough trouble for us, boy," Lucille said.

"Yet you've given us such a lovely gift—ridding us of Dracula's influence. Now it's a city ripe for the boiling," Camille added, grinning through a mouth of missing teeth.

I placed a calming hand on Natalie's shoulder since she looked ready to rip the two old women to shreds with her bare hands. She kept darting her head back to Agatha, who was steadily making her way closer to us, not seeming to be in any hurry.

"What do you want?" Natalie growled warningly. "Even three of you don't stand a chance against us."

The twins chuckled ominously. "You underestimate our resolve, child," Camille said. "All we wanted tonight was the shaman, but you stuck your nose in where it didn't belong."

"We will be taking you to our Black Sabbath, of course," Lucille added, her hands fiddling with her walker. She released it and shuffled a few steps closer to us, her back bowed like she was carrying a boulder over her shoulder. "Blasted potion is a nuisance," she cursed. "My tits are practically touching my knees, sister," she muttered to her twin.

"It will wear off soon," Camille said, releasing her own walker. "Once you get enough fresh blood on your hands to wash it off, of course."

"I do love getting my hands dirty," she cackled, bobbing her head up and down—which looked chilling combined with the bulging hump in her back. "But I hate having to give up my magic, even for pleasure."

"Then slice swiftly, sister. Bite deeply. Bathe your arms in their blood and you'll get your magic back. I think I would rather take my time." She eyed us like slabs of meat at a butcher. "With one of them, anyway."

Then they were both shuffling closer at a limping pace, not having their walkers to aid them.

I shot Natalie an incredulous look. "Is this some kind of joke? Let's just *hobble* away from them. We don't even have to jog."

Natalie was staring at their hands with her lips pulled back in a snarl. "This is bad, Sorin. Very bad."

And I realized the twin hags were clutching wickedly curved daggers in each hand, both stained with a dark substance.

I heard a sharp grunt from the alley, and I spun, almost having forgotten about Agatha—the witch who still had her magic. She had made a sound upon lobbing a glass vial up into the air. I yanked Natalie back in case it was more of the intense green flame.

The glass broke and a thick blanket of black fog suddenly crashed into the street. Every single lamppost for a hundred feet abruptly winked out as miniature orbs of black fog zipped upwards to cover them, plunging the street into complete darkness.

My eyes instantly adjusted, shifting my surroundings into a tapestry of light and dark grays—as if the colors of the rainbow had been replaced with all the possible shades of lethal blades.

The twin hags stared at us, and their suddenly pointed teeth glinted like polished, sharpened steel despite there being no light to cause a reflection. Their eyes had also changed, now glowing like green flames in the darkness—the only spots of color in my vision.

Agatha, likewise, featured the same metal teeth and fiery green eyes.

Whether the two old hags had magic or not, they were obviously more dangerous than they appeared, having ingested some potion to trade away their physical forms and their magic for these hunch-backed beasts.

But Agatha still had her magic—whatever that meant. Were their powers limited to these potions they kept flinging about in those glass vials, or could they actually do something directly?

A sudden chorus of angry meowing sounds rose up, making the hair on the back of my neck stand on end as the black fog eddied around my feet. I noticed at least a dozen pairs of glowing, feline eyes now surrounding us, trapping us inside a circle with the witches. Making things even worse, they didn't remain still long enough for me to accurately assess the size or scope of our new boundaries. Instead, they prowled left and right, back and forth, in a jarring, unsynchronized tempo, disorienting me so that I had to force myself to look away from those yellow eyes or risk tripping over my own feet.

"Fucking cats!" Natalie snarled, her forearms suddenly covered in golden fur and ending in long, black claws where her fingers had been. "Something is preventing me from fully shifting! I can only call upon my claws!"

I wondered if that was the purpose of the circling felines. Canines and felines were often depicted as mortal enemies in my day. Was their presence keeping Natalie's full werewolf form restrained?

As if my thought had been a summons, an offended yowl was all the warning I received before one of the vermin abruptly struck me from behind, latching onto my head with a maddened, coughing hiss. I cursed, snatching at it with my claws and violently flinging it away. The creature's claws scraped my cheek in the process and I instantly knew we were not dealing with typical cats. I grunted, feeling suddenly dizzy as my cheek burned like fire. "Silver. The cats have silver claws," I snarled, forcing myself to fight through the pain.

Natalie swore, comprehending just how dangerous that was to us. "Kill *everything*."

One of the hags laughed delightedly but I couldn't tell which one since both of their shawls looked the same in the darkness. "Oh, not my pretties. They came here for a meal and they are *so* hungry, the poor dearies."

I saw another pair of eyes gleaming at me from an alley, attempting to slink closer while I was distracted. I tapped into my blood reserves and tried to call forth my shadow and blood cloak to shield us from the felines, but I gasped in pain as a sharp warning pain bloomed in my chest. I gritted my teeth and snarled. I didn't have enough blood inside me to call it up—not with me using so much of my reserves back at the restaurant and my body fighting to heal the silver-claw wound on my cheek.

Instead, I went back to the basics. I formed a crystallized dagger of blood and shadow to hang suspended in the air before me. Even that small of a task was alarmingly difficult, and I knew I would have to end this fight fast or hope Natalie could save the day. I flung out a hand, hurling the blood crystal to impale the creature—the witch's familiar—to the wall.

It yowled and screeched loud enough to make me flinch, and I watched in horror as a darker, inky black fog drifted out of the dead familiar and then zipped towards three nearby allies.

All three of them abruptly grew larger, absorbing the soul of the familiar I had killed.

"We have a problem," I snarled at Natalie, trying to count how many familiars we had to deal with, and trying not to think about just how large the last cat standing might end up being.

"You have *many* problems," one of the hags cooed.

"We can take you dead or alive, but either way, you will lead us to the shaman and his tomahawks. Our mistress would prefer you alive so she can make your death slow," Agatha said in a sweet, strangely cheerful tone, licking the tips of her pointed teeth.

"And meat is so much better after it's been tenderized," one of the hags said.

"And easier on the teeth. The few I have left, anyway," she said, grinding her mismatched teeth together hard enough to emit sparks. Which made her old snaggle-toothed Camille.

"What have I done to offend your mistress, and why does she want the shaman?" I asked, knowing I wouldn't be able to get an explanation after I killed them all.

"That is not our concern. We obey!" they hissed in unison.

Then the two hags were scuttling forward like crabs, darting from side-to-side with stunning speed. I let out my claws, ready to spill some blood. Natalie risked a quick glance my way, her lip curling up at the corner in a macabre smile. "I'm more than enough bitch for three witches," she said in a surprisingly calm tone, revealing the reasoning for Stevie choosing her as a werewolf lieutenant. "You take the...Pussy Witch Muffs, or whatever we're calling the cats," she smirked in amusement at her nickname for them.

"What does that even *mean*?" I asked, dodging a flurry of attacks from Lucille before she slipped out of my reach.

"*The Three Billy Goats Gruff* fairy tale," Natalie said as if it explained everything, keeping her eyes on the other two witches as they circled us. "Beat down one and their bigger brother comes after you. A cat is sometimes called a pussy—"

Ruining both her explanation and her suggested enemy allocation, three cats suddenly lunged at her back. She managed to sidestep at the last second, slicing the three of them in half in one brutal swipe. Camille barely missed Natalie's spine with her dark dagger as she scuttled past the werewolf, trying to get in a cheap shot.

The same inky orbs zipped through the air from the three dead familiars, making the surviving familiars bigger—the size of large dogs now.

She pointed a bloody claw at them. "Pussy Witch Muffs," she hooted with a satisfied grin.

"I'm not calling them that," I muttered.

11

I pivoted to dodge another dagger swipe from Lucille's poisoned blade as she caught me staring at her familiars and their constantly shifting boundary. I struck her hunched back and it popped like a balloon, startling me as it began spraying a thick, pungent smoke. I coughed and wheezed, my vision suddenly going dark—no longer able to see in the blackness.

Lucille laughed delightedly—the sound whipping from behind me to in front of me and then gone again, but I couldn't see anything. Cats yowled and screeched in the darkness, but I couldn't see them either. I couldn't see *anything*, and my counterattack hadn't even seemed to harm the witch. In fact, she was toying with my blindness. If she'd wanted me dead in those few moments of confusion, she easily could have done so. My body was already beginning to ache from lack of blood, and some of Natalie's wounds must have opened as she fought, because it suddenly took every fiber of my being to restrain myself as the sweet scent of her blood struck my nostrils. Panic coupled with hunger was a great way to turn me into a mindless beast.

I took a calming breath to clear my head, and I heard their taunting laughs, and breaths, and footsteps dancing around me like a whirlwind of dead leaves—always just out of reach.

That's when it hit me. I didn't need my eyes. The gifts I had received from Artemis had made me a vampire, but they'd been given to me to become the world's best hunter. They had not been limited to my *sight*.

I also had enhanced *hearing*.

I immediately focused on heartbeats, distinguishing Natalie's from my foes so as not to accidentally kill her the moment I chose to go on the offensive. I heard a faint rustle before Natalie roared, slashing harmlessly at one of the cackling witches. "I can't see!" she snarled.

"Use your nose!" I snapped. I heard a faint pattering of feet rapidly approaching and I locked onto the thudding heartbeat just as one of the familiars struck my leg. Thanks to my hearing, I managed to stab it with my claws the moment it touched me, impaling it before the silver claws reached my flesh. I swiped wildly, hoping to destroy the inky orb that I knew was escaping the dead familiar—even though I couldn't see it. I felt no resistance, so I had either missed entirely or my claws were ineffective against it.

"I can't smell anything but that fucking smoke!" Natalie shouted, sneezing.

I gritted my teeth, successfully leaning away from a slashing dagger just in time to avoid contact. "Pick another sense! Hear their pulses! You're a goddamned hunter, Natalie. HUNT!"

"Gladly," she snarled. I heard Agatha suddenly let out a gasping scream, followed by a hollow, wet *splat* that reminded me of a bursting melon.

I heard the twins shriek as if they shared in Agatha's pain, but a gurgling cough cut one of those screams short. I didn't waste a moment, lunging towards the last witch. My claw tore through flesh at what I hoped was throat level for the hunch-backed hag, resulting in a moist, bubbling gasp and a spray of hot blood over my face. Luckily, I'd kept my mouth closed, expecting as much if my aim struck true.

The blinding smoke slowly began to dissipate. I took that as a good sign, relieved to find my vision incrementally returning.

Before I could verify my kill, I sensed a deep thumping heartbeat leaping through the air behind the hag, intending to hit me head-on from over her shoulder. I flung one hand up just in time to see my claws tear through the chest of a large feline the size of a panther. It snapped its silver fangs at me, showering me in sparks. I reared back and stabbed through its throat with my other hand, not daring to bite the familiar for fear that the blood was somehow tainted. Hot blood poured down my arm, but it smelled foul, confirming my assumption that the blood was poisoned.

Which meant that I couldn't risk taking a drink to restore my blood reserves. Still left with just my claws and my heightened senses. I shoved off the massive familiar and narrowed my eyes as I watched a much larger black orb zip out of the dead body. I had no idea how large the last familiar would be, but it wasn't looking promising. I already felt like sitting down and calling it quits.

But I couldn't quit. I never quit. Stagnation was death, movement was life.

So, I focused my attention, counting the remaining enemy heartbeats. I was stunned to find that the two hags were still alive, although one was bleeding profusely from her neck and the other had a nasty gut-wound that would kill her very slowly if she didn't find help soon. What really shocked me was that they were both squaring off against Natalie, on the verge of one final attack. Natalie crouched warily in a silent challenge.

She no longer had her claws out, letting me realize how exhausted she must be.

Seeing that Natalie was unarmed against her foes, I gritted my teeth and formed the last of my blood reserves into foot-long daggers of shadow and blood. I was only able to form two of them, and even that almost failed.

"Get down, Natalie," I whispered, feeling suddenly dizzy at the aggregate of energy I'd used. Knowing I couldn't wait any longer, I weakly flung out my hand, sending the crystals at Lucille and Camille. The blood crystals struck them between the eyes like spikes hammered into stone, sinking entirely through their skulls. They died before they could even make a sound, crumpling to the street.

I felt a sudden sense of vertigo and stars had begun to twinkle at the edges of my vision when an unseen hand suddenly grabbed me by the back of my neck and yanked my head downward.

I expected pain, opening my mouth to cry out.

Instead, my lips met the feverish flesh of a graceful, familiar neck as an even warmer, lithe body backed up against my torso, contorting to press every inch of her against me like the missing piece of a puzzle. The sweet taste of cinnamon and salt exploded across my tongue in a tantalizing pairing and I managed to let out a heady moan of pleasure, wondering if I was dreaming. My vantage from over her shoulder allowed my gaze to rove over her slick, silky skin and feast on the swell of her breasts only inches away from my nose.

"Drink *deeply*," Natalie purred, angling her head high to rest against my opposite collarbone so as to give me plenty of exposed shoulder and neck in which to feast upon. "I *need* you."

I hesitated, understanding the need—hers and mine—that we would soon be killed by the familiars if I didn't regain some power from her blood. We would both die. Here. Now.

But It would leave us momentarily vulnerable while I feasted. I also knew how dangerous it was in our current weakened states—my control was practically nonexistent. It was a risk to take time for a drink, but we didn't stand a chance unless I did.

"I *told* you," Natalie demanded, sounding annoyed by my reluctance. "You're going to have some fucking dessert tonight, Sorin, even if I have to force-feed you myself." True to her word, she took matters into her own hands.

Literally.

Her right hand wrapped around me to squeeze my ass like an anchor, trapping me in place. Then her free hand abruptly untucked the front of my shirt, snapping the buttons in her haste. Her sweaty palm trailed down my abdomen and slipped below the waist of my pants, her deft fingers dancing as they hungrily explored my skin in search of only one thing.

Before I knew it, she curled her silken fingers around my manhood, grabbing onto me and squeezing in a fever-hot grip that almost made my eyes roll back in my head, banishing all thoughts of concern.

I instinctively sunk my fangs deep into her neck with a desperate moan, encouraged by her shuddering whimper as her grip on me clenched tight enough to almost hurt. As her hot blood streamed down my throat, rapidly strengthening me, I realized that she had made an excellent point earlier in the car.

She was indeed a *great little dessert place.*

I suddenly remembered the familiars still circling us. Luckily, the deaths of their witches must have staggered them. Either that, or they were waiting for me to become too distracted by my feeding to notice a sudden coordinated attack. My fear of them trumped my carnal starvation.

Kind of.

Even as I guzzled Natalie, I immediately partitioned some of her blood to call up a rapidly rotating circle of dozens of blood crystals to surround us in a threatening ring of violence, daring the surviving familiars to interrupt us. They yowled in outrage. I hadn't ever done that before—using my victim's blood for my powers without fully absorbing it into my body.

It was more than Natalie could handle as the first orgasm ripped through her body in a convulsive tremor. Her fingers squeezed my rock-hard manhood and I cradled her tighter against me so her legs wouldn't give out.

I refused to let her fall. I wasn't finished yet.

Despite her weak knees, Natalie's hand remained fully functional, and she had no intention of releasing her prize anytime soon. In fact...

Her hand began to squeeze and stroke in a slow, sensual rhythm that matched the speed of me gulping down her blood, and her breathless panting was rapidly fanning the tender flames of our budding passion into a blazing inferno that would not be easily or quietly doused.

I sucked harder on her neck, hungrily trying to keep up with the increasing tempo of her desperate stroking as I drew her blood into me, joining us as one being. A strange foreign power began to grow between us, bringing us closer than merely a vampire and his nourishment.

A man and a woman.

Something...different...was taking place in addition to her frenzied passion and my frantic feeding. She panted hoarsely, writhing her body up and down against mine, still squeezing my ass with her other hand to hold me close and prevent me from separating. In response, I wrapped my arm around her waist, locking her in place as I guzzled her blood.

The tips of her breasts hardened as she arched her back, and I watched her bosom flush red from inches away.

MINE! my inner demon crowed within my head. *TAKE HER NOW! IN THE STREET!*

I managed to restrain myself from his demand—but only barely, and only because I knew we were still in grave danger, even with the protective ring of daggers circling us, warning the familiars back.

My pulse thundered in my ears as that strange magic continued melding us together, reminding me of something else I'd recently felt, but it was all I could do to keep drinking and force myself not to rip her clothes off and follow my inner demon's suggestion.

It wasn't love. It wasn't even lust. It was a *necessity*, fueled by that strange magic binding us together. Even more bizarre, tendrils of that magic seemed to be reaching out into the ether, searching for something unseen—a third anchor point in which to take root, bringing us all together as one.

Another climax caused Natalie to whimper huskily and redouble her efforts, fighting against me and herself for a better grip—torn between not wanting to break contact and desperately needing to briefly separate so as to find a more mutually beneficial body position.

I could now smell her lust in the air—an intoxicating perfume that threatened to shatter my tentative hold on rationality. As much as my body wanted her, some other part of me did not.

And above even those sensations, I knew we were still in very real danger despite my protective ring of blood crystals warning the familiars back.

12

I sensed the precise moment that the familiars chose to act, their heartbeats rapidly speeding up as they bolted towards us. I threw my hand out as I continued to lap up Natalie's precious life fluid —again, I used her blood to directly power the daggers' flight rather than tapping into my own reserves.

My blood daggers—easily two feet long now and covered in sinister thorns and wicked barbs of more crystallized blood—whipped out, ripping through every single enemy heart around me. With my enhanced senses, I felt and heard each of the hearts shatter and explode in a crescendo of carnage, an orchestra of obliteration, a symphony of screams as the familiars wailed and died.

But this macabre music was accompanied by Natalie's screams of pure rapture, because the moment I'd used her blood again, a trio of orgasms had roared through her, making her legs buckle as her cries of euphoria rose triumphantly above the sounds of shattered hearts, creating a hellacious harmony.

The only thing keeping her upright was my grip around her waist as her body bucked and writhed against mine, her whimpering instinctively making me bite deeper and suck harder.

TAKE HER! my demon screamed, incoherent in its desire. *HERE! NOW! MAKE HER VERY SOUL SCREAM WITH PLEASURE!*

The strange—unseen but definitely felt—vines of magic entwining us together doubled in thickness, the roots now reaching out from both of us to search for our missing third part. I felt like a sword thrust into the fires of the hottest forge and I knew I was only moments away from crossing the point of no return.

Natalie regained the use of her legs and I could tell by her sudden strength that she was about to make the decision for me, even if the price for attaining that pinnacle of bliss was her life.

Two simple words managed to finally slither past my primal urges, and they stopped me like an icy waterfall, momentarily snapping me out of my depthless hunger. With a choked gasp, I released Natalie from my bite and shoved her away before I lost that flicker of rationality.

I flung my head back and screamed, needing an outlet before I exploded. Natalie's powerful werewolf blood and our strange new bond raged within me, frothing and foaming as it soaked my insides like hot, sensual oil. My arms shot down to my sides and every muscle in my body locked rigid.

Natalie cried out, having fallen to the ground on all fours with her back to me. I lowered my head, panting as I stared down at her submissive posture—fighting back the dark urges that swamped over me. Her hair hung down her jawline like sinister wings, dripping with blood and sweat and raw, undiluted passion. She slowly glanced over her shoulder at me, her eyes blazing with a fiery green glow as she bit her lip hard enough to make it bleed.

In that look, I knew there would be no sating her. Whatever that strange magic had been between us was permanent, and it wasn't going to be stopped by mere words.

Especially not the two words that had ultimately stopped *me*.

Victoria Helsing.

"Take me," she pleaded in a hoarse whisper, slowly swaying her hips at me.

I shuddered at her tone, fighting against every primitive bone in my body as I repeated Victoria Helsing's name in my mind like a last-ditch prayer. Natalie's eyes were filmed over with mindless lust—literally unable to control her wild desire to be ravaged here in the middle of the street.

Because her blood had already been burning up from our fight with the witches. Although having been unable to fully shift, she'd been forced to call her inner wolf closer to the surface in order to survive, needing to rely on instinct rather than rationality.

And our two inner monsters were of the same opinion. They had earned a reward for their hard work and demanded payment.

Only Victoria Helsing's name had managed to snap me out of my mindless lust, and Natalie didn't have such a totem to bring her back under control.

She had saved our lives by offering me her blood, yet I had been too hungry to properly establish a buffer between our inner monsters. Instead, I had unwittingly bonded us together, actively using her blood to empower my blood daggers rather than calling upon my own reserves. I hadn't even known such a thing was possible.

And there had been those exploratory vines searching out to a third party. I knew they had somehow latched onto their target, joining the three of us together, because I could sense faint echoes from both Natalie and another person far off in the distance.

And I was almost certain that it was Victoria Helsing.

Thoughts of our new bond evaporated as I sensed a massive force leaping towards me from the side. I lunged forward, yanking Natalie up by the arm to toss her out of harm's way.

One last familiar—somehow it had evaded the attack that had ended its brethren—struck the pavement where I had been standing, pulverizing the concrete with its silver claws before momentum sent it careening off into a lamppost, bending the metal and shattering the bulb above. I was surprised to see that the black clouds were still covering the streetlights—thinking they should have dissipated when the last witch died. Glass showered down over the hulking feline, and I grunted to find that it was now the size of a small car. It had long, thick fur and paws as wide as tires as it hissed at me with silver teeth the size of small swords. Its tail swished back and forth overhead as it hunkered low, preparing to pounce.

Natalie lay in a heap, unable to stand or snap out of her fervent lust.

I squared my shoulders against the familiar, stepping between it and Natalie as I tapped into my now pregnant blood reserves to call upon my cloak of shadows and blood. "Just you and me," I said, baring my teeth as my cloak whipped and snapped around my shoulders like a nest of disturbed vipers.

The familiar leapt into the air from twenty feet away, easily capable of closing the distance. I heard a furious honking sound behind me as two beams of light struck the familiar's eyes, making its pupils dilate. My own eyes widened in recognition and I instantly changed tactics. I shifted into a cloud of crimson mist, and an overloaded dump truck ripped through me without causing any harm—although it was extremely uncomfortable to suddenly be displaced by such a large force.

The massive truck had been driving entirely too fast—likely not seeing us in the darkened, deserted street—and it struck the familiar with an explosion of snapping bone, screaming metal, and the damp splash of blood and gore. The dump truck slammed on its brakes too late, and the smell of burnt rubber filled the air, fighting for dominance over the putrid stench of offal and smoke from the damaged engine.

I heard a terrible squealing sound as the driver tried to force the warped metal door open, and I instantly coalesced back into my typical human form, diving for Natalie. I covered us both in my cloak, mentally shifting it to the blackest of shadows so that the driver couldn't see us. Natalie latched onto me, taking my sudden embrace as an invitation to pick up where we had left off moments ago. I tried to remain as still as possible while protecting myself from Natalie's eager hands and mouth, needing all my attention to conceal us from the man who suddenly fell out of the dump truck, cursing up a storm.

"What the FUCK was that?" he shouted to no one in particular. "Was it a fucking kid? Oh my god, tell me it wasn't a fucking kid. HELLO?" he called out, cupping his hands around his mouth. His wild eyes swept over us without notice, only seeing a smear of shadow on the already dark street as he tried to find whatever had destroyed his truck. I wanted to be gone before he found it—or the dead witches.

I panted hoarsely as Natalie began tugging at my pants hard

enough to almost snap the button. Instead of fighting her and possibly drawing the driver's attention, I held my breath and let her work freely. The moment the driver looked the other way, I instantly leaned back and punched Natalie in the jaw, knocking her unconscious. Then I hoisted her over my shoulder and ran into the alley, hoping it was in the direction of Mr. Hyde's place that Natalie had mentioned—*Tequila Mockingbird*.

I heard the driver shout out in surprise, but I was already down the opposite end of the alley, leaping over a parked car before crossing the next street. Strangely enough, it had rained on this street, even though the one with the witches had been dry. Natalie hung slumped over the back of my neck, her body hot to the touch. I used one hand to hold her head steady over my left shoulder and the other to grip a handful of her naked ass over my right shoulder.

Because at some point, she had started tugging down her pants before I knocked her out.

I bit down on my lip, hoping that the pain would distract my mind from both the feel of her sweaty flesh and the heady perfume of her earlier arousal. Being a vampire, the smells of sex and desire were as strong a scent as freshly-cooked bacon was to humans.

And even more enticing.

I bit my lip harder, ignoring every sensation but the pounding of my feet on the damp pavement. Even those wet slaps taunted me, reminding me that I still held a pleasant handful of Natalie's bare ass.

I bit my lip hard enough to pierce skin this time and adjusted my grip on the werewolf.

Natalie moaned absently, still unconscious but coming to.

I felt that faint echo of our new bond in the distance and let out an uneasy sigh. "It really was just dessert, but Victoria is definitely going to kill me," I added, thinking of the times I had so nobly chosen *not* to take the vampire hunter to my bed. If I had done so, Victoria might have been able to give me the benefit of the doubt about tonight's adventures. As it stood now, I didn't like my odds.

I imagined my gravestone.

Here lies Sorin. Nobility killed him, but sex would have saved him.

13

I had covered at least six blocks before I found a relatively quiet street far away from both crime scenes we had left behind. Natalie had murmured *Poole Street* a few times as I ran, so I'd stopped here upon seeing a sign of that very name, hoping she hadn't been dreaming about something else that was located on Poole Street. I set her down and pulled her pants all the way up, hoping that Victoria didn't choose this exact moment to find me. Natalie was slowly coming awake, mumbling unintelligibly to herself as if dreaming. I gently shook her shoulder. She murmured sleepily before opening her eyes and blinking at me.

"It's okay," I reassured her. "We're safe."

Her eyes widened and she swept our surroundings, realizing we were in an entirely different place. She let out a nervous breath, licking her lips. She carefully touched her jaw where I had punched her. "Tell me it wasn't one of the old hags who clocked me."

I kept my face blank, shaking my head. "It was Agatha. I think you returned the favor by breaking her head open like a melon."

Natalie nodded with a faint smile. "I think I remember that."

"Do you remember anything else?" I asked hesitantly.

She rolled her neck, loosening up stiff muscles. "Bits and pieces. I made you bite me—" She suddenly went still, meeting my eyes with a familiar hunger. "Tell me we had sex."

I shook my head firmly. "No. Absolutely not."

She frowned playfully. "Damn." She lifted her hand as if trying to pinch something out of the air before her. "What is this? I can feel something between us right here," she explained, pinching at the empty air again.

I sighed, sensing the bond between us as well. "I'm not entirely sure, but we somehow bonded when I bit you. Could be because we were both severely weakened or it could be something else," I admitted with a shrug.

Natalie licked her lips, sniffing at the air curiously. "But it's not just us, is it? There's another person in this bond," she said, testing out the word. She indicated another unseen cord stretching off into the distance—the same direction where I felt our third member.

"I think so, but we'll have to wait to find out more. We need to get to Tequila Mockingbird," I reminded her. "You mentioned Poole Street while you were unconscious," I explained, gesturing behind me.

She nodded, squinting her eyes. Then she grunted, pointing over my shoulder and giving me a suspicious frown, as if she thought I was trying to trick her. "That's Tequila Mockingbird."

I glanced back to see a nondescript building across the road. A set of stairs led down to a level below the street, and an aged, peeling sign read, *Tequila Mockingbird*.

I grunted, shaking my head. "Oh. Then I found it."

She chuckled, holding out her hand for me to pull her to her feet. I did and she immediately paused, glancing down at her unbuttoned pants. Then she shot me a sinister grin.

I held out my hands, shaking my head. "You took them off. I didn't know how to button them back up without waking you—only to suffer you decapitating me on reflex."

She grinned, nodding her agreement. "Now is when you tell me what really happened," she said dryly. "Why you punched me in the jaw and blamed it on Agatha. I think I can sense your lies with this new bond."

I stared at her, wincing. "Well...it happened pretty fast..." I explained quickly, doing my best to recount the whole affair without making her sound like a sex-crazed lunatic. She stared at me with wide eyes, listening to every word. I could feel her focusing on our bond as if testing it for lies, so I stuck to the pure truth.

I was very concerned about the new bond. In some ways, it was similar to me making a human blood slave, but where they would have been openly submissive, nothing about Natalie felt submissive. She was definitely agreeable, but I knew she was still herself.

I was simply learning that *herself* was very interested in sexual escapades—at least with me. Despite now having her mental faculties restored—unlike earlier when she'd been overcome by instinct—I knew what her answer would be if I asked her to have sex. Right here in the alley.

A resounding *yes*.

In a way, this revelation was much worse for me. Natalie wasn't brain-washed, she was simply determined to get what she wanted from me—which would result in Victoria killing me. I couldn't tell if it was a direct consequence of our new bond, or if our new bond was simply forcing her to openly admit her personal feelings.

And Natalie was well aware of my feelings for Victoria.

I wondered if Natalie was willingly submitting herself to me, much like an alpha controlled a subordinate werewolf. Submission meant something else entirely when it came to werewolves. They were independently dominant with a complicated hierarchy. By their definition, submissive meant *respectfully obedient*. If they wanted to argue with their alpha, they would—and he would bite back hard to put them in their place if they stepped out of line.

I was very concerned that I had accidentally blood-bonded her. I'd done it to willing humans before—my old blood slaves.

But never a willing werewolf.

Because there was the very strong chance that I had just stolen her from her alpha, Stevie, and I didn't know how to break it. If she was entirely agreeable with her new vampire master, then I stood no chance of breaking it. Stevie was nowhere near strong enough to overpower my control over Natalie because she wanted me *more*.

Much like I had bonded Hugo, Aristos, Valentine, and Renfield to my command. Except she was a female werewolf and we'd shared blood via a hypersexual bond before.

Only someone stronger than me could take it over, and Stevie was the strongest werewolf in New York City. But was he capable of breaking our bond? I knew beyond a shadow of a doubt that he couldn't best me in a fight, but he might know another way to fix the problem.

One problem at a time, I thought to myself.

"Let's go find a phone and get off the roads," Natalie said, tugging me across Poole Street. It looked like the rest of the area was mostly residential and that someone had converted their basement into a restaurant. "You just jogged through town with a naked werewolf slung over your shoulder. Imagine how that must have looked."

I grunted. "You weren't naked," I argued stubbornly.

"I have a bruise on my right cheek that says otherwise," she said, swatting her rump playfully to clarify that she wasn't talking about her face. "In the shape of a horny vampire's hand."

I narrowed my eyes at her, and she burst out laughing. "Maybe I should have just dragged you by your hair," I muttered.

She cast me a hungry grin. "Sounds kinky. Let's do it."

This time I actually blushed. "Just stop, Natalie. Victoria is going to kill me."

She nodded thoughtfully, pulling me down the stairs. "Don't worry, Sorin. I'll talk to her. Woman-to-woman." I nodded gratefully. "But I mean every word, Sorin," she said, squeezing my hand. I looked into her eyes to let her know that I was paying attention. "You. Me. We're going to break a bed together, Sorin. I *promise*." She noticed the startled look on my face and rolled her eyes. "I'm not looking for your eternal love. Victoria can have your heart—I just want to be a part. I just want this," she said, seeming to indicate our shared bond.

Then she was turning away, leaving me to gape at her with a stunned look on my face. I was pretty sure that was not how things worked. And we didn't need to have sex to maintain our bond. "We will talk about it," I said, running a hand through my hair.

"We just did, Sorin. We just did."

I was entirely sure that her supposed woman-to-woman talk with

Victoria was going to be a bloodbath, and that it would somehow be all my fault.

I let out a defeated sigh. Then I leaned close to the door, listening. I could hear faint violin music playing inside, so I was assuming it was open for business—even at this late hour. I tugged open the door and motioned Natalie to enter ahead of me. I warily glanced back at the street before following her inside and gently closing the door behind me. Luckily, I had been paying attention, because six wide wooden steps led down to the floor.

Lively violin music played from unseen speakers, but it wasn't loud enough to be distracting. The place had a heavy, pleasant aroma of old cigar smoke, reminding me of a thick, comforting blanket. The room was dim and full of heavy wooden tables and rickety chairs—not quite a tavern from my era, but definitely a place out of time. A bar, as they called drinking establishments these days.

Everything consisted of exquisitely carved wood, complete with beauty scars and worn edges, from the rather high ceiling to the solid flooring. A bar stood against the adjacent wall, and a man in a crisp, white, dress shirt with rolled up sleeves stared at me. He wore suspenders and had a large, bushy, curled mustache that looked as thick as a broom. His hair was slicked over to one side, not a single strand out of place.

"What'll it be, lass? Lad?" he asked in a brusque, no-nonsense voice as he absently polished a glass with a white hand towel. His forearms were layered with corded muscle, thick hair, and impressive scars, letting me know that he was no stranger to violence. He was an old lover of that macabre mistress—maybe even her first.

A mirror covered the wall behind him, and shelves of dusty liquor bottles hung from the reflective surface. My lips thinned, realizing that I didn't want to stand in front of that mirror. Not with this quietly dangerous man as the barkeep. The calm, silent types were often the deadliest of foes.

We seemed to be the only patrons in the room besides him.

"Barkeep's choice," I said with a carefully polite smile. I wasn't here to make friends, but I wasn't here to make enemies either. I just needed to get to a phone to check on Victoria, Nosh, and Isabella. I had a lot of work left to do yet tonight and dealing with the witches hadn't been on that list. Despite my plans, I knew I hadn't seen the last of them. They wanted Nosh's head—and probably mine after tonight.

The barkeep kept his eyes on me, setting the glass down as his curled mustache rose above his amused smirk. "Is that so?"

I slowly nodded. "It is."

Natalie piped up, sounding relieved to get a drink. "I'll take three fingers of your finest tequila. Neat."

This amused the barkeep even further, judging by his deep chuckle. "No offense, but it's not every day that a werewolf walks into the bar," he said in a jovial tone. I waited, but he didn't say anything about me being a vampire. Was that good or bad? "I've only got one other customer, so step right up." He held out his arm, indicating the row of stools.

14

Upon hearing about another customer, I immediately tensed, scanning the room in case it happened to be a witch. The small space had a very high ceiling, making it feel like a cavern rather than a tavern—or the hull of an aged ship at sea. Booths lined the walls, and not a single television hung above the bar—which was strange, even in my limited experience.

Having been too distracted by Natalie's indomitable persistence over our future sexual relations, I hadn't noticed the semi-solid cloud of smoke hovering in the back corner of the room, emanating from a shadowed booth. The nearby light had gone out and never been replaced. I saw a red ember floating within that cloud, flaring brightly off and on before the smoke thickened again in lazy puffs.

A cigar.

A thick glass pitcher of beer sat on the aged wooden table, and a massive boot rested on the bench—easily as large as my torso. I felt a flash of concern as I saw a hunk of scarred meat snatch up the pitcher, momentarily escaping the smoke and shadow, only to realize that it had been a hand.

One big enough to grab my head and squeeze it like an apple.

He chugged the pitcher of beer in one pull before slamming it back down on the table with a contented sigh. Then he resumed his puffing, the red dot flaring brighter until he exhaled another plume of thick smoke.

I nodded politely. A deep, basso chuckle rolled out of the unseen man's chest as I turned back to the barkeep. He had already poured a glass of tequila for Natalie and was setting a wineglass down on the bar beside it, except it didn't contain wine. It was a glass of fresh blood. The heady aroma made my nostrils flare, but I kept my face composed.

"You own a fine establishment," I said carefully, wondering why he'd served me blood yet hadn't mentioned me being a vampire like he'd done when he'd called Natalie a werewolf.

The barkeep pinched one end of his mustache, curling it between thumb and forefinger. "I just work here. That's the owner over there," he said, pointing in the direction of the floating red ember and the impossibly large man. "And my permanent customer, of course."

"Oh?" I asked politely as I walked up to the bar to accept my glass. "And what might his name be?" I asked conversationally, alert for any sense of movement behind me.

He paused, glancing in the direction of the man. "His name might be Dr. Jekyll. Or it might be Mr. Hyde."

"Might?" I asked, ignoring Natalie's sharp intake of breath. She'd known where to find Hyde but hadn't known who he was? How dangerous was this man, and why had Dr. Stein told me to come here for safety? The tension in the room didn't indicate safety at all. Quite the opposite.

The barkeep nodded—not hostile but no longer welcoming. "Just like you might not have a reflection." I froze in the act of reaching for the glass, and he nodded satisfactorily. "We don't take too kindly to vampires. You walked into the wrong bar."

"We should leave," Natalie murmured. "Thank you for the drinks." she said apologetically, even though we hadn't touched them.

"Oh, lass. I think we are well beyond that," he said, folding his arms and leaning back against the bar with a resigned sigh. "It would be better for everyone if you went and introduced yourself. No one should die without a name, after all. That would be a shame."

Despite the obvious threat, the barkeep looked as calm as ever.

I heard old wood squeal and creak behind me, and I glanced back to see a giant emerging from the cloud of smoke, the wood gasping in relief as he came to his feet. He had a large cigar clamped between a set of gnarled, yellow teeth that were four times larger than they should be.

One of his eyes was slightly larger than the other and glowed with an inner light, making it sparkle like a sapphire. The other was a dull, swampy green. The man's face had more scar tissue and hair than unblemished skin, and his bulging lower lip was a grotesque slug compared to the upper lip. He wore a round-topped, brimmed hat, and it was perched to the side, unable to fit over his colossal cranium. His shoulders more resembled that of a bear than a man, and he had to slouch so as not to destroy the high ceiling with his head.

When it came to his clothes, they were all torn at the seams in some form or fashion, not initially designed for his bulk. It was almost as if he had shifted into this monster, having once been wearing clothes designed for a larger than average man. Except now he had to be the size of two larger than average men—if not more.

He wore a wrinkled and ripped white shirt with a vest that strained the buttons to the point of snapping, and his fists hung like lead weights, each arm practically the width of my waist. His pants ended in ragged tears at the knees, and his gnarled toes had burst through the front of one of his boots, revealing toenails that were thick enough to be confused with ancient bones.

"What a horrifying visage," I murmured instinctively, taking a step back.

"What a puny little vampire," he grumbled in a voice so low that I could feel it more than hear it. His heartbeat was an incredibly deep thumping sound, and the amount of blood coursing through his veins instantly made my fangs extend—even though I wasn't hungry.

Natalie stepped up beside me, fur bristling over her arms and hands as she narrowed her eyes at the hulking man towering over her —he had to weigh ten times more than her dainty frame, but she didn't seem to particularly care. "Unlike those who feel the need to overcompensate by whipping out their pride and joy on the first date," she said, eyeing him up and down with a derisive snort, "Sorin is more of a *grow-*

er than a *show-er*. I've always found them infinitely more impressive. Especially compared to present company."

I had no idea what she meant by a *grow-er* versus a *show-er*, but I understood the part where she'd said he was overcompensating. The barkeep's muffled cough sounded suspiciously like laughter.

The beastly nightmare of hair and gristle narrowed his eyes at Natalie, his eyebrows bunching up like fur hoods as his face darkened.

I gently shoved Natalie clear of his reach, not breaking eye contact with him. "Keep your eyes off my wolf before I take it personal." I felt a delighted sensation from Natalie through our strange new bond, almost making me gasp in surprise. Thankfully, I managed to keep my face hard and merciless.

Hyde shifted his attention to me, clenching his cigar in his saucer-sized teeth. "Fair enough. I don't like strangers."

I nodded. "So I've heard." I paused for a moment before shrugging dismissively. "The thing is, I really don't care what you like, Hyde. I'm just here to use your phone."

Hyde grunted, slowly extracting his cigar to point a thick finger at his horribly asymmetric face. "Does this look like the face of a man who shares his things, you mouthy little shit?"

I felt a slight tugging sensation on my new bond, but I didn't dare take my eyes off Hyde. It hadn't come from Natalie. "It looks like a face that not even a mother could love."

The barkeep cleared his throat politely, drawing Hyde's attention away from my insult. "I think this is the man from the news. The one who killed the Griffins." I risked a glance to find the barkeep still leaning against the bar, seemingly unconcerned about the impending violence.

"Is that so?" Hyde grumbled thoughtfully, turning to assess me up and down with a drooling sneer as he replaced his cigar, puffing smoke into the air between us. "This cute little thing?"

"I *am* the man from the news," I admitted, waving away his smoke, "although I didn't kill the Griffins. I was framed by Mina Harker—"

Hyde abruptly lost his cool composure and slammed a fist down onto a nearby table, obliterating it in a shower of splinters. "*Never* say that name around me," he sputtered warningly.

I smirked arrogantly, deciding that I didn't much feel like obeying his demands. My teasing hadn't seemed to bother him, but now I knew what did get under his skin.

"What name?" I asked innocently. "*Mina Harker?*" I mused, drawing out her name.

Hyde growled ominously, his fist clenching to the sound of snapping bones rather than popping knuckles. "I'm warning you, vampire—"

"*Mina Harker* was a tramp, but she gave me a wild ride."

His scowl deepened at my repeated use of her name, and his cigar puffed brighter, inhaling the stub of tobacco fast enough for me to watch it shorten by a third from one intake. "Unless you came in here to die—"

"I *killed* Mina Harker for her efforts to frame me."

Hyde froze, blinking at me and almost dropping his cigar from his teeth. I nodded, smirking matter-of-factly.

"Then I went and killed every vampire under *Mina Harker's* control—"

His massive fist hit my chest like a charging horse shouldering me off a busy road. My back slammed into a wooden pillar, almost sending me entirely through it. I felt a bloom of concern and wild rage from Natalie through our new bond, but I waved her off. I growled viciously as I unencumbered myself, brushing off wooden splinters. "I warned you," Hyde growled, "not to say that name, even if it is to brag about murdering her."

"I don't think I like your tone," I told him. Then I glanced over at Natalie. "What about you? Do you like this beast's tone?"

"Not particularly," she said, squaring her shoulders. "And he ripped your suit jacket," she said, pointing at my sleeve. "I liked that jacket."

I checked my sleeve and clucked my tongue in displeasure before turning back towards Hyde. I flexed my fingers into claws, and let a faint, ominous purring sound bubble up from my lips. I drew deep on my blood reserves, making the claws longer and bloodier until they were the length and shape of scythe blades.

They rippled like liquid blood because that was what they were made from. I masked my sudden joy, even though I sorely wanted to do a little dance. I'd been waiting for this ability to return—the power to manipulate the blood within me into actual weapons. The crystallized blood knives that I threw around when I needed projectiles was simple by comparison.

My powers were returning after my long slumber, but nowhere near as fast as I would have preferred.

The barkeep made a strangled sound and I sensed his pulse doubling in speed. Likewise, Hyde's pulse suddenly sounded like a steady drum. They were both staring at my claws in utter disbelief. Hyde tugged the cigar from his mouth, pointing it at my claws. "The fuck is *that*? You the goddamned Devil or something?"

I bared my teeth in a deadly grin. "Oh, I'm a different shade of devil," I chuckled. "Much worse than anything you've ever read about in the Bible."

"I tried to warn you," Natalie said. "He's a grow-er, not a show-er."

15

Hyde didn't necessarily look frightened, but he did look immensely wary—realizing he had stepped into a much deeper puddle than he'd originally thought.

A puddle with no bottom.

"Why are your eyes red?" he demanded.

Again, I bit back my joy to hear about another facet of my old powers returning. "It happens when I get aroused," I purred, the sound now a steady hum, like a cat. "It's a pity," I murmured, taking a step closer to my foe.

"What's a pity?" he demanded, shoving his cigar back into his mouth and puffing nervously.

"That I won't be paying for my drink, and that your barkeep is about to pay for my jacket. We could have been friends."

"I highly doubt that," he said, clenching his fists and regaining some of his confidence.

I lifted my claws, drawing them down one of the wooden pillars. Slivers of wood curled down from the tips, falling to the ground in long spirals.

Natalie suddenly jerked her attention towards the door with a curious frown. I felt something outside the bar as well, but I trusted

Natalie to watch my back. If more witches had found us, things were going to get messy fast. Which meant I needed to wrap this up.

Natalie turned back towards Hyde after a moment. "All you had to do was let him use your phone and you could have kept your blood on the inside," she said sadly.

Hyde cocked his head abruptly, staring at Natalie with intense interest. "You said that before. Who tricked you into thinking you could walk in here and borrow my phone?" he sputtered.

I shoved my claw entirely through the wooden pillar with an explosive, splintering, cracking sound, jerking his attention back towards me. "Keep your eyes off my wolf, Hyde. I won't warn you again."

I felt another tug at my bond from beyond the door, but I couldn't tell how far away it was. Victoria? Or was I picking up on something that Natalie was sensing—some inbound danger? Because I sensed her studying the door again.

Hyde also noticed Natalie's wandering attention and pointed a huge finger at her, shifting his focus from me. "Why do you keep looking at the *door*?" he demanded. "What are you two planning?" he roared, his voice dripping with paranoia.

Quicker than a whip, I lashed out with my blood claws and severed the offending finger. It fell to the ground with a heavy *thud* and the stump spurted blood onto my face. Hyde bellowed in surprise, thumping his massive boots a few steps back, causing dust to fall from the ceiling.

"I told you," I said softly, licking his blood from my lips with a grin —even though he tasted as disgusting as he looked. "She isn't your concern."

Hyde's face was entirely purple now, and he stomped a thunderous boot my way, apparently infuriated that I'd made him instinctively retreat. He plucked the cigar from his mouth as he glared at me. He extinguished the cigar on his bleeding finger stump, the pain not even registering as the fresh wound sizzled and smoked.

"Oh, you're going to be fun, boy," he said, stomping another step closer. "I'm going to shove each one of those claws up your—"

I felt a sudden yank on my bond, and the door to the bar blew open behind me. I risked a glance back to see a vision of death staring at us from beneath a white hooded jacket. She wore a little black dress with white polka dots under her long white coat, and she was barefoot. She looked like someone might have ruined her dinner date, and that she thought that someone might be here.

Victoria Helsing.

The only other difference between now and then was that she had added a leather harness across her chest that held suspicious bulges beneath her coat, and she wielded a long double-barreled shotgun with both hands—the same new shotgun that she'd shown me before getting ready for dinner.

I realized that had been a prophetic moment.

Without saying a word, she swung the shotgun my way and pulled the trigger.

I dove clear from the blast, hissing as I snatched Natalie out of the way.

I realized that the strange sensation I'd felt a few times outside the bar had been Victoria drawing closer. That it had been our shared bond—which was why Natalie had kept looking at the door as well.

The blast struck Hyde in the shoulder, but he didn't stop, shifting his attention to the new customer with a hungry grin. She fired again, hitting him in the thigh with a splash of blood and shredded cloth.

Still, he didn't slow down, stomping towards her and making the entire room shake.

Victoria dropped the shotgun as she hopped down into the bar proper, slamming the door shut behind her and drawing two alarmingly large pistols that gleamed like liquid metal. She pulled the triggers one at a time and my ear drums popped at the sudden explosions, easily as loud as cannons in the wooden box of a room. She took her time, shooting one hand after the other, managing the powerful recoil.

The bullets tore through Hyde, ripping through his chest and out his back—proving just how powerful her guns were to be able to pierce that much flesh and muscle. Still, Hyde didn't stop. The ceiling shook and a few bottles fell from behind the bar, shattering on the ground with each thunderous stomp as he closed in on Victoria, laughing maniacally.

And...she was suddenly laughing as well, tossing the guns as she flung her arms wide. "Get over here, you sorry excuse for a rhinoceros."

I froze, blinking in confusion as Hyde wrapped her up in a hug, enveloping her entire body. "Vickie!" he boomed. "I missed you, you skinny runt!"

"That's skinny bitch, to you, Hyde!" she said, her words muffled by his bulk.

He set her down, shaking his head as he laughed. "I was just wrapping up some business. We can talk when I'm finished—"

"No," Victoria said, grabbing him by the beard and giving it a stern tug. "Sorin is my friend. Dr. Stein sent him here to lay low for a while. Witches were hunting us."

The giant man blinked at her, utterly silent for a few moments. "*Dr. Stein* sent him?" Then he glanced over at me, his hideous face contorted in confusion. "This little shit?"

Victoria nodded. "He's the world's first vampire. Killed your favorite person, but he's really here to kill Dracula."

He grunted, glancing down at me again. "He cut off my finger. And he made me put out my cigar," he grumbled unhappily, shooting me a withering look.

"You ripped my jacket," I said, allowing my claws to dissipate as I rose to my feet and folded my arms.

"You were rude."

"I was incredibly *courteous*."

"You—"

"ENOUGH!" Victoria snapped, clapping her hands together to halt our bickering. "Did you rip his jacket? Because that is uncalled for," she asked, giving Hyde a stern glare.

He hung his head. "Yes," he muttered guiltily.

I snorted triumphantly. "Ha! You owe me—"

"Did you cut off his finger?" she snapped, rounding on me.

I frowned at her sudden shift in blame. "Well, yes, but he was pointing—"

She narrowed her eyes at me, and my words simply cut short. Then she turned back to Hyde. "I warned you about pointing your fingers at people. It's rude."

"Sorry, Vickie," he grumbled. "He kept saying her name."

She arched a cool eyebrow and began tapping her foot. "And what have I taught you?"

His shoulders slumped in resignation. "Sticks and stones can't break my bones, so words definitely can't hurt me."

She nodded. "Who swung first?" she asked, pointing at the barkeep —who I'd almost forgotten about.

He shifted from foot-to-foot anxiously. "I wasn't really paying attention—"

"Mr. Poole," she warned, drawing out his name with murderous intent.

Hyde grumbled guiltily. "I did. But it was just a little shove."

I scoffed, pointing at the broken pillar. "A shove that almost brought the roof down—"

"And *you!*" Victoria said, riding right over my argument as she directed her anger at Natalie. "You were supposed to keep him out of trouble, not get him into more trouble. Why didn't you tell Hyde that Dr. Stein sent you?"

Natalie frowned. "The second band of witches ambushed us on our way here. Once Hyde learned Sorin was a vampire, things went to hell."

Victoria pursed her lips. "I saw the aftermath of your fight on my way over here. I thought I would find you both dead," she said, her voice breaking slightly. Then she cleared her throat. "It looked pretty messy," she said in a softer tone. "Thank you for keeping him safe."

Natalie nodded faintly, and I hoped she had enough sense not to bring up the bond right now.

Not ever, if I could help it. But I knew that wasn't going to happen. If we could sense her through the bond, she could sense us—and she probably had a long list of questions about it.

I heard a sloshing sound and turned to see that the barkeep—Mr. Poole, apparently—was drinking straight from the bottle. Natalie had silently slipped over to the bar and I watched her guzzle her own drink.

Victoria was tapping her bare foot, folding her arms across her chest as she eyed Hyde and me with a judgmental frown. "I want you to hug and apologize to each other."

I blinked incredulously. "You can't be serious."

"He's *mean!*" Hyde complained. "And he never mentioned Dr. Stein. How was I supposed to know?" He folded his arms stubbornly. Victoria slowly turned to give him a stern look and I watched as he visibly wilted. What the hell kind of power did she have over this man? He was easily big enough to crush her head between two fingers. She'd unloaded enough firepower to halt a charging cavalry and he'd hardly seemed to notice. In fact, it made me realize that our scrap might have leveled the building over our heads.

Quite literally.

"I didn't realize that I *needed* to mention Dr. Stein's name, or that you'd try to *kill* me after I bought a drink," I growled, glaring at him.

Victoria considered my words before turning to Hyde. "Is that true? You tried to kill a guest?"

He scratched at his jaw, hissing upon realizing he'd used his stub. "Ow!" he whined.

"Oh, for fuck's sake, you baby!" Natalie snapped, pointing a bottle of tequila at him—the barkeep must have handed it to her. "Victoria just unloaded a dozen bullets into your gut, and you shrugged it off. No one's buying your pathetic sympathy tactic, you big brute!" Her words made me frown, vaguely reminding me of something, but I couldn't quite place it.

Hyde shrugged guiltily. "Worth a try," he admitted with a shameless grin. He finally turned to look at me, his smirk fading. "Well, *I'm* not walking over to *you.*"

I rolled my eyes. "This is ridiculous. I am not—"

"Meet in the middle," Victoria snapped.

Hyde defiantly lifted his finger stub to the ceiling, cracking the wood. "Absolutely not! This is my business. I will not be made to—"

"Then I'm calling Dr. Stein," Victoria said, pulling out her phone.

Hyde froze as if he'd been shot in the groin by a cannon. "You *wouldn't...*" he rasped.

I flinched in sudden recognition. Dr. Stein had hired a brute to destroy the evidence at the police station, and I'd just seen Hyde shrug off bullets like they were buzzing gnats. She must have hired Hyde. That was why she'd sent me here for protection.

Victoria lifted her phone and hit a button. Then she hit another. And another. "I'm dialing her right now..." she warned.

Hyde and I rushed towards each other in a hurry, nodding stiffly like old enemies at the gallows, finally forgiving each other in the face of certain death. I could only reach his waist, and his massive arms swamped over me like freshly shoveled grave-dirt, burying me under his bulk. Too late, I realized that this only served to get his blood all over my face and chest, thanks to the bullet wounds Victoria had given him. Hyde patted my back hard enough to rattle my spine and I tried to do the same, only able to pat the sides of his belly.

"Sorry," we said in unison, but mine was more of a muffled grunt.

We stepped apart and Hyde smiled down at me, his bulbous lower lip wobbling as he spoke. "You've got balls, tiny vampire. Great big balls."

I nodded, wiping his blood from my face and neck with my sleeve. "Thank you. I think. Also, thank you for destroying the evidence at the police station," I said, watching him for a reaction.

He hesitated, cocking his massive head. "That was for you?" he asked, confirming my theory.

I shrugged. "Dr. Stein did it for her own reasons, but it greatly bene-fited me since all the evidence was false, framing me as the man who murdered the Griffins." I chose my next words carefully. "The woman you hate," I said meaningfully, "set it all up. I killed her for it."

He studied me for a long moment before nodding. "Then I guess we're even, tiny vampire."

"Men," Victoria muttered, striding past us. "Pour us drinks, Mr. Poole. I think we'll need a lot of them."

Hyde clucked his tongue loud enough that it sounded like a wet blanket striking the floor. "This should be fun," he grumbled, smiling grotesquely at me.

I found myself smiling back. "Sorry about the finger."

He grunted, lifting his hand to show me the stump. I blinked, surprised to find that a new, shorter fingertip had grown over the wound, looking comically small in comparison to the others. "It's no big deal. It will grow back to normal in a few hours."

I arched an eyebrow, suddenly reconsidering our fight. "Interesting..." I said, extending my hand to shake his.

His palm enveloped my entire forearm, jarring my teeth as he pumped it up and down. "The name is Dr. Jekyll. Well, Mr. Hyde, currently."

I nodded, freeing my hand from his. "The name is Sorin Ambrogio. Well, the Devil of New York, currently," I said, matching his phrasing.

"I think we're going to be friends, Sorin."

I glanced back at Victoria to see her smiling approvingly. "It seems that way."

16

We sat at the bar with our drinks in hand, the silence growing uncomfortable. Victoria had caught me up to speed on her own evening, letting me know that Nosh and Isabella were safely tucked away in Dr. Stein's laboratory and that no one had followed them. Isabella had woken up and was in the tender, loving care of Dr. Stein, while Renfield, Nero, and Stevie were on alert to prevent either of the lovebirds from leaving before I had a chance to talk with them. That's when her story had taken a turn for the worse.

Stevie had become suddenly irritable and hot-tempered, but he had refused to explain why. At the same time, Victoria had suddenly felt a strange sensation in her chest, urging her to go back out into the city. Following that sensation, she'd been drawn to the scene where we had fought the witches and their familiars. Then the same tugging sensation had led her to Hyde's bar, Tequila Mockingbird.

On that note, she'd turned to face me and had demanded an explanation.

With no other alternative, I had told Victoria about our new bond, knowing it was best to be completely honest with each other, especially since we were all bonded together, now.

That, and she'd already used up all her ammunition and dropped her armament of guns, so it seemed to be the safest chance I would get.

I hadn't provided any extra details, though. Just that it had accidentally happened when I bit Natalie.

Natalie was seated on the stool beside me, but she was using the
counter like a pillow, resting her chin on her forearm as she listened
with a sharp frown. She hadn't reacted upon mention of Stevie, but I
was pretty sure that his sudden anger was a result of me stealing his
wolf, just like I'd feared.

"You did *what?*" Victoria finally asked in a low whisper.

Hyde grunted, hurriedly making his way behind the bar to increase
his chances of survival. He stood beside Poole, the pair of them
studying us in disbelief.

I sighed. "I was almost out of blood and we were ambushed by the
witches. Natalie offered me her blood so we could finish—"

"No!" Natalie abruptly shouted, jumping to her feet and shooting
me a withering glare. "That's not what fucking happened, Sorin!" she
snapped, her shoulders trembling violently. Her eyes were brimming
with tears as she shook her head back and forth in denial.

And part of me began to panic, wondering how much worse this
night could get. It wasn't that I didn't want to tell Victoria the truth
about the more sensual moments of the bond, but that I didn't think it
was fair for Victoria to judge Natalie for her drastic measures while in a
magical haze or fighting for her very life. Trying to recount the events
with mere words didn't truly encapsulate what had transpired.

Before I could explain, Natalie cleared her throat and began to
speak in a rasping, emotional tone. "Sorin *sacrificed* himself to *save* me.
He's my goddamned *hero!*" Her words hung heavily in the air, and
everyone turned to stare at me with surprised looks—silently
wondering why my version of events hadn't admitted any heroism.

Part of me wanted to jump up and call her a liar so that I could
redirect the unwanted attention, but...Natalie hadn't lied. The reason I
hadn't mentioned my last use of blood was because I hadn't done it
with any thoughts of heroism in mind, and I *definitely* hadn't done it for
later recognition at Hyde's bar. I'd simply made the best call from the
options available to me—either we were both captured or killed, or I
took the chance to possibly save Natalie's life.

It was as cut and dried as that.

In my personal opinion, the ability to grant proper recognition was reserved only to those poor bastards who had stood shoulder-to-shoulder with you in the screaming fields of war, the men who had watched over you while you fitfully slept in the mud and the blood, the men who had seen you both at your very best and your very worst. The poor bastards who had somehow been lucky enough or stubborn enough to make it out alive with you. They were the only ones who truly knew what had happened, so they were the only ones truly qualified to condemn or to praise your decisions.

And to true warriors, genuine recognition was as simple and as heart-wrenchingly raw as direct eye contact followed by a slow, silent, unblinking nod—and only when no one else was looking. It was private, not public.

Meaningful recognition was not given with flowery speeches and applause, and certainly not with a medal or promotion—although those heartfelt attempts were incredibly kind and appreciated.

The problem with those attempts was that only true warriors knew that the cost of being a 'hero' was that you couldn't honor the good outcome without dredging up the grim horrors that had forced your 'heroic' action. Each well-intended act of recognition brought with it a reenactment of both the good and the bad—a curse that already plagued heroes every night when they closed their eyes, reserved for their dreams and nightmares.

The curse of a hero was to live with both memories weighing him down.

And the only respite was the final peace.

For me, I had done entirely too many horrible things to ever accept the hero title.

Hearing the term applied to me made me feel like I had robbed one neighbor of his gold only to be praised as altruistic for giving that stolen gold to a different neighbor.

Natalie and Victoria were studying me with raw anguish on their faces, their eyes moist with unshed tears. I suddenly felt terrible, fearing that my grim thoughts had translated through our bond, that I had accidentally given them pain.

Natalie wiped at her nose, turning to address everyone else. "Sorin used up the last *drop* of his blood to kill the witches before they managed to kill me," she whispered, sounding almost angry at my decision. "I caught him about a *second* before he went down for good, and I had to *force* the idiot to feed from me before the familiars had time to overwhelm us, because they were preventing me from shifting. I wasn't strong enough to get us out of there on my own," she said, sounding ashamed. Natalie blinked through her tears, looking incredibly guilty. "If he hadn't bitten me, we would both be dead right now. So, if anyone has a fucking problem with our new bond, we can have it out right here. Right. Now." She was panting, clenching her jaw tightly.

Thankfully, she kept her eyes downcast rather than glaring at her obvious target—Victoria.

With tensions running this high, I decided it was best to calm everyone down sooner rather than later. I cleared my throat. "Thank you, Natalie. If you hadn't forced the *idiot to feed*, we would be dead. I guess that actually makes you the hero, eh?" I said with an appeasing smile.

An emotional laugh stubbornly bubbled out of her mouth, and she blushed in embarrassment, hanging her head with a trembling sob.

Just like that, the tension dissipated. I had more to say to the both of them, but it was a conversation to be had in private—because I had a feeling that remnants of Victoria's blood in my system might have had an important part to play in our new bond.

It was the only logical explanation for why Victoria had been roped into it when she had been miles away from us.

Victoria slowly approached Natalie, not even attempting to wipe the guilty tears from her cheeks. She stood there in an awkward attempt at support, seeming unsure whether she should simply leave or embrace the crying werewolf.

Before she had time to decide, Natalie flung her arms around the vampire hunter's neck, burying her sobbing face into a shoulder. Victoria did the same, and soon they were leaking all over each other. Victoria clutched the weeping werewolf's head, holding it close, while her other hand rubbed her back reassuringly. "I'm so sorry, Natalie. I should have given you the benefit of the doubt."

Natalie squeezed Victoria tighter, murmuring something back that made Victoria spout even *more* tears. Hyde was shooting me a panicked look from over their shoulders as if asking me what we were supposed to do.

In answer, I lifted my glass of blood in a silent salute. Hyde and Poole each lifted an entire bottle in the air, returning the gesture. Then we took healthy gulps and tried our best not to disturb the women in any form or fashion, pretending that we were entirely unaware of their strange ritual.

It was safer that way. I knew that much, at least.

Anything else was akin to an innocent kitten trying to break up a vicious dog fight.

It didn't matter how precious and fluffy the kitten might be.

Dead was dead. Period.

I waited a few moments before I turned to Hyde. "How do you two know each other?" I asked Hyde, pointing my glass at Victoria. The two women were still wrapping up their ritual, so I knew it was best to speak quietly.

Hyde grunted. "She helped me get out of London a few years back. When my experiments grew out of control."

I frowned at his considerable size, eyeing the torn and stretched clothes. "Is that what this is?" I asked, gesturing at him. "An experiment gone wrong?"

He nodded. "I made a serum to help me understand the duality of mankind—their ability to be good or evil. I was once Dr. Henry Jekyll, but when I took the serum, a darker version of myself came out," he said, holding out his huge hands. "Mr. Edward Hyde."

I stared back at him, shaking my head. "A potion did this to you? Why didn't you stop taking it?" I asked curiously.

"I had to keep taking the potion to *control* the change—like a were-wolf involuntarily shifting. Pretty soon I grew immune to it, though. I had consumed enough for it to become a permanent part of me. Locals caught onto the truth and Poole and Victoria helped me escape town." He smiled fondly at the mustached barkeep.

"I almost turned against him, working with law enforcement," Poole said. "Victoria convinced me otherwise."

Hyde set the empty liquor bottle down and folded his massive arms over his chest. "She helped me learn to control it, but I'm more Hyde than Jekyll most days. I have to try very hard to become him. I can't have a lick of anger on my mind to do so."

Then he took a deep breath and closed his eyes. I watched his body relax muscle by muscle, and then he suddenly began to shrink. I gasped and even Natalie looked up in disbelief as Hyde's skin simply sloughed away, disappearing as if it had never existed.

An entirely new man stood before us, holding his clothes up to keep them from falling from his shoulders and waist since they were better suited for the much larger Hyde.

He opened his eyes and blinked slowly. His piercing gaze arrested me, and I was stunned at how handsome he was—like a perfect carving. He smiled at us. "I really don't have much need for this form anymore," he said in a firm, musical voice. "Unless I'm going out into town, which is risky. If someone cuts me off in traffic, I'm liable to lose my control on Hyde."

I shook my head in awe. "That's amazing."

He shrugged. "Mr. Hyde used to be a mindless beast, but I've gotten the hang of how to harness that rage and rein it in. It's why I run this bar. Closed to the general public and open to monsters like us— although precious few take the chance. It lets me relax, at least."

"And no one dares piss you off, granting you some measure of security," Victoria added with a smile, having finally regained her composure. "Except for Sorin, of course." She stood beside Natalie, close enough to touch shoulders. I smiled at the pair of them.

The handsome Jekyll nodded with a grin, turning to face me. "You really ticked me off, Sorin. Not sure I've been that worked up in a hundred years."

"You're immortal?" I asked, caught off guard.

He shrugged. "Not sure, to be honest. But I'm not dead yet, and I look the same now as I did back in 1890. Well, Hyde has gotten uglier, I guess."

Victoria scoffed. "That's an understatement. And he's gotten much bigger. When you first changed, you were just a small, violent man. That changed the more frequently you consumed your potions."

He puffed up his chest proudly. "I got bigger and nicer."

I studied him thoughtfully, wondering how I could best use him to my advantage in the days to come. "Which side were you on? Wolf or vampire?" I asked, even though they'd shown particular distaste for vampires when I'd first walked in.

"Definitely not vampire," he chuckled. "No one was on their side. But to be honest, I wasn't on *any* side. I just kept to myself and everyone else kept me out of their politics. You seem to have fucked that right the hell up. The witches will know you came here, so now I've got that to deal with."

I winced. "My apologies."

He shrugged. "Not necessary. I haven't felt this alive in a long time."

I finished my drink and set it down. "I need to go visit Dr. Stein and check on Isabella and Nosh."

"I'll drive," Jekyll said, suddenly shifting back into his larger form between one moment and the next.

Victoria frowned at him as he struggled to adjust his clothes back into place. "You just drank four fifths of whatever was in those bottles."

He frowned. Then he deftly scooped up another bottle and downed it. "There. Now I've had five fifths." He scratched his beard with a pensive frown. "What does five fifths make?"

Poole sighed. "One gallon. But I'll drive. Just to be safe."

I eyed Hyde warily. "Do we have a big enough car?"

Poole grinned, thumbing his mustache. "We have a big enough vehicle."

"We have a big fucking *truck*," Hyde clarified. "I like to feel the air in my hair."

I smirked at the two of them. "I guarantee you that mine is bigger. Hands down."

They stared at me suspiciously.

Victoria rolled her eyes, scooping up her guns. Natalie and I both watched her to make sure she didn't strain a muscle. We watched her very closely.

And I was confident that Victoria knew it, judging by how slowly she moved.

17

O ur footsteps echoed across the marble floor as we entered an expansive lobby. Hyde let out a long, slobbery whistle, his fat lower lip flopping up and down in a sickening fashion.

"Never thought I'd see this place," he rumbled, smiling excitedly. It was an improvement from his almost immediate pout upon seeing my vehicle. Granted, I'd cheated.

Boats were bigger than cars.

Nero was waiting for us, watching me specifically. He looked both excited and uneasy, but I knew it wasn't something to figure out with so many people present. After all, most people still thought he was my prisoner. In a way, he still was.

His metal collar gleamed around his neck, but he pretended not to notice. So I did the same. He was earning back my trust by working with Dr. Stein, but he had a long way to go before he was back in my good graces, because I had no real way to verify his story. And he hadn't told me his whole tale yet anyway, holding much back for some reason.

So, the collar stayed on.

Dozens of wooden crates lined the wall, waiting to be moved or opened by the next shift. There was still a lot of work to do. I turned to

Nero with a wary frown. "Almost finished?" I asked, pointedly eyeing the crates.

He nodded easily. "Most of those are empty, but we still have a lot of work to do upstairs. Definitely on schedule for tomorrow, though," he reassured me. "Just waiting for a storm." I noticed him eyeing Hyde warily, probably concerned about his massive size causing a problem.

I nodded, hoping he was right. "Where is everyone?" I asked, thinking primarily about Isabella and why her nose had started bleeding back at the restaurant—just like the witches. She also had some information to give me, since our dinner had been so rudely interrupted.

No one else knew about that, though.

"On the tenth floor."

"Ten floors? That's it?" Hyde frowned.

"The pedestal is ten stories tall," Nero said. "The crown is twelve stories above *that*."

"How does no one know you're here?" Poole asked, shaking his head in disbelief.

Nero chuckled. "Friends in high places granted a reputable construction company—Sorin—a permit for *critical structural repair*, I think they called it," he said with an amused smirk. "And we enthrall anyone who gets too close, of course."

Hyde scoffed, glancing left and right in disbelief. "That's what all the scaffolding was outside?"

Nero shrugged. "Have to keep up appearances." He motioned for them to follow him up a flight of stairs at the end of the room. "Follow me. I'll give you the tour."

Victoria grabbed my hand, preventing me from moving, although she didn't look at me. "Go ahead. We'll be with you in just a minute," she said to the others, staring down at the floor.

Natalie nodded, ushering Mr. Poole and Mr. Hyde, following behind Nero, up the stairs to our final destination—Dr. Stein's strange new laboratory. Even I hadn't seen it yet.

"Remember me!" I called out, making it sound like the last words they would ever hear me speak. Natalie burst out laughing at my intended eulogy, but she shoved the others ahead before they could comment. I thought I caught her flash me a thumbs up gesture before they rounded the corner to continue up yet another flight of stairs.

Victoria waited until their echoing voices faded before releasing my hand and lifting her attention from the ground. She took a leisurely step forward, obviously not in a hurry but needing to be in motion. She was wringing her hands together as she pointedly stared ahead. "I had several surprise orgasms through the bond," she whispered abruptly, not making eye contact.

I missed a step, wondering if I was fast enough to escape. "Um..." I said stupidly.

"I'm not angry, Sorin," she said in that same soft tone. One thing I did know was that when a woman said she wasn't angry she was telling the truth. But what she really meant was that she had flown far past angry several emotions ago, and that you were on borrowed time.

Angry was safe.

Not angry was a death sentence.

"I talked to Natalie about it," she continued. I blushed, suddenly realizing that my life had just become incredibly complicated if they were going to share things like that with each other. "Apparently, you left her high and dry," she said with a faint smile. Oh, so faint.

"Y-yes," I stammered. "The...feelings she had—"

"Orgasms, Sorin," she interrupted firmly. "Supernatural, mind-bending orgasms."

I raked a hand through my hair, blushing profusely. "Yes...those. They happened when I bit her. Not...from anything else. We didn't—"

She set a hand on my forearm, finally meeting my eyes. "I know, Sorin. I know."

I sighed in relief. "What I feel for her is nothing like what I feel for you, Victoria," I said honestly. "There *is* a serious physical spark between us, and I care for her deeply," I admitted, knowing she could feel it through our bond. "I feel that same intense physical spark with you, too," I said, meeting her eyes so she could see my resolve. "And. So. Much. More."

Victoria bit her lip, nodding uncertainly. "Thank you for admitting that," she whispered. "About your physical chemistry with Natalie."

"And my physical chemistry with you," I reminded her. "It is no different in that regard. Where you two differ is...on a deeper level," I said, struggling to find the words. "I feel like my very *soul* is connected to you. If I had one, anyway," I muttered.

She smiled, looking both saddened by my last comment and relieved by the others. "Since we're being honest, I feel I should admit that I spent a significant portion of my life in the company of women," she said, gauging my reaction. I frowned, scratching at my head. "Romantically." My eyes widened and her cheeks flushed with embarrassment. "I feel an intense physical connection with Natalie, too, so I can't take out my frustration on you."

My mouth worked wordlessly, having no idea what I was supposed to say.

"In a way, this bond gave me an excuse to be honest. For each of us to be honest."

I slowly nodded. "It...seems complicated," I admitted, not entirely sure how I felt about her interest in Natalie. It wasn't that I had a problem with it but...I felt slightly jealous, as ridiculous as that sounded. I knew the double standard was unfair, even as I thought it. And I suddenly began to comprehend how Victoria must feel. And Natalie, for that matter. Did she feel like she was just our plaything to be dragged into bed when the mood arose?

"The fact that you bonding Natalie somehow crossed a vast distance to also entangle me in your web..." she murmured, smiling, "says more than anything else. I don't know how I would have felt if I had been left out."

I licked my lips, nodding slowly. "I thought about you," I whispered. "I think some remnant of your blood inside me helped bridge the gap," I admitted, having no idea if that was the reason for her inclusion in our bond.

She smiled. "We will have time to talk soon, Sorin. The three of us." She squeezed my hand warmly, leaning up on her toes to kiss me on the cheek, holding it longer than necessary. She settled back onto her heels, smiling up at me. "Natalie was wrong. I don't think you'll be difficult to manage at all, Sorin," she grinned, lightly tapping her finger on my nose in a playful gesture.

Then she was walking away, looking as if she had unshouldered some great burden that had been weighing her down. "What do you mean, Natalie was wrong?" I called out, confused as all hell.

Victoria spun on her heel, grinning wickedly. "She said you were a real...*handful*." She clearly enunciated the word. Then she licked her lips and winked at me in a way that made my pants bulge, confirming my suspicion. "But I'm sure I can handle it. That *we* can handle it."

My eyes widened and my heart thumped in my chest. Was she really talking about what I thought she was talking about? Was I reading too much into her words, thinking like a lecher?

She laughed at the look on my face. "I believe Dr. Stein is waiting for you," she said before twirling around to continue up the next flight of stairs and rejoin the others, leaving me...

High and dry.

"Women are going to be the death of me," I muttered to myself.

Then I began stomping after her, clearing my head for whatever Dr. Stein needed to talk about. She'd been busy lately, so I hoped she had some answers for me.

Because I had a lot more questions now.

It took me a while to make it up the stairs, but it gave me plenty of time to internally debate who I wanted to interrogate first: Dr. Stein, Isabella, or Nosh.

I finally stormed onto the tenth floor, wondering why I hadn't just taken the elevator. Hyde and Poole grunted as they noticed me, and I saw Hyde hand Poole a wad of cash, grumbling unhappily. I narrowed my eyes at the pair. They had placed a bet on me?

For what?

Stevie stood beside them, casting an arctic glare my way before he shifted his attention to settle on Natalie, his thoughts obvious. I added him to my list before dismissing him.

Natalie and Victoria were seated on a nearby couch against the wall. They were speaking in hushed tones, obviously wanting their privacy. I eyed them suspiciously, wondering if I should be a part of their conversation. They noticed my attention and smiled mischievously before putting their heads back together.

Hyde gently elbowed Stevie, knocking him back a step. "You have anything to drink here? You look as sober as I feel."

Stevie regained his stance and nodded, motioning the two over to a large table where I spotted a few coolers, a shelf laden with boxes and bags of snacks, and a few dozen bottles of water. Stevie opened one of the coolers to pull out a bottle of liquor, and then he scooped up some red plastic cups from the shelf before carrying it all back to the table. Hyde obviously wasn't able to sit, so the three of them remained standing as Stevie poured the liquor into the cups and handed them out.

I turned away, scanning the rest of the space in search of Nero, but he was absent. This floor was much more crowded—the far half of the room was littered with more stacks of unopened crates, but a lot of the medical equipment was already up and running. Several glass-doored refrigeration units hugged the back wall, and I could see they were all filled with the bags of blood I had stolen from the blood bank with Victoria. I'd come up with a good use for them.

I'd accomplished a lot. Getting the necessary permits, arranging all the logistics of transporting the required materials, and scheduling the work of so many people to accomplish a single task...

It almost felt like a war. In a way, it was. I silently congratulated myself, feeling like I was getting back to the man I had once been. The most powerful man in the world—

Something cracked me in the shin hard enough to make me curse. "Gah!" I instinctively bent down to cradle it. Stein suddenly appeared beside me and grabbed me firmly by the ear, taking advantage of my vulnerable stance.

Then she was dragging me by the ear towards a side room, muttering unintelligibly under her breath, forcing me to hobble along after her or sacrifice my ear.

18

I noticed the wooden spoon hanging out of her white lab coat, proving her guilt in the random shin strike. I ignored the muffled laughter from my friends, knowing they wouldn't have fared any better in my position.

I wasn't going to hit an old woman, and she was doing important work for me anyway.

One rule for managing a proper household that I'd learned over the years was that you couldn't kill the help. I convinced myself that it was the true reason for my obedience as she opened a door, jerking me by the ear again. She released it at the last second and swatted me on the ass with her wooden spoon for good measure—like she was corralling livestock into a pen.

I spun towards her with a stern glare only to find her standing in front of the door and holding out her hand in a calming gesture. I froze in confusion. A large glass window beside the door allowed me to see my friends in the main room—and for them to see me as well. Case in point, Hyde and Poole were craning their necks to get a glimpse at me.

"I didn't want to raise any suspicion," Dr. Stein said, "so I gave them what they expected to see." She walked over to stand in full view of the window but turned to address me in the center of the room with her back to the glass. She lifted her arms angrily, but her face was entirely calm.

"Are...you okay, Dr. Stein?" I asked warily, wondering if this was worse than her waving her spoon—the calm before the storm.

"Make sure they can see you, and act like I'm yelling at you. We need to talk about the blood."

I pursed my lips nervously, not liking this at all. "Okay."

"Excellent. You are very good at pouting. Keep looking like that."

I narrowed my eyes. "I'm not pouting. I'm—"

"Even better!" she said, pointing at my face. "Just like that!" she snapped, still waving her hands. Then she began to pace towards the center of the room, forcing me to retreat so our apparent audience could see both of us through the glass.

I folded my arms stubbornly, still annoyed by her comment, but I was even more concerned about her anxiety. I'd never seen Dr. Stein like this. Never. "What did you find?"

She stopped and waggled a finger at me aggressively. "The usual way to run a blood test with modern science provides very detailed results, but it takes too long—days or weeks to get a full analysis. So, I had to go old school. Nero knew a tracking spell—using a strand of someone's hair to find them if they go missing, for example." I nodded, having used one before. "Nero was able to adapt the spell to my needs. A way to attract like to like."

"And it's reliable?" I asked. "If it attracts like to like, wouldn't it connect any vampire to any other vampire? How specific is it?"

She blinked at me, then slowly nodded her approval. "That is exceedingly clever of you, Sorin. It's like an inert crystal I was studying under my microscope suddenly began to sing to me."

I narrowed my eyes. "Are you calling me—"

"As dumb as a rock, yes," she said, waving a finger at me for the benefit of our audience—who were pretending not to be watching us. "Now. More listening, less speaking. I stress-tested Nero's spell in every way imaginable. My first subjects were two unrelated vampires— Gabriel and Renfield. Thankfully, Nero's spell showed no connection."

I nodded grimly, considering the ramifications if it *had* shown a connection. It would have meant that any vampire could be used to locate and hunt down any other vampire. I shuddered. Magic was terrifying sometimes.

"Nero's spell is quite limited in what it will allow you to connect. In fact, it is eerily reflective of what a full DNA test would have shown in a lab—something I'm very interested in exploring at a later time, by the way," she said aggressively, as if I had tried to tell her no. "When I used Nero's spell to test two siblings, it was noticeably weaker than a parent to their offspring."

I waited for more, but she just watched me. "Okay. So why did you pull me in here? Did you test Nosh's blood against mine?"

She licked her lips, looking suddenly uneasy. "Listen closely and pick up a piece of paper from the table. Any paper." I frowned, choosing one at random from a nearby stack. "Okay, now angle your back to the window and pretend to read the paper, but what I really need you to do is watch the floor and listen closely."

I followed her advice, leaning against a table with my back to the window. "Okay."

She began to pace about the small tiled room. "On the floor, I've spread out various samples of blood—you, Victoria, Natalie, Stevie, Gabriel, Renfield, and mine."

Pretending to read the paper, I used my peripheral vision to scan the room. Directly across from me, I noticed a small clear plate the size of a large coin on the tile floor. It had a drop of red in the center. As I casually swept the rest of the room, pretending to stretch my neck to either side, I noticed more of the blood samples equally spread out around the perimeter. One was only a few feet away from where I stood.

"That one is yours," she said, discreetly pointing at the sample by my feet. "Now, watch closely because it doesn't last long," Dr. Stein said, pulling out a pad of paper and a pencil from her long white coat. Her hand was shaking, and I suddenly felt nervous. "I'm going to cast Nero's spell and drop a sample of Nosh's blood at my feet. You'll see a strong connection to his blood relative. The person who shares his DNA. I've limited it to only connect to the *samples* rather than the actual *person* or we would have mass panic outside. This room is warded. What happens next is only for us—unless someone takes a closer look through that window."

I shifted uncomfortably. "Can't you just tell me?" I asked in a soft whisper.

She shot me a stern glare and shook her head firmly. "This is something you need to see for yourself if you're going to believe it. Make sure to maintain your composure. I suggest you keep leaning on that table," she muttered. Then she began furiously scribbling on her pad. I felt a faint hum to the air the moment her pen stopped moving, making the hair on the back of my hand suddenly stand up. I saw a tiny strip of fabric fall from her pocket and she whispered a sinister word.

I flinched the second the fabric touched the floor, almost dropping my paper as my eyes shot wide open. Remembering Dr. Stein's warning, I forced myself to appear calm as I stared down at the tile floor.

Crackling, golden beams of light, no thicker than a pencil, radiated outward from the strip of fabric—Nosh's blood sample—emitting a faint, audible buzz.

Not just one beam like I'd anticipated.

Nosh's blood sample looked like a star, casting lines of golden light to...

Every sample in the room.

None were thicker or brighter than another, which was impossible. I realized my heart was racing. Through my new bond, I noticed Victoria and Natalie suddenly coming to attention, picking up on my anxiety. I forced myself to calm down and met Dr. Stein's eyes. She nodded ever so slowly before drawing a harsh line across her pad, hard enough to snap her pencil. The lights winked out, leaving us in silence.

"What does it mean?" I whispered.

Dr. Stein shrugged. "That Nosh has some serious explaining to do, because it's impossible for him to be related to every sample. I tried to find a way to break my test, forcing a false link between two samples, and I failed. Nero tried as well, using magic to try and trick the spell. He failed. Repeatedly. The spell does not lie."

I carefully set down my paper, regulating my breathing as I mentally went over my every encounter with Nosh, looking for some possible explanation. A chilling thought came to mind, and I froze. Nosh had worked for Deganawida...

Dr. Stein noticed my reaction, taking a slow step forward. "What is it?" she asked. "What did you just think of?"

I lifted my head to meet her eyes, hoping I was wrong. "What do you know about skinwalkers?" I whispered.

She dropped her pad of paper, staring at me in shock. "Nothing good...but I'll do some research," she murmured, sounding both shaken and angry that she hadn't known.

I nodded. "You do that, Dr. Stein. And make sure everything is ready for the next storm. We don't want to be caught with our pants down." My eyes settled on the fabric with Nosh's blood and I gritted my teeth. "Not again, anyway," I muttered.

I turned towards the door.

"Where are you going?"

"To figure out what the hell he's really doing here and get some goddamned answers. He's being hunted by the witches, and I think we just found out why. We're the only friends he has right now, like it or not."

"I don't think skinwalkers have friends," she said warningly. "They are soulless monsters."

I shot her a look from over my shoulder, allowing the blood in my reserves to completely cover my eyes in a rippling crimson pool. She gasped in surprise. I slowly nodded. "Then maybe he will feel right at home with me, because I am a soulless monster, too, Dr. Stein."

"Take Hyde with you—if for no other reason than as a shield."

I thought about it and shrugged. "Is his girlfriend awake? Isabella?" I asked.

"Yes..." she said, obviously confused by my change of topic.

"Good. Then I have multiple points of leverage," I said, opening the door. "Find out whatever you can. Quickly, Dr. Stein. And get rid of this evidence. No one can know about this, because if he's a skinwalker, he could be any one of us."

"Y-yes, Sorin," she stammered, sounding suddenly alarmed.

I let the door close behind me, clearing my eyes of the blood. That was the first time I'd come out on top with Dr. Stein, rather than her making me feel like an unruly child.

Things were looking up.

19

Questions zipped through my mind, and I honestly had no idea which one to focus on.

How had the infamous Medicine Man, Deganawida, not known that Nosh was a skinwalker?

Why hadn't Nosh told me?

And what the hell was a skinwalker doing helping *anyone*?

As I'd heard it—from Deganawida, no less—skinwalkers were bad news. The tribe hardly ever talked about them for fear of drawing their attention—

"We've come to an understanding," Natalie said, making me jump in surprise.

I turned to see Victoria and Natalie studying me intensely. I knew they had sensed my anxiety in the room, but they didn't look very sympathetic right now. They looked predatory.

"About?" I asked, suddenly wary.

"Our bond," Victoria said. "There are rules until we figure it all out."

I scratched my head, struggling to switch my mentality from how to survive a skinwalker incursion to negotiating a legal document outlining apparent rules for our bond. I decided that going on the offensive was the best tactic. It had worked with Dr. Stein. "I *made* the bond. I get the final say."

They turned to each other with matching baffled looks. Then they turned back to me, shaking their heads firmly. "No. Majority rules," Victoria said.

I folded my arms, realizing that I should have hired representation. "Now, wait a minute—"

"We will share you," Natalie interrupted, clapping excitedly.

"And each other, of course," Victoria added.

My eyebrows almost jumped off my forehead.

Hyde choked loudly, spewing liquor all over Mr. Poole in a powerful stream of alcohol.

The barkeep let out a curse, wiping frantically at his face. "Ah! My eyes!"

Hyde quickly made his way over, doing his best to help his friend. I hadn't even noticed they were still in the room! Thankfully, Stevie had left or this conversation would have become even more awkward.

"What about Stevie and the Crescent?" I asked, not wanting to talk about sharing in front of Hyde and Poole.

Natalie frowned. "I can no longer sense the pack. I don't feel the bond to Stevie anymore. You dethroned him in that regard."

"I became your alpha?" I asked, having feared that outcome—especially after seeing Stevie's warm welcome a few minutes ago and hearing about his sudden temper the moment Victoria had first felt the bond hit her. I'd hoped to learn that my bond had just nudged his to the side, not that I'd broken it entirely. "I'm not sure Stevie will accept that so easily."

She shrugged. "Then we will convince him. It's not like you're usurping his place in the werewolf hierarchy, and you didn't *try* to take me from him, so there is no dominance challenge. It was an unanticipated consequence of you saving my life. He can't argue with *that* unless he wants to indirectly admit that my life wasn't worth saving— which would infuriate the pack."

I stared at her woodenly, not entirely convinced that Stevie would see it that way—or that he would appreciate Natalie's entrapping argument. Also, I *needed* his werewolves. Desperately.

Victoria glanced from me to Natalie. "We have agreed to a temporary truce. We can share you, and *only* when we are together. In the same room. Neither of us is permitted to take a more...intimate step, alone, without the other's prior permission."

I stared at them incredulously, wondering if I had just heard her correctly.

Hyde sputtered incredulously—thankfully not with a mouthful of liquor this time—drawing our attention again. He stiffened, apparently not having anticipated that we could hear him as well as he could hear us. I was beginning to realize that he wasn't the sharpest arrow in the quiver. He snatched up the liquor bottle on the table and simply bit off the top, guzzling and crunching the glass in equal measure. I winced, imagining what glass would do to his guts, let alone his gums.

Poole stared at me in stark wonder, as if he was seeing a holy miracle in the flesh.

Hyde finished the last of his bottle and lowered it in confusion, blinking at it. Then he flung it at the wall—where it shattered—before crouching down over the cooler to see if he could find a refill, grumbling under his breath all the while.

He finally found a replacement and bit the top off of that one as well. "Thank you," he said, raising the broken bottle my way.

I frowned. "For?"

"Walking into my bar," he muttered, shaking his head.

Poole gave me a solemn nod of agreement.

Rather than commenting on any of the insanity, I turned and walked away in search of a skinwalker to interrogate. At least that made sense to me.

"He's hardcore," Hyde rumbled.

"A man's man," Poole agreed. "So stoic."

I rolled my eyes and walked faster. I didn't even know where Nosh was, but I decided that I'd rather find out myself than getting stuck in another bizarre conversation. Even if Hyde doubled as a dependable shield.

20

After searching the entire tenth floor with no success, I'd chosen to use the elevator to check the lower levels. I hadn't wanted to circle back to the stairs and risk encountering Victoria and Natalie again. They had probably already determined more rules that they expected me to obey, and I didn't have time for any more distractions. As it was, half the night had already been wasted as a result of the witch attacks, and I still had private business to conclude with Isabella—business that had been interrupted by the attack at dinner.

Nosh wasn't going to be pleased to learn that the entire dinner had actually been a carefully orchestrated ruse that served multiple purposes. *My* purposes.

Only Isabella and Victoria had known that.

Once I got what I needed from Isabella, I would need to confront Nosh about his lies. I hadn't decided which lies I wanted to address yet, but I knew how I intended to soften him up.

This floor featured a vast open space in the center that was deco-rated with pedestals and displays depicting the history of the colossus above. Pictures of its various stages of construction and design process hung on the walls, along with biographies of the men and women who had been involved in the conception of the astonishing structure.

The moment I'd seen the iconic landmark from a distance, I'd agreed with Dr. Stein's assessment that it was a perfect location for her new laboratory—for multiple reasons, including the practical, principled, and superstitious. Although it wasn't easy to visit, the multiple benefits of its location far outweighed the inconvenience. And Hugo had been eager to spend some of Dracula's cash on a new asset. I smiled, satisfied at our progress—at the successful collaboration of Nero and Dr. Stein, to be precise.

Offices lined the walls, each featuring glass windows that opened towards the center displays. Since all but one was dark, it took me no time to find Nosh and Isabella. I didn't care to modify my stern countenance to appease their concern, so they watched my approach through the window with hesitant smiles.

I did lift my hand in a polite gesture so that they didn't think I was here to murder them—which I thought was incredibly courteous of me.

I opened the door and paused at the entryway. The carpeted room featured a desk and chair, a bookshelf, a couch and armchair, and a coffee table. Isabella was reclined on the couch, propped up by pillows and her arm was hooked up to an IV drip like those Dr. Stein had set up on the floor above—except this one held a bag of clear fluid rather than blood.

I smiled politely at Isabella, ignoring Nosh entirely.

"Hello, Sorin," she said nervously, lifting a hand to self-consciously fix her red hair to the side. "Thank you for getting us to safety." Nosh sat in the armchair beside her, resting a hand on her shoulder. He echoed her greeting, but in a warier tone, clearly reading my body language. Despite his concern, his pulse was as slow as ever, because Nosh knew how to remain calm when the figurative house was on fire. And his house was on fire, alright. It was a raging inferno.

I nodded at Isabella, waiting.

Nosh cleared his throat. "You were about to ask me something before all hell broke loose at the restaurant."

I glanced at him briefly, not bothering to hide my annoyance. "I was."

His polite smile faltered. "I heard you did something to upset Stevie—"

"I need to speak to Isabella," I interrupted. "I'll let you know when I'm finished."

Nosh's pretense at civility disappeared. "Okay. Let's talk outside. Now."

I gave him a cool, dismissive look. "When I'm finished, boy."

Isabella lifted her untethered hand, snapping her fingers to prevent Nosh from lurching to his feet. "It's okay, Nosh. I do have something for him. I was unable to give it to him at dinner."

He jolted, slowly turning to stare at her with a somewhat betrayed expression. Because he hadn't known about it. He shifted his attention to me, and his eyes danced with fury. "I see."

He calmly stood, brushed off his pants, and exited the room, closing the door behind him.

I took his place in the chair with a contented sigh, crossing my legs. Isabella shot me a slight frown. "I don't know what is going on between you two, Sorin, but I hope you are not the type of man to be cruel for no good reason—especially to a friend."

"I am not," I reassured her, considering whether the term *friend* still applied.

She sighed wearily, realizing that I would not be entertaining other topics until our business was finished. "They have agreed to your request for a meeting in the underground—the same place you originally suggested." I nodded, masking my sudden excitement. "Tonight. Two hours before dawn. Alone." She reached up to unclasp a golden necklace from around her neck and then handed it over to me. "Show them this crucifix as proof of both your identity and that you have spoken with me. Otherwise, they may mistake you for one of the other underground residents," she said meaningfully, alluding to my vampires.

I dangled the necklace before me, watching it swing back and forth in the lamplight. "You told them about my immunity from touching holy items," I commented. "Smart."

"Necessary," she corrected. "Otherwise there would have been no meeting."

I nodded. "It wasn't a criticism. It was a compliment. Thank you."

She let out a sigh. "Don't thank me yet. I can't guarantee a peaceful outcome, because I don't know your intentions. I hope you know what you are doing. They are not fans of vampires, but they were intrigued by your immunity—and me vouching for you."

"And you didn't mention anything to Victoria? Or anyone else for that matter?"

She shook her head. "I keep my word, Sorin. Always."

I nodded, letting the silence stretch for a few moments. "When were you going to tell me that you were a witch?" I asked gently, so as not to intimidate her.

She leaned her head back into the pillow. "At dinner, as a matter of fact. But to be completely transparent, I was only going to tell you because I feared how you would react if you found out on your own— feared you jumping to the false conclusion that all witches are the same. The truth of the matter is that the Cauldron is mortal enemies with the Sisters of Mercy. Witches of the dark arts hate our focus on healing and nurturing. We disgust them—an offense to the title of witch, since all they care about is power and control."

I listened intently, having hoped as much. "You hide behind religion to prevent open war."

She nodded. "We aren't prepared for war. Our magic is in healing, not harming. Our magic works against many other monsters but is sorely inadequate when facing the black sisters of the Cauldron. So, yes. We hide behind religion—and do wondrous things for the world in our cowardice."

I set an appeasing hand on her shoulder, picking up on her obvious offense to my comment. "I did not mean it in that way. I think it's a clever tactic. The Cauldron doesn't dare stand against the entire might of the church, which allows you to continue your good work without fear of persecution." She relaxed, nodding proudly. "Does the church know what you are?"

She grew still and I sensed her pulse steadily increasing. "No," she whispered.

I squeezed her shoulder reassuringly. "Your secret is safe with me, Isabella. I swear it."

She finally turned her head to meet my eyes, and I had a difficult time forcing myself not to stare at her vulnerable throat. I wasn't hungry, but the angle of her head emphasized the intoxicating pulse of blood beneath her thin skin. And she was injured. My prey drive was instinctual, something I always had to dominate.

"Until you overthrew Dracula's hold on the city," Isabella said, "the Cauldron maintained a respectful distance, only peppering the vampires and werewolves with minor attacks as if to keep up appearances. They have never dared such a risky mission as they did at the restaurant tonight. I'm still trying to wrap my head around it—what did I do to suddenly make them so bold?" She sighed, closing her eyes for a long moment. "Families, right?" she said tiredly.

I grunted my agreement of her last comment. "They were not after you, Isabella. They just wanted you out of the way. They wanted Nosh, or maybe something he has in his possession. According to the second assault I endured, anyway. I'm confident they have since added me to their list," I said dryly.

Her eyes snapped open and she spun to face me with a thoughtful frown. I watched as the white witch's gaze flicked to the door and then back to me, her suspicion brewing. "So, *that's* what this is," she said, blinking slowly. "You knew that our private talk would bother Nosh. You're trying to get under his skin. To find out what they wanted from him."

I smiled faintly. "An added benefit. I was also fishing for information from you about witches in general."

She snorted lightly, shaking her head. "Nosh is going to feel overprotective and hurt, wondering what we are discussing right now and why he wasn't welcome, making him easier for you to manipulate. He thinks our talk is about what happened tonight, not the secret meeting I arranged for you."

I lowered my eyes. "It is difficult to get Nosh to open up, Isabella. I'm not trying to hurt him."

"As long as his interests align with yours."

"I hope to help him realize that our interests *do* align, but first I must get him to *listen*. Hence the façade."

She shuddered. "That is...devious."

I nodded. "It is better than direct conflict and shouting at each other for hours while the Cauldron circles closer. His stubbornness could get him killed."

She frowned thoughtfully, processing my words. She finally turned to give me a nervous nod.

"What else can you teach me about the witches? Both the Sisters of Mercy and the Cauldron."

"We oppose each other. We white witches want to heal and give blessings, but the black witches want to harm and take. We are powered by love; they are powered by hate. Two sides of the same coin. It's why our noses bleed when we get too close to each other."

"But they didn't pass out," I said, frowning.

Isabella pursed her lips. "I accepted a drink from a waitress when I was talking to Victoria. She set it next to me and walked away. I didn't think anything of it. She left so quickly that my nose didn't even have time to bleed. I took my first sip as you and Nosh were walking back from the bar. I passed out a few seconds later. Dr. Stein said I'm fine, but she's got me on fluids to make sure," she said, lifting her arm with the IV. "It is why I thought the attack was focused on me, because I saw you rushing back to the table with panicked looks on your faces."

"Well, I am glad that you are okay. I want you to stay here where it's safe—even if you're feeling better. It's only going to get more dangerous outside in the next few days."

She studied me as I rose to my feet. "You're not just referring to the witches, are you?"

I shook my head. "No. I have a few dangerous ideas of my own," I admitted. I dipped my head at her. "Get well, Isabella. I think you are good for Nosh. He shines brighter in your warm light."

She gave me a surprised smile. "Well. I guess you aren't all that bad."

I smiled. "I'm not sure there's a warm enough light out there for me. The sun is off limits, so I manage as best I can."

She studied me curiously. "Be easy on him, Sorin. You've already delivered the first salvo before he was ready."

I smiled politely and left the room without agreeing. That was entirely up to him.

Nosh stood beside a display case in the center of the room, reading a placard within. His body language was tense, but his pulse was steady. Now it was time to see how convincing I could be.

21

Hearing my approaching footsteps, Nosh turned to face me. He was wearing a t-shirt that depicted a Native American man's face and, below it, the words *"Fighting terrorists since 1492."*. I didn't know what a terrorist was, so I dismissed it. Nosh's face was calm, but his eyes blazed like stoked forges. I nodded at him in greeting. He didn't nod back.

"I had my own reasons for going to dinner tonight, Nosh, and you were only one of them."

He gave me a hard stare. "What are you talking about?"

"Isabella had obtained valuable information for me. I made her promise not to tell anyone, so don't be upset with her. It quite literally had nothing to do with you."

He clenched his fists angrily, but his pulse remained steady. "How dare you? She isn't your soldier, Sorin. I didn't wake you to watch you build a brand-new empire."

"That's what emperors *do*, boy."

"Your secret put her in unnecessary danger."

I arched an incredulous eyebrow, unable to stop the ear-to-ear grin that split my cheeks. "Oh, that is rich! Are you *really* sure you want to go there, boy? To talk about secrets putting others in danger? Please, say yes."

He stiffened, turning back to the display case.

"That's what I thought," I muttered. I gave him a few moments to calm down, eyeing him sidelong. "The witches were after you, but I'm sure you already knew that. Isabella didn't, though. She blamed herself for the attack."

A flash of guilt crossed his features, letting me know he hadn't considered that possibility.

"A second band of witches ambushed Natalie and me after we fled the restaurant. They were able to prevent her from shifting," I said, letting my fishing statement hang in the air for a few moments, wondering if he would admit to being a skinwalker on his own. He didn't, so I continued. "I'm guessing they also have measures in place to counter your powers as a shaman."

Nosh pursed his lips in a thin line, still not answering.

"They intended to kidnap and torture us until we took them to you —and your tomahawks. Apparently, they sensed them when you called them up inside the restaurant. The same tomahawks you used to kill those vampires at the auction, remember?" I asked jovially. "Turned them to red dust." I waggled my fingers in the air dramatically, but he didn't look over at me. "Though at the time, I thought they were just elemental constructs—some kind of shamanistic light—because I *specifically* remember putting a pair of magical, antique tomahawks inside a box to hide them from Mina Harker. We even gave them to a friend of yours for safekeeping. That's an impressive sleight of hand, Nosh."

He didn't respond, continuing to study the display case.

"Perhaps you'd like to comment on why you created such an elaborate lie—because I wouldn't have given two shits if you tucked them into your belt the moment I pointed them out."

His jaw clenched. "It's personal," he rasped. I folded my arms, waiting for more. "You weren't supposed to notice them. It was inconvenient for me. I'd hidden them at my parents' penthouse a long time ago so that no one would ever find them. I'm confident that they were the real reason Mina Harker killed my parents, but I couldn't tell you that."

I winced at the pain in his voice, but it was just another factor that proved my point. "Just to clarify, are the Griffins your parents or not? I get easily confused when blood tests contradict what my friends tell me."

He froze, slowly turning to stare at me. "Blood tests..." he repeated in a flat tone.

"I got the crazy idea that you might be my son. Then a test shows me you really are a Griffin. Makes a man wonder..." I trailed off, giving him another opportunity to come clean.

He stared at me for a long moment. And then he simply burst out laughing. "I am not your son, Sorin. That's just *ridiculous*."

I watched him in silence until his laughter faded. "We'll put a pin in it. The witches want these tomahawks something fierce, Nosh. Your parents died for your lie. Isabella almost died for your lie. I almost died for your lie. Victoria almost died for your lie. Natalie almost died for your lie, and she wasn't even in the restaurant!" I shoved him forcefully. He rounded on me with a pained snarl—both furious and heartbroken. "Give me one good reason I shouldn't hand you over to the witches right now, because your fucking secret is going to get us all killed. And think *very* hard before you answer, because I already know!"

"Fine!" he snapped, panting harshly. "I'm a skinwalker! And before you think there is some grand conspiracy, no one knew. That was the whole damned point! I hid by placing myself—and my tomahawks—within the Griffin family. They wanted a son; I needed a safe haven."

I studied him pensively, unable to discern whether he was telling the truth. "The witches never mentioned anything about wanting a skinwalker. They just wanted the shaman and the tomahawks," I said, thinking out loud. "Something involving the Black Sabbath."

He nodded stiffly. "The tomahawks *make* the skinwalker," he hissed. "Which is why I *hid* them. I picked up the shaman powers long ago. But I'm not here to write an autobiography."

I blinked at him, having about a hundred new questions, but he was right. Neither of us had time for that right now. "Fine. So, the witches may or may not already know that you're also a skinwalker, but they definitely know the significance of the tomahawks—either way, they'll kill you to get them." He nodded in frustration. "Any idea why?"

He stared at me for a long moment, debating his answer. "The most obvious guess would be so that they can make a skinwalker of their own. Which would explain the Black Sabbath. It's a power ritual for them."

I raised an eyebrow. "They can do that?"

"With the tomahawks in their possession and me dead, yes."

I frowned. "I'm going to say this with all due respect, Nosh, but that means it's an incredibly stupid idea for you to hold onto the tomahawks. You're giving them everything they need."

He flung his hands up. "Some dumb idiot decided to be nosy and point them out," he muttered, glaring at me. "Maybe it would be a good idea to hide them. Maybe even keep their existence a secret," he said, deadpan. I could practically taste his sarcasm.

I waved a hand, trying to think of a beneficial solution. "Fine. We're both at fault."

Nosh sighed tiredly, pointing a finger up at the ceiling. "Trust works both ways. I told you my secret, so how about you tell me yours? What the hell are you doing with a laboratory inside the Statue of Liberty? It looks like a hospital."

I glanced over at him. "Why didn't you just change your appearance and find out for yourself?" I asked, genuinely curious.

He narrowed his eyes. "For the same reason you don't drink the blood of every person you see. Just because I have this curse doesn't mean I have to use it for every little thing. It feels nice to have people see me as a man rather than a monster."

I grunted, understanding him completely. I gestured dismissively at the ceiling, "I'm raising an undead army of vampires to take on Dracula. I'm transporting my old castle here tomorrow because he's hiding inside it," I said absently, still thinking about Nosh's tomahawks. I couldn't risk the witches making another attempt at him—and certainly not here. I needed a distraction.

"WHAT?!" he demanded.

An idea hit me and I grinned, clapping my hands together. "The witches would need both of your tomahawks, right?" I asked him excitedly. He nodded, still looking pale after hearing of my own plan against Dracula. "So, give *me* one of them."

He tensed, suddenly leery. "Why? What are you going to do with it?"

"Nothing!" I chuckled. "But the witches are hunting me too, now. If I see any, I'm going to whip it out and show them. That should help draw their attention away from you and Isabella—since now they know she's the way to get to you."

He considered my words in silence for a good ten seconds. Then he reached into his pocket and pulled out a flint arrowhead, hefting it in his palm a few times.

"That," I said, frowning at it, "is not a tomahawk."

Nosh grunted, slamming it into my palm as he whispered a strange word. He looked up at me with an uneasy frown. "Not sure if you can make it work. Try imagining a hatchet—gah!"

A crackling crimson tomahawk flared to life in my grip, almost slicing his stomach open before he managed to leap back a step. "Sorry!" I said, but I couldn't hide my proud grin. "This is *way* better than yours," I said, referring to the cool blue color I'd seen when he'd held it.

He narrowed his eyes, folding his arms. "Yeah, well, that's your opinion, isn't it?" he said, obviously disagreeing. "Just keep the flint in your pocket. You can't break it or lose it, so don't be afraid to have some fun with it. I bonded it to you, so even if you drop it you can always summon it back to your pocket with a thought." He held up a finger of warning. "And I can summon it back to *me* with a thought."

I nodded, even though he'd just threatened to take my new toy away. "Okay." I imagined it disappearing and it was suddenly gone. The flint was also inside my pocket rather than my palm.

"What can I do to help with your insane plan?" he asked, eyeing the display case with a concerned look. "You're not going to break the statue, are you? It's very important to a lot of people."

I hesitated long enough to make him frown. "We should be fine," I said, waving my hand reassuringly. "But I'm going to need you and Isabella to remain here where it's safe. If the witches had a way to nullify a werewolf's abilities, I imagine they have something cooked up for a shaman—possibly even a skinwalker. And they already despise Isabella. There will be plenty of monsters here to keep you safe, but Mr. Hyde will be your new bodyguard. Do you know him?"

Nosh shook his head with a frown. "Sounds familiar for some reason, though..."

"Oh, he's great. Knows how to take a beating, though he doesn't look like much."

Nosh nodded with a regretful sigh. "That's it? Just hide here?" he asked, frowning in disappointment.

"Just through tomorrow night. Then I'll be free to help you come up with a permanent solution. The arrival of Dracula and his vampires will give the Cauldron plenty more important things to worry about. Might even solve your problem for you."

"Fine."

"I need to head off to a meeting," I told him, "but I'll let Dr. Stein know you want to help. She knows what you are, but I haven't told anyone else, and I don't intend to. I'm extending some trust in that regard, just like you did with the tomahawk."

He nodded gratefully. "Thank you, Sorin."

"But I would advise you to tell Isabella before she hears it from someone else. No matter how bad the news, it's always better that way."

He grimaced. "I'll think on it, but I know what you mean."

I extended my hand. Neither one of us was completely happy, which meant it had been a true compromise. I could live with that—for now. He probably felt the same. Having heard the very beginning of his story, I felt much better, even though I knew there were plenty of gaps to fill in.

I hadn't told him my life story either.

He traded grips with me, and we shook hands. I turned around to make my way back upstairs, hoping to find Renfield because I needed a driver. Victoria already knew about my intended meeting with the Nephilim, but not that I'd solidified it for tonight. She would want to come, as would Natalie, but the Nephilim wanted it private.

"Hey, Sorin!" Nosh called out. I turned to look at him. "You sure you don't need backup?"

I shrugged. "Probably, but you've got a pretty girl to kiss. That's way more important."

He watched me with a thoughtful frown before slowly lifting his hand to wave goodbye. I returned the gesture with a faint smile, not entirely sure how I felt about our talk.

I spotted Renfield making his way towards the elevator and rushed to catch up to him. He was carrying a cardboard box that held rolls of thick gray tape, rolls of opaque plastic wrap, several strange metal tools, a hammer, a candle that said *Christmas Morning*, and an avocado. I stared at the box for a moment. "Busy?" I asked, peeling my eyes away from his bizarre collection.

"Of course not, Master Ambrogio. I was just heading back to the city to run an errand, but it can wait."

"No. That's perfect. I need a ride back as well. Do you have a car available?"

He smiled eagerly, jingling a pair of keys. "Excellent." The elevator door opened, and I saw Nosh still watching me with a slight frown, looking deeply hurt that I had asked for Renfield's help but not his.

The doors closed and we began to descend. I told Renfield why I was heading back, and he almost dropped his box.

22

I walked through the vast open tunnel of the underground, retracing my steps towards the rendezvous point that Renfield had helped me find a week ago. I'd wanted to have a quick escape route in the event that my discussion with the Nephilim went...Biblical.

All in all, it was a straight shot—maybe a five-minute walk from the alley where Renfield had parked to where the Nephilim waited for me. Renfield had even made me leave the water drain open so that his car's headlights could illuminate the tunnel's entrance.

I'd quizzed Renfield about Nephilim as he drove one of our recently purchased boats back to the mainland. He hadn't known much more than me: they were the offspring of angels and humans; they were known as giants—although Renfield had never personally confirmed this—and they were merciless foes.

When I'd told him what I intended with them, he had almost rammed the boat into the dock. He had quickly recovered from his near crash and successfully managed to dock the boat before leading me to his vehicle with his box held in his arms. I had frowned as he unlocked the car, because the vehicle was bouncing up and down and I heard muffled screaming coming from the trunk.

Renfield had then turned to me with a thoughtful look on his face.

"Would you, by any chance, be needing two warm bodies? Gabriel caught a pair of Dracula's vampires lurking in the underground."

The muffled screaming continued from the trunk, the vampire prisoners hearing our voices just outside. "That all depends on how my talk goes, and how many there are."

"How fortuitous," he had murmured, opening the rear door to set his box down in the backseat. He then straightened, holding the avocado in his palm with a pleased smile as he closed the door. "I guess I can eat the avocado, then."

I had stared at him, and then the avocado with a leery frown. "Renfield, what did you originally intend to do with the avocado?"

He had grinned wolfishly, climbing into the driver's seat and motioning for me to get in. "It's something you truly need to see to believe," he chuckled, putting the vehicle into drive and exiting the parking lot. "I'll show you sometime. Gabriel beat these two morons silly and then slapped some of Hugo's nullification cuffs on them before calling me. Figured I would have a little fun in our downtime, but your plan is much more rewarding. And now I can enjoy my avocado another way."

I didn't think I would ever eat an avocado again but having the nullification cuffs on hand could end up being incredibly helpful, depending on how my meeting went. The cuffs worked on the same principle as Nero's collar. Put them on and your powers were suddenly muted. We often used them on new vampires until we confirmed they had control of their bloodlust, which was probably why Gabriel had them on hand when he found the spying vampires.

But listening to them screaming and thumping around in the trunk as we drove to our destination had been rather distracting. At least to me. Renfield hadn't seemed to even notice.

Once we arrived, Renfield wasn't pleased about me making him wait in the car with the crying vampires, or the fact I'd told him to call Victoria and break the news about my meeting and its contingency on me coming alone, but Renfield always obeyed. Even when it put a noose around his neck. I would meet them back at the museum where I intended to rest for the day. He had handed me a new disposable phone so I could call him the moment my meeting concluded. Because with the meeting so close to sunrise, we were running against the clock. I was entirely sure that he would provide my number to Victoria in the event that his life was in imminent danger from her wrath.

I'd turned it on silent mode.

I had also made him promise to give Dr. Stein an immediate call —*after* I got out of the car, thank you very much—to alleviate her concerns for Nosh's medical condition, and to inform her that I agreed with her suggestion to hire Hyde to guard both Nosh and Isabella for the next three days.

Obviously, Renfield didn't understand the true context of my message—which meant that he would also be keeping a close eye on Nosh over the next few days, whether I wanted him to or not.

Which had been my intention—a third, silent bodyguard to keep Nosh honest.

While I had been speaking to everyone at the statue, Renfield had been working at calming Stevie down over the Natalie situation. The werewolf had ultimately agreed to shelve it but had told Renfield that I would owe him a small favor. I hadn't liked the sound of that, but I also hadn't agreed to any such thing.

All that mattered was that I would have werewolf assistance tomorrow night, which would be necessary if the witches, or more of Dracula's vampires, tried anything.

I strode down the tunnel, reaching out with my senses for any sign of ambush or betrayal. I had no reason to suspect such a thing, but I had no reason not to either. This was a gamble, but for what I had planned tomorrow, I would need allies.

As many as I could get.

The tunnel opened up as I walked further from Renfield's head-lights, widening so that three subway trains could have fit side-by-side, making it feel like an abandoned warehouse. On my left, I spotted metal rungs that had been hammered into the wall, climbing up to reveal manhole covers in the ceiling above. The ground was covered in a shallow film of water, and I was careful where I stepped, thankful that I didn't have to walk through raw sewage. It still smelled terrible, but at least the smell of rot wasn't spiced with the perfume of human excrement.

I soon came upon the arched opening of an adjacent tunnel and I paused, taking a steadying breath. I had no idea what Nephilim were capable of, or if they simply intended to murder me the moment they set eyes upon me.

All I could hope for was that they had agreed to Isabella's request in good faith, and that I didn't do anything to overly offend them. They already knew I was a monster. I needed to show them that I was a *man*, and that I wanted what was best for this city—and the world.

I cocked my head as I sensed a steady hum of power in the air—something very old. They were already here.

I dangled Isabella's crucifix from one hand and held out my other palm so they could see the branded crucifix on my flesh. Then I stepped into the new tunnel, ready for anything.

Two orbs of cool blue light pierced the darkness, hanging from each wall of the tunnel.

Two statues at least twice as tall as me occupied the center of the tunnel, seemingly made from pristine white marble. One was a true beast of a man and the other was a thin, lithe woman with a body shaped like an hourglass, easily half his width and bulk. The pair were unashamedly naked yet also regal, like warrior angels without wings. They stood with their shoulders almost touching, yet angled slightly apart from each other, and their grim, stoic countenances promised death to their foes. They looked so realistic that I doubted they were statues at all. Especially since no one else occupied the tunnel, and the ancient power I had felt in the air was emanating directly from their chests.

I planted my feet and held my arms to my sides, facing them squarely as I spoke. "My name is Sorin Ambrogio, and I have come to speak with the Nephilim of Central Park."

The statues suddenly moved as fluidly as real flesh, and even their hair shifted and bounced as if it was as real as mine—despite maintaining the look of polished marble. They turned to face me, mirroring my posture, and their eyes blazed with blue fire as the orbs on the wall winked out of existence.

I stood steady under the intensity of their scrutiny, forcing myself to look directly into the fire of their eyes. The power I had sensed earlier had doubled the moment they moved, and I felt my pulse rapidly increase as my survival instincts screamed for me to flee. I denied my instincts, feeling strangely at peace.

I dipped my chin to the woman and then the large man with the utmost respect, careful not to gawk at their nudity—especially the woman's flattering curves. "Thank you for meeting with me, Nephilim."

The pair of Nephilim continued to stare at me. "Speak your need, Sorin Ambrogio. We will pass judgment," the man said.

I kept my face utterly calm at his words. "There will be no judgment upon me, Nephilim. I did not come here to seek your approval. I came here to befriend a potential ally. We share a common enemy, one whom I wish to eradicate. Dracula."

The woman's lips twitched in amusement at my dismissal of her compatriot's judgment. The man narrowed his eyes ever so slightly. Finally, he nodded. "Isabella claimed that you needed us to grant you a section of Central Park. Is this true?"

"I do not need a *section* of Central Park. I believe I will need *all* of it. I could have taken it at any point in the last few weeks, but I chose to honor your prior claim on the consecrated land. Because following my decision, the land will become cursed. With your partnership, however, I believe the land may be saved. That its very consecration may be our best weapon."

The pair of Nephilim giants clenched their fists with a resounding crack, an instinctive response to my words. I stood firm.

"You dare much, vampire," the man said in a low, threatening tone.

"My fellow Nephilim is considering smiting you where you stand," the woman said.

The man nodded stiffly, pursing his lips. "It is more than a consideration. It is a foregone conclusion."

And then he began to advance, storming towards me with the inevitability of an avalanche.

23

The woman cleared her throat with a warm smile, and the man abruptly halted, having only taken two steps. His anger had shifted to thoughtfulness between one moment and the next, and then he gave me a respectful nod.

Watching their different reactions—her amusement and his curiosity—I realized I had just passed a test. They had expected me to respond with instant violence and now seemed intrigued by my calm demeanor.

She gave him a meaningful look, confirming my suspicion, before turning back to me and eyeing Isabella's crucifix. "Isabella told us very little about you, Sorin Ambrogio. She told us the rumors and stories that everyone whispers on the streets about your attack on the vampires and what you've done since. That you were once called the Devil of Italy, or Greece, or Europe, even. And that they now call you the Devil of New York. That things have been better since your arrival in spite of the blood spilled."

I considered her words and then nodded carefully. "That is true."

"That you claim to be the world's first vampire..."

"I do not *claim* it. I *am* the world's first vampire," I said firmly.

"Then I would hear your story. I cannot validate rumors, but I can tell when a man is lying. Tell me your tale, Sorin Ambrogio. No embellishments. Only the basic facts."

"Enough to convince us not to destroy you where you stand," the man added with a polite smile. "If you are the first, then is this not all your fault?"

I met his eyes, careful not to take it personally. He had a solid point. But it was wrong.

I considered their request, silently weighing how much they needed to know to make a decision about my character. I decided they needed quite a bit, given my reputation, so I let them have it. "I grew up in Greece as an orphan. Upon reaching manhood, I traveled to the Oracle of Delphi in hopes of hearing my destiny was to be brighter than my past," I began in a soft voice. "I didn't know it then, but that was the day my life would be changed forever. That was the day the Olympian Gods cursed me to become the world's first vampire, and I'm confident that it was out of pure spite."

The Nephilim listened with open astonishment, especially at my mention of the Olympians. As I continued my brief but honest reiterations, I carefully noted their reactions as I told them about meeting Selene, hearing my various curses, my eventual conquest of Europe, my friend Dracula, the Americas, my betrayer Dracula, my slumber, and then waking up hundreds of years later, learning I had been forgotten, and all that had transpired from then through to today—here, standing before the Nephilim. I told them everything significant—even my failures. I paused for a few moments, watching them digest my story, before I began speaking again. "And then the brave male Nephilim said he would love to help me, and that all would be well. And then the beautiful female Nephilim said I was the most honorable man she ever—"

"That will be *quite* enough," the female Nephilim said, trying to hide an amused smirk. The male Nephilim had flashed me a warm grin, chuckling softly.

"It was worth a try," I said with an innocent shrug.

She studied me curiously. "You did not lie." She sounded...surprised.

The man watched me. "We too know what it is like to be forgotten underground, vampire," he said, gesturing angrily at the tunnel. Then he clamped his lips shut, looking surprised that he had spoken his frustrations out loud—especially to me.

I dipped my chin, a gesture of thanks for his openness. "Does that mean my extra bit at the end is as good as your handshake?" I asked with a hopeful smile.

The man grunted. "Nice try. We don't even know what you are requesting of us yet. What we have now is a foundation on which to begin." I nodded. "Although I must admit that I am more open to persuasion now that I know the cursed Olympians are behind it all."

The woman nodded her agreement. "The Olympians have much to answer for."

"I get first swing at the ones I mentioned in my story," I said. "Let's get that clear right now."

The man chuckled, shaking his head. "I do not think punching a minor god would go well for even you, Sorin Ambrogio, but it would be entertaining to witness."

The woman cleared her throat pointedly, bringing us back to business. "Show me the brand where the crucifix burned you," she said. "When you banished Dracula from possessing the necromancer and took over the city."

I held out my palm, advancing a few steps for them to get a clear view. "Religious items have never harmed me, but they do harm other vampires. Perhaps it is due to my origins in Greece long ago." I lifted Isabella's crucifix in the air and then placed it on my forehead, showing them that it caused me no discomfort whatsoever.

They nodded thoughtfully, still looking like they couldn't quite believe it.

Finally, the woman spoke. "If witches like the Sisters of Mercy can fight on our side, I see no reason why Sorin couldn't do the same."

I dipped my chin graciously. "Unless you have a lot more friends than I see right now, a numbers game is not in our favor. Dracula likely has hundreds of vampires across the ocean, and however many he has snuck back into the city since I defeated him. Then there is the Cauldron. Seven of their witches died this evening after attacking me and my associates. For all I know, the

Cauldron and Dracula are working together, or at least in concert."

The woman shook her head. "The Cauldron hates Dracula almost as much as we do."

I shrugged. "Unfortunately, they have found a common enemy in *me*. War makes for unlikely allies," I said, gesturing at the three of us as an obvious example.

"Then what do you suggest?" the man asked, sounding intrigued.

I took a deep breath, wondering how best to answer his question. I could tell from our interaction so far that they valued open honesty above all else, and that the only way forward was to speak plainly. Especially after the man mentioned being abandoned and forgotten underground. "Dracula allegedly controls the travel industry, preventing me from going to him. So, I intend to bring his castle—my castle—*here*. I have the ability to do this with surprisingly minimal effort. My only issue is that I need a very large open place to do so. My spell would transport Dracula, the entire structure, and its inhabitants, here, cutting him off from his allies in Europe."

The Nephilim scoffed outrageously. "Absolutely not! Bringing his entire castle here to the middle of New York City? Inviting Dracula directly into our bosoms? That's like telling us that the best way to fight a plague is to stab ourselves in the heart."

I nodded, having already thought about it at great length. This was where I had hit a brick wall. "Which is the second reason I wanted to speak with you—and any other Nephilim you may know. I believe it is possible to bond the castle not only to me and Central Park, but to the Nephilim. To turn his fortress into a prison."

They stared at me, their eyes wide in disbelief. The man spoke first. "Preposterous. How would you—" He cut off abruptly, his body stiffening in sudden understanding. He stared at me, his fiery blue eyes flaring brighter as his mouth hung open.

"I wish to turn you," I said. "Turn you into Nephilim vampires."

The woman gasped, lifting a hand to her mouth in shock.

The man had managed to close his mouth, and was now staring at me in open disbelief, looking torn about whether he should feel offended or...honored.

I pressed on, taking advantage of the silence. "If you are bonded to me and to the consecrated land, we would be trapping the castle and Dracula within. Holy artifacts destroy evil and harm vampires, yet you have seen that I suffer no such affliction. What if bonding you to me and the castle allows us to taint the very walls? Turning Dracula's fortress into a prison? Enough of a prison for me to enter and at least stand a chance of destroying him once and for all."

The woman held a hand to her breasts, licking her lips. "Such a request could have disastrous consequences to us," she whispered, but I could tell that she was merely making a comment, not an impassioned argument. My hopes began to rise ever so slightly, but I kept my face neutral.

The man didn't bother hiding his emotions, openly revealing his bitterness. "Consequences?" he repeated in a cool, clipped tone. "We have been living in a sewer for hundreds of years with no one coming to take us home or give us a quest. We have been forgotten. Truly."

The woman met his eyes, slowly gathering her courage. Then she gave him a slow, firm nod. "Perhaps it would be considered martyrdom if this grants us the power to one day make the Olympians pay for their history of crimes."

I nodded sincerely. "I can't promise when, but I will do everything in my power to make the Olympians pay. One day soon, I hope."

She licked her lips. "Then I am agreed. I can do no good for the world from down here."

The man nodded as well. "I grow weary of hiding underground. I think it's about time we made an appearance above, and if you're bringing a castle to Central Park, I doubt anyone would have cause to look twice at a pair of giants walking the earth."

"Compared to my castle, you won't look like giants, of that I can assure you." I studied them thoughtfully, wondering how I was supposed to sneak two giants into Central Park without drawing every eye. "How do we get you out of here?"

They smiled pompously. Then they suddenly shrunk to the same height as me. "We can maintain this form for a day or so at a time. But what are we to do in Central Park?"

I closed the distance between us, standing before them in momentary silence. They still looked made of marble, yet their naked flesh looked soft enough to caress—like poured milk. "First, I wish to thank you for making such a difficult decision. As I told you, I could have attempted all of this on my own, but I realize that would just be bringing a bigger problem to New York City. With your help, I hope to change everything. Thank you for believing in me," I said, extending my hand.

The woman smiled at me. "I can't remember the last time I did anything worthwhile for mankind. I'm ashamed to say that you have done more in the past few weeks to help them than I have in the last few hundred years." She grasped my hand and shook it. I was surprised at how incredibly soft her skin was—and how insanely strong her dainty grip was. "It was not as hard a decision as you think, Sorin Ambrogio."

The man nodded, swallowing my hand in his. "I second what she said. And I want to square off against the Olympians one day. I'm holding you to that promise."

"We are Nephilim," the woman said. "What if your bond is not strong enough to hold us? It could destroy you," she said, studying my face for a reaction.

"That is a risk I am willing to take. I am not entirely responsible for what I became, but I am responsible for bringing Dracula into power. I have vowed to pay for that mistake."

They nodded approvingly.

"Do you two have names?" I asked.

They studied each other intensely, seeming to have a silent conversation. The woman finally turned to me, smiling excitedly. "You will call us Adam and Eve, for I fear we find ourselves in a new garden full of temptations."

The man nodded with a matching grin. "I agree."

"It is appropriate, really," the woman continued, holding out her arms and spinning in a slow, sensuous circle to show off her nudity. "A naked woman and a naked man are entering into a brave new world, making a deal with the Devil."

I understood their reference. "Hopefully to *save* Eden this time," I reminded them.

"So said the serpent," Eve said with a shrug.

Adam grunted dismissively at her comment. "If our choice to fall on this blade can make the world a better place, I see no difference than if we were to die in a pointless battle with no hope of change. Or to die down here, forgotten. Our brothers and sisters have tried infiltrating Dracula's Castle in the past, and they have all perished in the attempt. I'm willing to try, but what makes you think your plan will be any different?"

I smiled at him, baring my teeth. I tapped my fangs. "Because now you're working with the landlord. The Castle is *mine*, and through our bond, you will have direct access to it."

He nodded slowly. "As long as it doesn't destroy our souls in the process."

I held out my hands. "I won't lie to you about the risks. But I can assure you that becoming a vampire doesn't change your personality. It might lower your inhibitions, but it doesn't *change* you. Men like Dracula change you. The only alternative is to continue living below ground and hope that I win. Otherwise Eden will die while you continue to eke out an empty existence in these tunnels. Until Dracula finds you, of course. And if I die, you will no longer have the chance to bond with the castle, to purify it with your blood."

Adam smirked, a strange, malevolent look on his stoic face. "I just needed to hear you admit it. The fact that you do not avoid unpleasant questions earns you my respect." He glanced at the woman. "What do you say, Eve? Ready to sell your soul to save the world from a worse monster than the Devil?"

24

She studied me in silence. "Will you limit how many vampires I kill?" she asked, her words sending a shiver down my spine, given her unassuming frame.

I shook my head. "As long as they are not *my* vampires, you may kill as many as you want."

"You speak of those sharing the underground with us?" Eve asked, discreetly eyeing Adam with a deep, passionate interest, as if suddenly entertaining a long-dismissed hope.

I kept this observation to myself, nodding at her question. "I personally interviewed them, carefully selecting only those whom I believed I could trust. Mostly old war veterans that the world left behind. Anyone with addictions or temperamental issues, I left as I found them. After hundreds of years, I've learned what type of person makes a good vampire and what type of person makes a terrible monster. Dracula is mine. The rest are fair game."

Eve nodded. "Then I can agree. I will buy back my soul in blood. This is a worthy cause."

"We will make our new garden thrive, growing rich off the blood of monsters," Adam said.

I nodded gratefully, trying not to show my level of excitement. I checked my blood reserves, happy to see they were still pregnant from feeding on Natalie earlier. I would have preferred to top it off with Victoria Helsing's powerful blood, just to be safe, but I knew I would need that for tonight, and I hadn't wanted to risk drinking from her twice in a row.

Turning a human into a vampire was relatively easy—not even requiring much power.

But I was playing an entirely different game here. I wasn't even sure if it was possible. It wasn't like I had a father to ask or anything. I was the first vampire, and no one had been crazy enough to try turning a Nephilim—or even crazy enough to try *convincing* a Nephilim to be turned.

As a precaution, I pulled out my phone and checked the clock. I was pleased to see that I still had plenty of time to wrap this up and make it back to the museum. That was surprising given all that had transpired: the retelling of my story and the subsequent negotiations. My only concern was if something went wrong and all three of us passed out from the attempt.

I called Renfield's phone—he had already saved it in the contacts, thankfully.

"Yes, Master Ambrogio?" he asked anxiously. "Is everything okay?"

I turned my back on Adam and Eve, hiding my giddy grin. "More than okay, Renfield. We are going to need those warm bodies after all," I told him. "The nullification cuffs might come in handy as well."

"Of course, Master Ambrogio. We will see you momentarily." Rather than waiting for my response, he simply hung up. I chuckled, pocketing the phone.

I thought about the work ahead now that it was more than just a vague wish. When turning from human to vampire, the transition could be brutal. The fledgling vampire often grew wild and erratic. We'd spoken at length about it to Hugo, wanting to find a way to minimize dangers when turning new vampires—and he'd told us about the collection of nullification cuffs they kept for just that reason.

I would have to be careful in how I brought the cuffs up to the Nephilim. The first introduction of restraints into a relationship was always a dicey exchange—especially for a relationship this fresh and new. It grew easier with repetition.

I turned to Adam and Eve. "Alright. Who wishes to go first?"

Instead of competing, they calmly stepped forward together, matching their strides.

"We will go together," they said in unison.

I smiled, approving of their choice—as long as it didn't overwhelm me to try turning two Nephilim at once. I'd turned multiple humans at once and it hadn't been any more difficult than turning one. Then again, these weren't humans. But Renfield was on his way, so he could save me if things went poorly.

I studied the two of them sternly, having forgotten to address something. "I need you to be completely honest with me. Typically, when a human is first turned into a vampire, the transition can be quite difficult. The bloodlust takes over and they have a hard time balancing the new powers and instincts they receive. Granted, they had no powers before being turned, so had no experience at managing abilities of any kind."

They nodded, looking as if they already realized what I was getting at. Eve spoke up. "We Nephilim live a life of balance and control. It is quite literally a part of us. We already have incredible powers that we must use responsibly. I think we will be fine."

I turned to Adam, curious to hear his response. "I agree with Eve. But I also see the dangers of hubris. If beings as powerful as us did *not* handle the change well, it would be unbelievably dangerous. The risk is incredibly high."

I nodded. "I think you are both right. And our whole goal here is to do some good, not destroy the city. Which is why my associate is bringing some bracelets that we use on humans and supernaturals to prevent them from harming anyone. We will put them on as a precaution only."

I turned from one to the other, waiting for their response. This command was only the first of many they would receive in the coming days.

"Agreed," they said in unison, and without hesitation.

"Thank you. While we wait for my associate, I will run through the steps we're going to take so you are not alarmed during the actual process." They nodded, almost looking eager—willing to do anything to once again serve a higher calling. "First, I'm going to bite you and drink a sip or two of your blood, so make sure you don't get hard on me —" I blinked, realizing how that had sounded. And then I coughed, noticing that I had glanced down at Adam's...well-developed Tree of Knowledge. "Don't let your *skin* turn hard on me," I corrected.

Eve let out a pure, chiming laugh before slapping a hand over her mouth. I ignored her, hoping I wasn't blushing. Adam, surprisingly, looked slightly self-conscious. Eve placed a hand on his arm when he shifted as if to cover himself. The warm smile she gave him seemed to shock even Adam, embarrassing him further. I pretended not to notice the virgin tension that bloomed to life between them in that single moment—for it was a pure, joyous tension.

"Then you will drink a few sips of my blood. I will use my powers to bond our blood together while you swear an oath." They nodded somberly as I recited the words for them.

Surprisingly, they didn't balk at the oath, and I began to wonder if I hadn't made this a larger problem than it needed to be.

I cleared my throat, hoping the last step wouldn't break their resolve. "The final act is to kill your first victim, consuming their blood." Renfield rounded the corner, making sure to move loudly enough that he caught our attention from a distance rather than causing a panic. Then again, he was herding two dazed vampires ahead of him. He must have already enthralled them, because they appeared to be in a trance. Adam and Eve watched them approach with wary frowns. "These are two of Dracula's vampires. They were caught lurking here in the underground, hunting my vampires and searching for weaknesses that their master could later exploit to destroy me. I can absolutely guarantee that they are heartless killers, for those are the only men Dracula turns. The only kind of men he would trust to send against me."

The Nephilims' demeanor changed between one moment and the next, and they eyed the vampires with sudden fury. They were also staring at the thick metal bracelets.

Renfield murmured a command, and the vampires calmly knelt on the ground, as docile as sheep. I sensed that Renfield was significantly stronger than the pair, even though he was outnumbered. Even Gabriel had been stronger. It seemed that Dracula had preferred quantity over quality when choosing his spies.

Renfield introduced himself, congratulating them on their decisions and welcoming them to our family. He briefly reassured them that the two vampires were enthralled, and that becoming a vampire wouldn't suddenly turn them into monsters.

"It might *temporarily* make you a...difficult person to deal with," I said with a disarming smile, "so we will put the cuffs on." I turned to Renfield and gestured for him to remove the cuffs from the enthralled vampires. He did, handing each of the Nephilim a pair so they could inspect them for themselves. I wasn't even sure if they were capable of restraining a Nephilim, but they were all we had. I waited until they looked up at me with satisfied nods. "Please cuff our new friends, Adam and Eve, Renfield."

His eyes twitched at the names, but he masked his reaction, cuffing the Nephilim with gentle words, easing any last-minute concerns they may have. I turned away, taking calming, steadying breaths. Victoria and Natalie were definitely going to feel something through the bond tonight.

I turned back around to find the Nephilim facing me, wearing their bracelets with mild frowns. That was actually a relief. "Are they blocking your powers?" I asked gently.

"Yes," they said, twisting the bracelets with mild surprise.

"Good. As soon as I see that you've got the change under control, I swear on my life that I will take them off." They nodded somberly, but I wanted absolutely no doubt in their minds. "Renfield, you have permission to kill me if I break my word and try to keep them prisoner without cause."

He paled, hesitating before giving me a sickened nod. The Nephilim studied me in open disbelief.

"Now, let us begin," I said, ignoring their reactions. "Kneel, Adam. Kneel, Eve."

They each bent down on one knee, looking up at me with their fiery blue eyes.

"Give me your wrists," I commanded.

They complied, lifting the wrists closest to each other like reflections in a mirror. I listened as their breathing grew faster and shallower.

I grabbed a wrist in each hand, took a deep breath, and chose Eve first. I met her eyes as I bit into her soft flesh, relieved that there hadn't been any resistance. My eyes instantly rolled back into my head as raw, icy power rolled over me, threatening to drown me in liquid light that felt strangely cleansing—purifying and refreshing, even. It was unlike anything I'd ever felt before.

Although it was shockingly intense, it still wasn't as potent as Victoria's blood—it was just...different.

And I didn't dare take more than a few sips, having no idea what possible effects that Nephilim blood might have on a vampire. I heard Eve whimper in bodily pleasure and I quickly let go, not wanting to accidentally be the first man to give the Nephilim that type of sensual experience—and definitely not after the way she had looked at Adam. Or the way he had discreetly appraised her when he thought she wasn't looking.

My head began to spin as I turned to Adam. I bit into his wrist before he had time to notice how much Eve's blood had affected me. He gasped as I drew two sips of his strangely clean blood before withdrawing. I had to fight to conceal the tingling sensation that began to dance across my flesh, making my skin suddenly feel tight and rejuvenated.

Renfield shot me a concerned look but I waved him off, thankful that Adam and Eve were too transfixed with their own sensations to notice mine. I bit into each of my wrists and then steadied my gaze on Eve. "Open your mouth and drink me, Eve," I told her.

She shuddered involuntarily, blinking dreamily, but remained coherent enough to obey.

"Open your mouth and drink me, Adam," I told him

He did the same, his shoulders trembling.

I extended my wrists over their mouths, marveling at the sight of my bright blood striking their white tongues and throats. They swallowed desperately, their eyes closing as they let out sounds of intense pleasure between fervent gulps of their new master's blood.

I almost gasped in alarm as crimson veins abruptly exploded across their flesh in beautiful striated designs from head to toe, decorating the pristine white marble skin in a manner that somehow only served to emphasize their muscles and curves, turning them each into works of art. Even more mesmerizing, the designs shifted and changed, expanding and contracting like growing root systems across their flesh.

I withdrew my wrists and their eyes shot open, now flaring with crimson flames.

I managed to maintain my composure even though I wanted to stare in wonder. I reached deep within our bodies and latched onto the blood we had each consumed, binding theirs to mine, and mine to theirs before our bodies had time to process it into power or nourishment. The Nephilim tensed, their backs suddenly arching as they flared their chests out, momentarily unable to catch their breaths. My ears popped and I suddenly felt like the room was slowly tilting from side to side.

I felt my bond with Natalie and Victoria suddenly vibrate like a struck gong, but I didn't know what it meant, having to use all my concentration to remain standing and in control of the rest of the process. I didn't have the energy to entertain any distractions.

"Swear your undying fealty to me," I said, using what remained of my focus to speak clearly and concisely, hoping I wasn't slurring. "That you will faithfully and loyally serve me, and only me, until death do us part."

They did, their voices dripping with pleasure and anticipation. "I swear my undying fealty to you, Sorin Ambrogio. I will faithfully serve you, and only you, until death do us part."

I felt the magic take hold of me from two different directions—one from Adam and one from Eve—hitting me like sudden storms of ice and fire that chimed like massive bells, tolling deep enough to make my bones vibrate and my teeth rattle. They gasped, trembling as the same sensations rocked through them. I felt light-headed, but they were too distracted to notice.

I stumbled backwards a few paces, suddenly feeling drunk. "Rise, my children. Rise, Adam and Eve. Welcome to House Ambrogio," I murmured, having to squint to see the room clearly.

I'd feared a strong response or a possible failure. I was turning two

Nephilim, after all. If a little dizziness was the price to pay, I would gladly pay it, because I could tell that it had worked. I had turned them!

My bond with Natalie and Victoria still hummed deep in my chest, feeling suddenly warm and...ticklish. I found myself chuckling dazedly. "Don't forget to eat your dinner," I mumbled tiredly. And then I fell, the world slowly fading to black. I heard a loud splash as Renfield shouted in alarm.

But I was more interested in who was tickling me, even though I was too tired to laugh...

25

I woke up with a start, panicking about an already dissipating distant dream. It took me a moment to realize that I was in bed, back at my chambers in the Museum of Natural History. The crackling fireplace served to calm my racing pulse, and I took a relaxing breath.

Then my eyes widened as a different panic settled over me. I wasn't alone.

Natalie was on my right, and Victoria was on my left, both sleeping soundly. I was extremely aware of this promising development because I could feel the tantalizing sensation of their hot flesh pressed against mine.

And it was enough bare skin for me to realize we were all naked, at least from the waist up.

I regulated my breathing, not wanting to disturb them yet.

Because I couldn't remember how I had gotten to the museum. Had they taken me here? Had...we done anything before falling asleep? My pulse quickened as Victoria murmured something in her sleep, sliding her knee over my thigh. Her head was swiveled in my direction as she hugged a pillow to her cheek, sprawled out on her belly. Her ripe, plump lips begged to be kissed, but I refrained for obvious reasons.

I remained still, wondering exactly how naked I was, and desperately trying to recall exactly how much fun I'd had getting that way.

With no memory coming to mind, I carefully lifted the crimson silk sheets to see that I wore silk pajama pants that were a darker red than the sheets. Rather than scoping out my bedmates, I dropped the sheets, triumphing over the temptation.

What *had* I been doing last night—

Thinking about my current temptation, the answer hit me with a blinding flash.

The Nephilim! Adam and Eve! I'd passed out after turning the fucking Nephilim into vampires! Oh no. Where were they? Who was watching them? Renfield? Was he strong enough? Had the cuffs been strong enough to hold them? Had they killed the two vampires—their first victims? Maybe they'd already overwhelmed and killed Renfield. I needed to get out of bed and call him. Call someone. Anyone who might know his whereabouts, because *someone* had brought me here.

Recalling the strange sensation of my shared bond with the Nephilim and the crisp, purifying taste of their blood, I decided to see if I could feel them through our bond. If successful, I would at least know if they had lost control—feeling a frayed, roughened rope connecting us rather than the smooth, tight wire that signified a healthy relationship with my offspring.

I reached out through my mind, prepared to struggle to find the entirely different breed of vampire. Almost instantly, I blinked in surprise. I immediately felt a solid, slick cable of cleansing light connecting the three of us together in a trinity—not just me to them, and them to me, but them to each other as well.

It was like spotting two lighthouses on a stormy night. They felt utterly dependable and reassuring as their steadfast beacons pierced my murkiest fears from a moment before.

My bond with Renfield wasn't even that smooth. How much of that was from them and how much of it was from me? Regardless, I finally allowed my shoulders to relax, knowing that the world hadn't ended after I passed out. Wherever the Nephilim were, I now sensed that Renfield wasn't far from them, and I felt zero cause for concern from any of them.

Even though one major concern was alleviated, two more tangled knots of seductive trouble dozed only feet away from me.

I slipped out from beneath the silk sheets—careful to keep the women covered up and decent—before I accidentally woke them up and initiated an encounter that I wasn't prepared to handle.

The most frightening aspect was that they seemed more accepting of our strange bond and apparent accompanying relationship than I was. Sure, it sounded glorious on the surface, but it was gods damned complicated. Not that they seemed conflicted or concerned about anything approaching the rational—other than how they intended to share me.

Either way, the situation stressed me right the hell out, and I wanted to clear my head before the other vampires in the museum woke up.

I silently slithered off the foot of the bed, biting my lip as a significant portion of my brain threatened to take over my body to see what kind of fun we could have with the silk sheets and a crackling fire to produce just the right kind of ambience. But that wasn't what I truly wanted. My inner demon wanted it.

Very much so.

I controlled my breathing, closing my eyes as I banished my almost overwhelming lust. Once composed, I crept out the large bedroom's open doorway and into the main salon of my suite. I walked past the coffee table near the second fireplace and picked up the phone Renfield had given me, before slipping out the door and into the main library. I closed the door behind me with a soft click and let out a sigh, leaning back against the warm wood.

I glanced down at the phone's screen to check the time and relaxed even further. I had a little while before the other vampires would wake up, giving me a few moments to sit down and think.

I walked over to a nearby couch and sat down with a huff.

This bond was going to take some serious getting used to. It was confusing as all hell, because as similar as the two women could be, they were also remarkably different, occupying two separate halves of my heart.

I truly cherished Victoria and wanted to learn everything about her. I had already started to believe that I might have finally found my soulmate. She was even immortal. We also shared Artemis' blood—something that could not be duplicated by any other person. Period. I'd felt that powerful resonance between us from the very first moment we'd met.

And her *blood*. I leaned my head back to stare up at the ceiling high above. Her blood made me feel stronger than I ever had in my entire existence. I had quite literally felt unstoppable the last time I'd fed from her—like I'd momentarily become a god.

Even without her incredibly potent blood, Victoria empowered me —not through compliments, but through confrontation and challenge, forcing me to consider all angles of any decision I made. She didn't agree to every little thing that I did. She pushed me, holding my decisions to the grindstone to force me to be better, wiser, and stronger. And I felt it working, even in the brief span of time we'd known each other.

Victoria seemed to feed my very soul, keeping me grounded and focused. A kindred spirit that understood me inside and out. Like she was a missing piece of me that I had finally found.

I could feel her fingers gently curling around my heart, slowly, silently stealing it for herself. And...I liked that feeling. Very, very much.

But then there was Natalie...

As much as I wanted to deny it, I felt an incredibly strong attraction to Natalie in the magical sense. Something about her werewolf spirit seemed to strengthen my own powers, drawing out the bold wildness within my heart. It didn't make me feel godly like Victoria's blood, but it seemed to ignite my heart with passion—as did Natalie herself. She made me believe that I had no limits, that I could reach higher, fight harder...that I was more than I let myself believe. That I could achieve more with her cheering me on.

Much like a general could deliver a rousing speech on the battlefield, inspiring the wounded, beaten soldiers into fighting one last time even when they faced insurmountable odds. Natalie was that general— feeding my inner dreams and making sure my heart was full and ready for the next fight.

Natalie desired to be my battery—to keep my passion, drive, and energy up without taking away from any loving feelings that I held for Victoria. She didn't want the part of my heart that Victoria was interested in, and she was perfectly content with sharing.

Because Natalie wanted to support me in any way I needed, and a large part of me desperately hungered for that—to have an unquenchable bed of hot coals to keep my heart blazing and hungry for the next conquest. I felt like a stronger man with her snarling territorially beside me.

Together, did that make them my heart and soul, or was I being idiotically romantic?

How could a man love two different women in two different fashions and not be considered a scoundrel? And for that matter, I had a hard time truly believing they seemed fine with it, let alone that they also had feelings for each other!

No matter the answers, I wanted both of them. I hated myself for it, but it was the truth.

Even though I'd never been able to handle even one woman, let alone two. Each time I'd fallen in love, my life had taken a drastic turn for the worse. The first time should have been the only lesson necessary—loving Selene had turned me into a vampire, cursed by the Olympian gods for my heart's desire.

It seemed to indicate that my current situation meant that I was setting myself up for twice the fallout. Was I supposed to love both of them equally? Differently?

It was all so confusing. I climbed to my feet, shaking my head. "You once ruled your corner of the world, Sorin. Stop whining about two women and get your head in the game."

My words fell flat in the large open chamber, doing little to inspire my confidence. Regardless, I had other, more serious, matters to address tonight. The sudden surprise of finding them in bed with me had served to wake me up faster than normal, but my mind was still sluggish, so I made my way over to the kitchen down the hall to get my usual drink.

After a few minutes of preparation, I had a drink in hand and was walking back towards the main area. I checked my phone again, realizing that only ten excruciating minutes had passed since waking. The others should be up soon. They already had their marching orders for tonight.

I swept my gaze across the empty catacombs, sipping my steaming mug of blood. Hugo had invented the beverage for us vampires to drink upon waking up at dusk, calling it *bloodee*—like coffee for humans.

"Bloodee puts the bang in your fangs," he'd told me a few weeks ago, extending a steaming white mug of strangely spicy blood. The cup had said *I Sucked Your Mother* on the front, with *and she liked it* on the back. He'd bought it online somewhere, obviously trying to find a way to suck up to his new boss.

Unfortunately, he had neglected to inform me of the key ingredients that he added to the blood to give it such a unique smell and taste. A dash of cinnamon, a pinch of cayenne pepper, and...

A full dose of cocaine.

I hadn't been able to rest for *days*. It was during this high that I had first come up with my bold plans for tonight, because I'd briefly believed that I could actually see into the future. I'd ultimately crashed down from my high and slept for two straight days and nights.

Upon waking, I had immediately informed him to stop putting cocaine in my bloodee, and I'd settled for the virgin version with just the blood and spices for my usual waking drink.

My bloodee had instantly triggered my mental alertness, and I found myself smiling as I scanned the shelves of books surrounding us. Nero had made his lair—now my lair—in a forgotten sublevel of the museum that only showed up in the oldest blueprints. He'd had to enthrall the elevator technicians so that they never remembered doing the work that extended the elevator to descend to a level that no one knew existed.

Far above our heads was a collection of almost thirty interconnected buildings that encompassed over two million square feet beside Central Park, all devoted to the history of mankind. Hugo had sat me down, telling me more than was absolutely necessary about the building's history—since I had been unable to sleep thanks to his cocaine—and I'd come to learn that there were more secrets to the museum than most of the legitimate workers above truly knew. Hugo had once lost a vampire after sending him out to explore several of the uninhabited storage levels. The vampire had gotten lost and ultimately starved to death.

The area we had taken over was filled with books on the occult and science apparatuses that were mainly used by Hugo and Nero—before I had imprisoned him. Aristos and Valentine had offices down the hall where they worked on the various business ventures that the vampires had run before I forced Dracula to kill them all. Stevie spent many days here now, working with the pair to accomplish peaceful transfers and the successful management of our various businesses throughout the city.

Aristos was the money man, and Valentine was involved with acquisitions and general management—and it was their lifelong mission to infuriate each other while working. Although after work, they could often be found snuggling up together on a couch with one of their willing blood slaves between them, sharing like the best of friends. I wasn't sure if they were romantically involved, but I didn't really care to pry. As long as they did their jobs and didn't attempt to betray me, they could sink their fangs into whatever body parts they wanted.

I'd outlawed murder unless it was a criminal—and even then, I had made sure that we had a system in place to check their family and make sure our final justice didn't leave behind an orphan. Or if an orphanage was actually a better option than the child's current life with a criminal parent, that they were set up with an anonymous, lucrative trust that would make sure they were raised in a healthy, loving home and that a significant portion of their future living expenses were taken care of.

My fervor on that topic had truly surprised Hugo, Aristos, and Valentine. Especially when I'd named the charity *Kassandra's Tears*, after both Renfield's daughter and the first true Oracle of Delphi.

Orphans were loved by the vampires. Full stop.

I'd managed to slip in quite a few of my new vampires as official employees of the museum so that we no longer had to worry about hiding our presence. We set up an employment agency—run by Stevie's werewolves—that catered specifically to my vampire offspring —the old war vets Gabriel and I had turned from the underbelly of New York City.

Come sunset, they, and a large number of werewolves, would have a vital job to do across the street in Central Park—working together to make sure the entire park and surrounding streets were devoid of all humans. Since most of my vampires had recently been homeless, they knew all the favored hiding places. A few hours from now, Central Park would be empty of everyone but my vampires and Stevie's werewolves.

I stiffened as I felt a violent...ripple to the air. That was the only way I could describe it.

Everything went silent—the air vents stopped pushing air and a ticking clock stopped ticking.

I remained motionless, slowly scanning the sub-basement floor for signs of danger, wondering if Dracula had sent more vampires or if the witches had somehow broken in past the security werewolves we had upstairs during the day. But nothing moved, and nothing else happened. I glanced down at the coffee mug in my hand, at the bloodee I had just finished.

"Son of a bitch. He put cocaine in it again," I hissed, dropping the mug.

It shattered at my feet and I winced at the loud sound in the oppressive silence.

I wondered how I was going to enact my plans while high on—

"It's not cocaine, Ambrogio," a silky voice said from a few paces away. I spun towards the sound to find a stunning, young woman with long white hair studying me from the open doorway leading into my chambers. But I knew that I hadn't left the door open.

She wore a pristine white toga that was clasped with a silver crescent moon brooch over one shoulder, leaving the other bare. The toga hung lower on the side with the bare shoulder, ending just above the knee, but ended just below her hip on the other side, flashing a long expanse of pale, almost silvery skin. She wore a belt made of connected silver rings, and silver lace sandals that extended up her calves. It was all very monochromatic. I stared at her in disbelief, knowing her face like the back of my hand. Better than my own face, even.

"Selene," I breathed in disbelief.

She slipped into my chambers without speaking a word, her long, silver fingernails glinting like razors. I remained motionless out of pure shock, wondering if I really was high on cocaine.

The first woman I had ever loved—a woman who had shared an entire life with me, even though we had never been allowed to touch.

And she'd just slipped into my rooms—where two naked women slept in my bed.

26

I hissed, chasing through the open door after her. Not finding her in the main room, I continued running towards the open door of the bedroom, beginning to panic as I imagined those fingernails slicing into Natalie or Victoria. I skidded to a halt upon seeing her standing at the foot of the massive bed, staring numbly at the sleeping women with an eerily calm, terrifying aura of jealousy radiating from her entire body. Her gaze subtly shifted from Natalie on the left side of the bed, to Victoria on the right, and back to the center where a third person had obviously been sleeping.

With a swift, violent motion, she gripped a fistful of the red silk sheets and tugged them down towards the foot of the bed, uncovering the two mostly naked women. They continued to sleep, not even twitching at the sensations of the sheets being torn away.

Victoria now slept on her right side, facing Natalie, and she wore only a pair of black, skin-tight underwear that resembled a pair of extremely short shorts. Her left leg was still bent and folded over the space where I had been sleeping, and her elbow covered her breasts as she hugged her pillow with both hands, sleeping soundly. The firelight danced over the deliciously narrow curve of her waist, revealing her utter lack of body fat and emphasizing the well-defined muscles of her back and shoulders.

Natalie slept on her back with her hands clasped behind her head, her short blonde hair covering one of her eyes. Natalie was noticeably leaner than Victoria, not having nearly as much muscle mass, although both were thinner than most other female werewolves or warriors. Natalie's ribs were visible, and I could clearly see the muscle definition of her stomach, broken into four sections as if drawn on with a pencil. She wore only a red, lacy thong—a thin triangle of fabric held in place by two lacy strings leading up from each corner to hug her prominent hip bones.

"Selene," I pleaded in a loud enough tone that I hoped it might wake my lovers, or at least draw Selene's attention away from them.

Selene tensed at the sound of my voice, but she didn't turn around. Instead, she slowly began to approach the left side of the bed where Natalie continued to sleep. There was no more time for talking. I took a sudden step forward, preparing to tackle her, but something unseen latched onto my wrists, halting me before I could take my second step. I snarled viciously, straining and pulling as hard as I could, but it was no use.

I glanced down to see that fragile, paper-thin glass manacles banded around my wrists, connected to glass chains as thin as a fine necklace that stretched behind me. I glanced back, but they continued on into the far room and out of sight. I tugged harder and watched in disbelief as the impossibly thin restraints flushed a deep wine color— the shade of the darkest blood in the body—as their strength was tested. I relaxed again, watching as they swiftly shifted back to become transparent.

Selene finally glanced over at me from beside the bed, mere inches away from Natalie. "It uses your own blood against you, my *beloved Ambrogio*," she said, clearly enunciating the term of endearment in a way that made me clench my teeth. "It is quite unbreakable. The harder you pull, the more of your blood reserves it absorbs, leaving you with *less* energy to pull. Hephaestus is rather clever and devious. But what else is a man to do when his wife, Aphrodite, is so openly..." she glanced down at Natalie and then Victoria, her lips curling back in a bloodless sneer, "unfaithful."

I snarled, chomping my teeth as I threw everything I had against my Olympian-made chains. Hephaestus was the Blacksmith God, known for all manner of breathtaking creations throughout history. Selene calmly lifted a lone finger and her wickedly long fingernail glistened like molten silver in the glow of the fire. She lowered it to finally touch Natalie's right nipple, which looked remarkably close to where her heart should be located.

The werewolf screamed as the silver touched her skin—but she didn't wake.

Victoria slept peacefully beside the werewolf with a dreamy smile on her face despite the agonized scream.

Like she was merely drawing on flesh with a marker, Selene trailed her fingernail upwards in a sinuous, curving line, arcing across the top of Natalie's chest and then gliding downwards between the center of her breasts, leaving behind a bright red line that oozed with steaming blood. Selene paused with her finger between Natalie's breasts to brush a loose strand of hair from my werewolf's cheek with her free hand, smiling down at her victim's nightmare.

"SELENE! STOP!" I roared as Natalie panted and hissed, struggling to regain her breath from the first heart-wrenching scream. Her face was contorted in agony, but she continued to sleep, her body twitching at the slow, sensual torture across her chest.

I felt the crystal chains emitting a strained ringing sound in the air, and my body draining of power only a hair faster than I could pull, tormenting me with its maddening design. Because I knew that was its intent—to give the imprisoned a false sense of hope.

If loving Natalie would save her life, I would love every square inch of her body. Every vice and virtue hidden deep within her soul. Every sorrowful tear and every belly laugh. I would love every *drop* of her blood if it would save her life from Selene. The emotion hit me like a bolt of lightning, momentarily surprising me.

Selene gritted her teeth, glancing back at me sharply—as if she had sensed my sudden surge of emotion. "*Two*, Ambrogio? Was *one* not enough to shame me!?" she hissed, turning back to focus on her sinuous artwork as she continued arcing her fingernail downward to loop into another rounded curve below the swell of Natalie's right breast. Selene was panting as she continued up over Natalie's breast, stopping right at her nipple before taking a step back to nod satisfactorily down at her work.

She glanced over her shoulder at me with a grim, ghost of a smile, pointing down at the sadistically artful wound over the whimpering werewolf's chest. "S."

I bared my teeth at the woman I had once loved. "Why?" I snarled, straining against my restraints even though I knew it was fruitless.

"For Selene. So that every time you touch this trollop, you will remember the woman you could not touch. The woman you said you loved. Although I'm counting on them thinking it stands for Sorin— that you marked your harem as the livestock they truly are. While they slept!"

"What *happened* to you?" I hissed, straining against the chains. I tried to reach out to the naked women on the bed through our new bond, to somehow wake them up from this slumber. I could feel them —Natalie's nightmare and Victoria's peaceful dream—but I couldn't get through to them.

"Do not waste your time. Your voice in their heads would only serve to make it worse for them. This will be over shortly, at any rate."

And she began walking towards me, pausing near the foot of the bed. I snarled, trying to lunge close enough to take a bite, but she remained infuriatingly out of reach—a mere hair's breadth from harm as my teeth snapped shut before her nose, strong enough to shift her hair. She didn't even budge.

She gripped my chin suddenly, preventing me from biting her or breaking free as her silver fingernails touched my skin and—

Did not burn me.

They were as cold as ice, but they did not harm me. I stilled suddenly, wondering what was really going on. Silver had almost killed me a few weeks ago. It was one of Artemis' curses. Selene stared at me, and I watched as her face crumpled in pain, dropping the mask of jealous rage as if it had never happened. Her eyes were full of anguished horror and she bit her lip in profound guilt as she spoke to me.

No. Not *spoke.*

It was hardly even a *breath,* but I heard words—so soft and faint that I had to hold my own breath to even *notice* them.

"*I don't want to do this, my love, but even I am watched by my fellow Olympians. They wish to destroy you, Ambrogio. You were supposed to die as an orphan. Then as a vampire. Then in the Americas. They have to kill you because of what you are. Who you are. Your curses were a conspiracy born in their jealousy!*"

I stared at her, dumbfounded, speaking back just as softly. "What do you mean?"

"*This was the only way I could pass along a warning without drawing their suspicion. They had to see me hurt you. Use your bonds to save them, my love. Remember your name and who hurt you, because they know your plans this night and will do anything to stop you, even turning him against you. Connect the dots before it's too late! Don't let me harm the other girl, Ambrogio,*" she pleaded, fighting back tears. "*I can't bear hurting the only lights left in your life when the Olympians have purposely taken every other from you! Use your bond. Stop me. NOW!*"

27

Selene abruptly sneered and she shoved my head, laughing viciously as she donned the supposedly false mask of spite again. What the hell had that been? Use my bond? I'd tried!

"You thought I would actually kiss you!" she crowed. "So broken. So weak." She continued circling the bed, coming to Victoria's side now. "If the werewolf didn't motivate you to be faithful, perhaps the hunter will. I wonder if Artemis would object to me spoiling her human protégé..." she trailed off thoughtfully. "Now would be the time to object, Huntress," she said dryly. "I know you are watching my sport. You always do."

I desperately reached out to my bond as Selene stopped beside Victoria, facing her unprotected back since the hunter was sleeping on her side.

I railed and screamed. Not Victoria! She was my soul! My fresh start. I needed her to keep me grounded. To knock me off my high horse when I wasn't thinking clearly. Our souls were one, and I would be gods damned if I let Selene—even as a charade—come so close as scratching her.

I called up my blood reserves, trying again to throw them at my women and wake them up—

The realization hit me like a blow to my face.

Not my *women*.

Not my *friends*.

Not my *allies*.

Natalie and Victoria were...my *lovers*.

Whether we had consummated anything or not. We were lovers far beyond the simple aspects of love or lust. We shared the same *spirit*. We were the backbone of the same cause—to rid the world of the true monsters.

Because only monsters could stand against that kind of foe.

We three were all *devils*. They were *my* devils. I was *their* devil.

Taking Selene's cryptic advice, I sent out one last clarion call through my bond, using all the power I could muster, and not just to reach out to my devilish lovers before me.

I reached out to my entire bloodline, infusing my desperate need into every drop of blood I held in my reserves. Rather than trying to force that imbued blood with destructive power...

I *sacrificed* it in one implosive force that made my own heart skip and falter off beat, causing my eyes to suddenly flash with searing pain, followed by an agonizing throb in the depths of my brain. My head hung limp before my chest as I panted shakily, trying to catch a full breath as all the power left my body, condensing into a single drop of blood that simply evaporated with a *pop* like a pricked bubble.

I felt an unseen wave of power clap deep within my chest like a constricting circle, and then that power ricocheted outward blasting forth in every direction—not guided by my will, so it slipped right past my glass manacles and chains.

Almost instantly, I felt a reaction—from much closer than I'd hoped, although the reaction was too far away for Selene to have noticed. I felt twin throbs of power come to attention from deep within the museum itself and they rapidly swelled with an alarming amount of energy. Then more. And more. And even more echoes heard my silent cry, from all over the city.

Their master was in danger. It was time for war.

Selene glanced up at me sharply, cocking her head as her eyes flicked to the crystal chains. "What..." she trailed off, slowly turning to fully face me. "What did you just do with your blood? I felt you do something, yet the chains show no tampering, and nothing happened as a result. The chains are immune to any force used against them..."

With agonizing slowness, I lifted my head, peering up at Selene through the curtain of hair hanging over my face. I had no idea which side she was truly on. Perhaps her little private conversation was yet another way for her to torment me. I didn't care. I was fixing this my own way, getting an idea from her last comment.

"They...are...MINE!" I roared.

And I abruptly *moved*.

Rather than pull *against* the restraints, I *twisted* my wrists harshly, directing my force in on myself. Because Selene had just admitted that the chains only prevented forces applied *against* them. And the call through my bonds had been successful because I had sacrificed my blood reserves, aiming my power inward rather than forcing them out of my body.

The resulting ricochet had slipped right through the glass restraints without even slowing.

With that simple twisting motion, the manacles sliced deeply into both of my wrists like razors, and blood began to spray outward and downward. My legs immediately buckled, and my feet slipped in my blood, forcing me to my knees. Selene gasped in disbelief, racing towards me. "What have you *done*, you fool?" she hissed, sounding both horrified and furious.

My vision began to tunnel, and I felt my pulse slowing at an alarming pace, much swifter than any human attempting to slice his own wrists open like I had just done.

Luckily, the glass had been so thin and sharp that it managed to slice through my tendons to reach the veins deep beneath my flesh. Selene had closed half the distance when the double doors to the room suddenly blew inwards, slamming into the walls and destroying one of the couches.

Selene gasped as two hulking marble vampires scanned the room with their fiery, crimson eyes. Their once pristine white skin was now decorated with the shifting crimson striations, resembling fingers of lightning arcing across their bodies in slow motion.

The Nephilim vampires, Adam and Eve. The twin throbs of power I'd felt deep within the museum, although I hadn't known they were *this* close.

Their focus latched onto Selene and they snarled. "OLYMPIAN!" they roared in unison.

Eve leapt into the air with her wicked crimson claws outstretched, aiming straight for Selene, while Adam crouched defensively in the now-open doorway, holding his massive arms out to prevent Selene's escape.

Selene's eyes widened and she shot me an incredibly horrified look before she promptly disappeared in a puff of sparkling silver mist. My chains evaporated in the same way and I fell forward, draped over the foot of the bed, unable to even catch myself since my wrist tendons were severed, and too weak to have done so even if they had been functional. I couldn't even manage to roll over or sit up as blood continued pulsing out of my wounds. All I could do was stare at my Nephilim vampires, blinking slowly as I struggled to remain awake. I couldn't even gather the necessary energy to call out to them—neither through my empty blood reserves or my actual voice.

Adam and Eve snarled murderously, their heads swiveling back and forth for any sign of Selene. I heard Natalie and Victoria come awake with astonished gasps to find the two Nephilim invading their rooms, and no sign of me sleeping between them.

Natalie's voice was tinged with pain, and I could tell she was clenching her teeth. "Where...is my Sorin. I can smell his blood," she hissed, sounding terrified at the implication.

In my position at the foot of the bed, they couldn't even see me with the bunched-up sheets forming a wall between us.

So close...

"Where is Sorin?" Victoria demanded, making my ears ring.

Adam and Eve raced over to me, shaking the floor with thunderous stomps before scooping me up in their incredibly strong grips and propping me up between them.

Despite Eve being half Adam's body mass, she was equally as strong. "What do you need, Master Sorin?" Eve whispered affectionately, nuzzling her cheek against mine.

Victoria and Natalie cried out in stunned shock to see me suddenly hoisted into view, openly bleeding from the wrists down and my silk pants drenched from the knees to the cuffs where I'd been kneeling in my own blood.

"My bed..." I breathed dazedly, not sure if I succeeded in actually making a sound.

The Nephilim gracefully lifted me up over the wall of blankets and settled me down onto my back between Natalie and Victoria. I was so weak that I couldn't move my neck or lift my arms. I couldn't even roll over.

"Guard that door with your lives!" Victoria commanded the pair.

Adam and Eve obeyed without hesitation as a flurry of warm hands trailed all over my body, searching for additional wounds. My vision was tunneling smaller, timed with my slowing pulse so that it expanded and contracted with each fading throb.

One of them stuck two fingers in my mouth, hurriedly scooping up my saliva to spread across my wounded wrists. "His saliva closes open wounds," Victoria whispered urgently. "He can't afford to lose any more blood." If I hadn't been so weak, I would have applauded her ingenuity. "My god!" she gasped, suddenly alarmed. "Who the fuck cut into your chest with a silver knife?"

"It's already healing," Natalie snapped, the pain in her voice proving her lie.

"No!" Victoria snapped lividly. "It's *spreading*! You're burning up!"

"He's obviously not able to help, so I'll just have to do it myself," Natalie growled. She was right. Natalie slithered her body over mine, straddling my hips. She supported her weight with one palm over my heart, and I was alarmed at how hot her skin was—a sign that the wound was overpowering her healing abilities as a werewolf.

She needed my strength as much as I needed hers. Without it, we would both die.

28

I stared up at the topless, werewolf goddess in delirious awe, feeling like I was gazing upon a dark angel. Because the light from the fireplace at the far end of the room limned her silhouette—the graceful neck, the delicate shoulders, and the perky swell of her breasts—with a warm, orange glow, leaving the details of her chest and face shrouded in darkness. Somehow, I could still see the familiar glimmer in her eyes.

Natalie wiggled her hips to get comfortable. "Got milk?" she asked with a sudden laugh, and then she shifted her hands to either side of my head as she descended over me, angling her breast towards my mouth.

"Open wide, Sorin," Victoria purred in amusement from only inches away as she leaned down next to me, using her thumb to gently tug my chin down so that my mouth opened. "You're saving each other's lives. Don't look so happy about it."

Natalie laughed huskily. Then she gasped as her nipple brushed my lips, momentarily shuddering before she continued on to offer me the outside of her breast—a larger biting area and one not marred by her wound.

She finally paused and I felt one of her hands scoop under my neck, getting a good grip. Then she let out a breath before simultaneously sinking her torso lower and lifting my mouth to her feverish skin. With the last of my strength, I sank my fangs into the side of her breast and sucked like my life depended on it.

Because it did.

Natalie cried out, her body stiffening as her thighs clenched my hips like a vise. Her blood raced down my throat, tasting like my happiest memory of safe sunlight as it exploded into my body like tendrils of lightning, making my toes curl. Natalie panted into my ear, urging me on as her hot flesh pressed firmly against my mouth. I lapped up her blood with my tongue, drinking her down with abandon.

Strength bloomed within me, and I was soon able to hold my own head up without Natalie's support, but she didn't show any signs of letting go as her fist clenched tighter, pulling at my hair. In response, I sucked harder, pleased at the sudden frantic rocking of her hips.

My wrists flashed cold, and I felt my tendons fusing back together with creaking pops, sending painful tingles shooting down my finger-tips as the fresh flow of blood was restored.

Natalie's panting rapidly grew into breathless whimpers as Victoria urged us on in a soothing, caring tone. "It's working! You're healing her, Sorin. The wound is shrinking! Keep drinking!"

As if her words had been a catalyst, Natalie shuddered in release, but her hips didn't stop grinding against me and my suddenly func-tioning manhood. She writhed like a demon, her underwear now hot and damp as they pressed into my silk pajama pants.

I did manage to notice that her skin no longer felt feverish. At least not in any bad way.

"Ohmygod, ohmygod, ohmygod..." Natalie chanted, directly into my ear.

My hands suddenly began to work again, no longer numb and tingling from their repair, and I couldn't help but grab onto her hips to keep her close, finally able to enforce some measure of control over my prey. I trailed one hand up, sliding my fingers over the sweat-slick muscles of her back to reach across and grab her opposite shoulder, pulling her breast further into my mouth as my other hand gripped a handful of her ass, my fingers brushing the thin lacy string between her cheeks. I growled into her breast as I hooked the lace thong with my finger, tugging it sharply against her—

Natalie instantly shoved her face into the pillow and screamed at the top of her lungs as her body rocked more violently than before. I didn't let up, instead sucking harder until a cascading trio of climaxes abruptly roared through her, catching her entirely by surprise and causing her body to spasm again and again and again, briefly unable to even breathe. I greedily lapped up every drop of blood that flowed from her breast.

I sensed a subtle change to her blood and I instantly extracted my fangs, lapping my tongue over her wound and pulling away, breathing heavily as her blood roared through my body. She collapsed atop me, nuzzling her face into my neck as she struggled to catch her breath, and I slid my fingertips down her sweat-slicked spine, shifting one hand to lightly trail down the side of her rib cage before firmly settling atop her hip and upper thigh with a firm squeeze. She spasmed again with a light whimper, and I chuckled while I lightly massaged her lower back with the fingers of my other hand in slow, sensual circles until I felt her body finally begin to relax.

She slowly sat up, raking her nails down my chest as she settled her feverish panties atop my aching groin, squirming absently as if she didn't know what effect it was having. In response, I gently scratched my fingernails down her ass, curving inwards across the backs of her inner thighs, dangerously close to that maddening triangle of hot silk. I laughed when her legs instinctively clenched and she let out a surprised gasp. Then I gently gripped her waist with both hands and set her down beside me, chuckling when it took her a moment to unclench her thighs again. Her body was otherwise compliant and sluggish as she allowed me to move her, never blinking or breaking eye contact as she sunk down into the mattress with a contented purr and a lazy smile.

"Are you okay?" I asked in a rough voice, propping myself up on one elbow as I stared down at her chest to find only a razor-thin, pale scar where Selene had cut into her. It almost looked like an artful tattoo, now, emphasizing the beauty of her torso. All I cared about was that it was healed, but I was concerned I'd continued drinking from her a second too long after I'd tasted the subtle change in her blood—a warning sign that it was time to stop. The first warning sign, thankfully.

It marked the final point where they would be able to function normally, post-biting.

Drinking beyond that might result in the victim needing to go sleep for a few hours to recover.

Natalie glanced up at me, lifting an arm to rest over her head with a lazy grin. "Oh, I'm way past okay, honey. But you are not yet fully restored. You've had your milk," she said, wiggling her chest playfully. "Now it's time for your *cookies*," she said with a wider grin before giving me a hard-enough shove to knock me down onto my back again.

I had no warning as Victoria deliciously slipped into place atop my lap, humming hungrily as she cruelly grazed her sex over my silk pants in an exploratory, sliding measure.

"Mmm...that's nice," she murmured, licking her lips. She leaned back, lifting both arms to adjust her hair over her shoulders.

I was more interested in the glistening sheen of her breasts in the ambient firelight and how her hip bones looked tasty enough to bite. She finished and set both hands on my abdomen, smiling impatiently. "You've got a big night ahead of you, Sorin. As much as I think we would all like this to continue, we need to make this a quickie."

She grabbed my wrists and flung them behind my head, making me smile. Then she gripped my biceps in each hand and slowly slid her breasts across my chest, making my skin pebble and my fists clench above my head. She slowly settled each of her elbows down beside my ears, still pinning my arms as her breasts grazed my parted lips, and then she rose up so that they hung just out of my reach. She stared down at me with smoky eyes, her hair falling to form a curtain around us as she licked her lips.

"Don't be gentle," she whispered, taking a moment to enjoy the frenzied lust and hunger warring in my eyes before she laughed and angled her torso low enough to offer my aching fangs the side of her left breast, still pinning my arms overhead.

My fangs sunk into her salty skin and an important part of me almost tore through my silk pants. Only the fact that Victoria was already grinding her groin into mine, sliding up and down with excruciating slowness, kept it at bay.

That first drop of blood hit my tongue and it tasted like...it tasted like...

It was like tasting frost-coated lava. With cocaine in the center.

Her blood hit me like a raging wildfire of liquid ice, and a silent storm of black lightning struck my brain.

My mind simply stopped making sense to me.

My ears popped as her Olympian-infused blood tore through me, destroying everything in its wake. I felt my bones groan, my cartilage bend to the tearing point, and my muscles rip with millions of flashes of fiery agony.

Yet...

An icy wind roared through immediately following the destruction, freezing everything in place with a sudden coating of thick frost. That frost expanded, cracking and snapping as it bolstered the damage, repairing every strain and crack within me and filling the voids and fractures so that I thought I might explode, or that I would see the spears of ice tear through my very skin.

I sucked harder, demanding more of the destructive pleasure as I managed to slip my arms free of her trap, desperately raking my fingers up the back of her neck and scalp.

I grabbed her by the hair, listening closely to her sudden breathless moaning as I tugged—careful to pull only hard enough to make her gasp in surprise and not in true pain.

She climaxed at that exact moment, crying out loudly as I held her head back.

I had to forcefully block out the sudden sweet, honeyed scent of Victoria's lust.

To me, the smell was akin to licking the first drops of juicy nectar from a freshly split peach.

Even though her frame was tiny, even someone as strong as Adam wouldn't have been able to unlock her thighs from trapping me to the bed. Heat bloomed over her sex and my free hand slid beneath the waist of her shorts to squeeze one of her cheeks before curling my fingers lower around the very peak of her inner thigh, close enough to feel the slick moisture that was definitely not sweat.

I almost lost my mind as she spasmed again, screaming as she slapped the headboard loudly with her open palm. "Yes! Yes! YES!" she cried.

And I continued to drink, devouring her blood as it bonded with my body, re-forging my muscles and bones and tendons into something new, something stronger.

Something unbreakable.

Like she was infusing priceless sapphires into my very bones. I even felt her blood bond with the blood I had taken from Natalie, instantly crystallizing into dense rubies that sunk into the well of my blood reserves.

I tasted that subtle warning tang in her blood and released her with a faint tug to her hair and a squeeze of her inner thigh, my fingers sliding alarmingly close to a veritable oven of hot desire. She gasped at another climax, her back arching as she flung her head back, grinding harder into me at the near touch of my fingers.

My own back was locked rigid as her blood continued to rock through me, making me want to scream as my ancient vampire powers poured into me—granting me the abilities that I was so sorely missing after my magical slumber.

Because they were taking so long to come back on their own.

Victoria's blood, on the other hand, made me feel as if my old powers had been a joke—powers that only a fledgling vampire would brag about to his old human friends. I released my grip on her hair, and Victoria slipped off me, collapsing to my other side in a quivering puddle. She panted hoarsely, her thighs squeezed together as one of her hands tightly cupped her breast—the one I had bitten.

"Oh. My. God." Her eyes were closed, and she was licking her lips.

"I'm pretty sure even He couldn't do you so well without actually *doing* you," Natalie purred, resting a possessive hand on my chest. I turned my head to see that she was lying on her side, facing me. She had draped her knee over my thigh at some point, and she was leaning on her elbow, propping her head up in her hand. She winked at me and then glanced over my chest at Victoria, who only just now seemed to be coming out of her haze. "You okay, Victoria?" she asked with a grin.

"I'm going to need a shower. Maybe reconsider my life's priorities, because I've been focusing on all the wrong things," the vampire hunter murmured in a sleepy hum.

Natalie let out a loud laugh, absently raking her fingernails across my chest—like a cat kneading a blanket. "Good. Because those two statues have been itching to get Sorin's attention for a while now. Either that or they are shy. Or curious. Or shy-curious."

I sat up sharply, my motion inadvertently forcing Natalie to break contact. I had completely forgotten that I'd told Adam and Eve to stand guard at the now-open door. Victoria tiredly lifted her arm up in the air to cast a vague wave at our audience, not bothering to sit up or cover herself, which sent Natalie into a fit of giggles.

29

Missing my werewolf's idle touch, I propped the pillows up behind me so that I could lean back at an angle. Then I silently grasped her hand and placed it back on my chest with a fond smile. She beamed brightly, obliging me with more attention. It felt...nice to maintain contact with my two devils, and it had nothing to do with lust. It was almost as if physical contact served to strengthen our bond. Victoria still needed time to recover, so I let her be.

I finally addressed the Nephilim. "Is everything okay?" I asked.

Eve was smiling warmly at me and Natalie, taking note of our silent exchange.

Adam nodded. "Yes, Master Ambrogio. Three vampires are waiting to speak with you outside of your chambers. Master Renfield refused to let them enter."

"We can all hear you since you destroyed the doors!" Aristos called out in an annoyed, distant shout.

Adam cast me a guilty wince, shifting from foot-to-foot. "It was a sturdy door. My compliments to the carpenter."

Natalie burst out laughing. "Please tell me that was a pun." The Nephilim stared back at her quizzically. "*The* carpenter," she pressed, glancing from one to the other. She finally sighed in grumbling disappointment.

I ignored Natalie's interruption, turning back to Adam. "Please call Renfield in here."

Adam nodded, cupping his hands around his mouth as he called out through the open doors in a booming voice. "Master Ambrogio requests your presence, Master Renfield."

Eve was eyeing the three of us on the bed. She slowly licked her lips, looking upon us as I'm sure her namesake had once looked upon the infamous apple in the Garden of Eden. "Will...you show us how to do that?" she asked.

I studied her in silence for a few seconds, knowing that this was a pivotal moment for the Nephilim. "Biting someone?" I asked.

She shook her head very slowly. "The...other part," she said quietly, her eyes discreetly flicking to Adam for the barest of seconds. He did the same thing, discreetly glancing at her a moment later. I hid my amusement at their apparent...well, whatever it was between them.

Natalie burst out laughing. "I *like* her! What's your name, babe?" she asked, eyeing the Nephilim's similar nudity with a nod of approval.

"Eve," she said, sounding self-conscious. "I am a Nephilim vampire. I think."

Natalie waved at her, unflustered by her answer. "I'm Natalie. And that lazy puddle of sex is Victoria—"

A pillow hit her in the face, barely missing me. "Fuck off," Victoria muttered, still lying on her back with her eyes closed. She lifted her arm again to wave in Eve's general direction. "Hi, Eve, the Nephilim vampire."

Eve waved back with a crooked smile. "Hi, Natalie and lazy puddle of sex, Victoria."

Natalie hooted, her fingernails digging into my chest at the motion. Victoria chuckled softly and finally rolled over onto her side to face us and join the conversation, propping herself up on her elbow. I draped my arm behind her, pulling her close enough so that I could rest my hand on her lower back. She smiled, wiggling even closer so she could set a hand on my stomach, her shoulders relaxing the moment she did so.

Then she stuck her tongue out at Natalie, laughing at the were-wolf's playful, territorial growl.

Eve watched us, fascinated. To be honest, it was fascinating to me as well—if I tried thinking about it too closely. So, I didn't. I simply knew that it felt better to be close to them. And it had nothing to do with any lurking darker desires that would have to wait until we fixed the door or found some other place with privacy.

Although I was confident that would make us all feel much better as well.

I realized Adam was discreetly appraising Eve with a hopeful, adoring smile. Thankfully, his display of pleasure remained limited to his face and not his open nudity.

Eve was as tall as Adam, but so much smaller that she looked tiny when compared to his sheer mass. He looked like a gladiator, yet I could tell that she had him in her thrall—and I hadn't even taught them about that yet! This was the natural kind of enthrallment. The innocent beginnings of potential love.

Eve was watching me intently, still expecting an answer to her earlier question about teaching her the ways of lovers. Natalie slowly grinned, turning to look at me with an arched eyebrow. As did Victoria, both on the verge of laughter.

I cleared my throat uncertainly. "Well, you see, Eve...the thing is..." I trailed off, struggling under the scrutiny of the three female preda-tors. I had no idea where to begin with the previously celibate Nephilim.

Victoria rolled her eyes before resting her cheek on my ribs to address Natalie. "When you find someone you like very much, you do things to make them feel good, to give them pleasure. And they return the favor. Then you try those pleasurable things without clothes," she said, eyeing their already nude bodies with a smirk.

"And the favors and pleasures get better with practice," Natalie said with a suggestive smile.

Eve nodded thoughtfully, pointedly not looking at her fellow Nephilim.

"My name is Adam," he said, because everyone else was staring at him, having already picked up on the apparent attraction between the two Nephilim. Eve's lips thinned, and she looked suddenly embarrassed.

"Hello, *likeable someone*," Natalie said with a grin, leading Eve to catch the obvious hint. Adam and Eve each tensed, pointedly avoiding looking at each other.

I wondered if they had ever been permitted to entertain romance as Nephilim. It didn't seem like it. They had lived underground together for hundreds of years, so it would have already happened long ago if they harbored such feelings for each other and were allowed to indulge.

I would have to change that—help them understand that romance wasn't an evil thing.

Renfield chose that moment to enter the room, striding past the Nephilim without noticing their discomfort.

Renfield smiled, looking relieved to find me healthy and hale. "Adam and Eve told me about the Olympian intruder. We are fortunate that they were so quick to respond to your blood alarm."

"We were already awake," Adam said with a light shrug of his broad shoulders.

I arched an eyebrow at Renfield, and he nodded. "It seems your new Nephilim vampires do not require rest during the day. The rest of us were still sleeping, so we were not as swift to respond. It will not happen again, Master Ambrogio."

"We do not require sleep at all," Eve clarified. "At least we didn't as Nephilim."

I nodded thoughtfully, realizing I had just promoted them to guards. "Last night is rather hazy to me—at least following the ritual," I clarified.

"We felt the ritual," Natalie said with a shiver. "It was different than our bond, though," she added, glancing at me curiously. I nodded without explanation, because I had no answers.

"You were singing," Victoria smiled, but her nails scratched my stomach to let me know she wasn't pleased about my deceit—that I hadn't included her and Natalie.

"We had fun getting you ready for bed," Natalie smiled, pointing down at my pajamas.

I blushed, studying the Nephilim. "Your blood is very...potent." Internally, I wondered about my new bond with them—how different it was from my bond with Natalie and Victoria. I was certain that I would find out tonight when we summoned the castle.

Adam smiled at my comment. "No other vampire in the world has ever been able to bite us without simply exploding upon contact, thanks to our Holy nature. A little singing is better."

I grunted. "Should I be concerned about you shaking hands with my vampires?" I asked, wondering if their very touch was poison.

They shared a long look with each other before Eve smiled brightly. "I do not believe that is a concern. We consumed the souls of the two vampires you gave us in the underground before Master Renfield brought us all here. They did not explode upon contact."

My relief was overshadowed by her other comment. "Consumed their souls? You mean their blood, right?"

Adam shook his head. "When we bit them, we drank down their spirit and power, along with their blood." He licked his lips fondly. "I must admit that I did not anticipate it tasting so pleasant."

Eve nodded with a shudder of pleasure. "It was...a first for me," she said. Then she abruptly averted her eyes, looking ashamed of her reaction.

Natalie slowly sat up, hopping off the bed. "Can you help me get some warm washcloths, Eve? So I can clean up the mess Sorin made?" she asked the Nephilim, stretching her arms out over her head and rising up on the balls of her feet with a sigh. Victoria watched Natalie's movements like a lion hunting a gazelle, humming absently, not seeming to realize her fingernails had dug into my stomach. I forced myself to look away before a much more direct reaction came over me and I ordered everyone but Natalie from the room.

Eve followed Natalie into the bathroom. I heard the two women speaking softly and smiled. Adam was in trouble, now.

Renfield cleared his throat, drawing my attention. "I thought it safest to bring the Nephilim here after you grew weary from turning them," he said carefully, rather than stating I had passed out cold. "Since it was their first night, I put them in the warded cells in the event they lost control while we slept." He eyed Adam with a reassuring smile. "Though it didn't do much good."

Adam lifted his wrist to reveal a charred mark over his wrist where the manacles had been. "When I felt your alarm, they just burned off. Then I tore through the ward, freeing Eve so we could come to your aid." He frowned. "I had to break quite a few more doors, Master Ambrogio. Otherwise, I would have been here sooner."

I burst out laughing, shaking my head. Good lord. How strong were the Nephilim? Neither the warded cells nor the nullification cuffs had held them back.

"How do you feel? You seem in control of your faculties."

Adam shrugged. "New powers, new day. I feel no uncontrollable urges." He frowned. "Well, I did when I saw the Olympian," he admitted with a growl.

Natalie guided Eve back into the room, tugging her by the hand. The Nephilim carried steaming washcloths over to me and Victoria. I dipped my chin, accepting one as I sat up. I used it to wash off my hands and wrists, knowing we would all need a long shower rather than just a washcloth. Victoria did the same, and Natalie watched us, perched on the edge of the bed.

I stared down at my hands, recalling my strange meeting with Selene. "The Olympian's name was Selene, although there is a chance she is not an enemy."

Victoria gripped my shoulder, turning me to face her. "Selene?" she asked meaningfully.

I nodded. "Yes. *That* Selene. The Goddess of the Moon. My...wife, once upon a time."

Natalie cleared her throat and I turned to see her studying her own chest and the almost invisible pale line that created a horizontal S over her breasts. "S...for Selene?" she asked softly, tracing it again with a finger before meeting my eyes. "Are you really trying to tell me that your ex-wife caught us in bed with you and tried to skin me alive, but that she might *not* be an enemy?"

30

I winced at her tone, reaching out to squeeze her thigh. "Enemy or not, I was trying to kill her while she had you. She bound me with powerful chains that nullified my powers."

Natalie continued staring at me, looking shaken. "I...was having a dream. It hurt in the dream, but I couldn't wake up," she whispered.

I nodded, the fear in her voice waking something very dangerous deep within me. "I was shouting at the both of you, but you couldn't wake up, and I couldn't break free of my chains," I said, my voice cold and dry as their blood boiled in my blood reserves, begging for release. "But as she was moving to Victoria, she leaned in close enough to whisper a secret message."

The whole room was listening now—especially the Nephilim.

"She said the only way for her to speak to me without drawing suspicion was to hurt me through you two, because the other Olympians were watching her..." I turned from Natalie to Victoria—the only two who really mattered in this conversation since they had been the victims. "She told me to remember my name. That they all want me dead, and that they would turn *him* against me—whoever that is. That I was supposed to die many times in my life but that I keep dodging it somehow. Which is why they collaborated to curse me. She...begged me to stop her from hurting you," I rasped.

The room was deadly silent. "Remember your name?" Renfield finally asked. "Sorin Ambrogio?"

I shook my head. "When I knew Selene, my true name was only Ambrogio. I adopted Sorin in bitter irony since it means *sun*, because Apollo cursed sunlight to harm me."

Victoria frowned thoughtfully. "What about Ambrogio? What does that mean?"

I grunted bitterly. "The root word is ambrosia—the nectar of the gods." I let out a breath, deciding that the details of Selene's private message didn't matter at the moment. I wanted to analyze them myself in private, not with an audience. My mind worked better that way. "Anyway, the restraints were designed to turn my power against me, making them unbreakable, so I turned them in on myself instead. I used them to cut into my flesh and drain all my blood. I used them to kill myself, hoping it would break them."

Natalie and Victoria stiffened in disbelief. "You *what*?" Victoria snapped in breathless fury.

Natalie was staring at me, opening and closing her mouth wordlessly. "You...killed yourself to try and save us?" she whispered, sounding both awed and confused. "How would that have helped?"

"The restraints were leeching off my blood, using its power to restrain me. The harder I fought, the stronger they grew, and the weaker I became. So...I turned their design on its head."

Victoria blinked. "Just...like that. While witnessing Natalie's torture and listening to Selene tell you a cryptic secret message, you were clearheaded enough to decipher how to break an Olympian's chains..." she said, sounding as if she thought she must have missed a vital part of my story.

I nodded. "I think clearer in times of stress," I admitted with a shrug.

Victoria mouthed my words, shaking her head. "Sorin, you are incredibly humble...and scarier than anyone I've ever met," she said, making it sound like a compliment.

Natalie smiled deeply. "And he's all ours. All. Ours." She suddenly leapt on me, wrapping her arms around me in a hug and kissing me on the forehead. "Thank you, Sorin. I thought I was going to die in my dream, and then I woke to find *you* almost dying!"

Victoria joined in, wrapping me in her own hug, but resting her cheek on my shoulder and squeezing long and tight in a silent thank you. "You amaze me, Sorin," she whispered. "Truly." Then she kissed me on the cheek and pulled away, wiping back a tear.

Natalie cocked her head with an emotional smile. "I don't think anyone has ever fought for me like that, Sorin. I think we both just fell in love with you. Even if you do bring home strays without discussing it with us first," she said, eyeing the Nephilim with a playful grin. "We'll have to add that to our rules."

The Nephilim smiled back at her. I noticed that Eve looked decidedly more confident after her brief talk with Natalie. Her posture had even changed ever so slightly. Enough to better emphasize her feminine form in minute ways. A fact which Adam hadn't failed to notice, judging by the startled look on his face and the almost panicked covering of his genitals with both hands. I glanced at Natalie suspiciously and she shrugged with false innocence.

Adam and Eve shared another of their private conversations before kneeling on the ground with heavy thuds. They lowered their chins and spoke in unison. "You almost died. We failed you, Master Ambrogio."

Renfield's eyes widened before flicking to mine. I waved a hand at him reassuringly. "No one failed me tonight. None of us expected an Olympian—let alone that they would have the ability to sneak in here undetected," I said firmly.

I scooted down to the edge of the bed and set my feet on the floor. I set a palm on both Adam and Eve's heads and gently tilted them to look up at me.

"I think you honored yourselves tonight. And you honored me. I do not think we have any concerns when it comes to your self-control or devotion," I said with a proud smile. "You sensed I was in danger and broke out of your restraints to come save me. That is not failure. That is dedication." They smiled faintly but didn't speak. "Your alleged greatest enemies are the Olympians, as far as you've told me." They nodded resolutely. "Which means your blood was up—your anger—and instead of losing control, you saved me. Then you guarded my door while we...put on a show. As Nephilim, this would have greatly offended you, adding to your already turbulent anger over the Olympian..." they winced, nodding guiltily. "But as vampires—especially vampires only a few hours old—it should have shattered your inhibitions completely. Even experienced vampires would have likely started their own...offensive celebration right here on the floor."

Eve's eyes flared brighter for a moment and Adam licked his lips subconsciously. "We...would never—" he cut off with a sharp flicker of his eyes to Eve. "Duty first," he said stiffly, focusing on me to hide his discomfort from Eve.

She frowned, looking slightly hurt by his comment. These two were going to be work. But pleasant, honest work—teaching them that love and affection were not crimes.

I nodded. "For which I am grateful. I am just saying that even if you had, it would have been totally acceptable. And understandable. Not only did you refrain, but you jumped to attention to guard my door against four vampires who desperately wanted to get in." I held up a finger, meeting each of their eyes for a long moment. "And you did not kill them."

Renfield nodded thoughtfully. "I can attest to how truly unusual that is. I have worked with thousands of new vampires in my years and I have never seen half their restraint. Even from many full-fledged vampires," he added meaningfully.

"Then it is settled. Welcome to the family, Adam and Eve. There will be growing pains, but we will get through them together. Tonight will be the hardest part."

I helped them to their feet, gripping their forearms firmly and meeting their fiery eyes. They nodded with grim anticipation, eager to trap Dracula in his castle.

I turned to Renfield. "Tell them I will be leaving soon, and that they should already be finalizing tonight's activities. You can finally tell Hugo the real reason he and Gabriel have been working so hard to clear out Central Park. Hugo will be the point of contact for whomever Stevie chooses to lead his wolves. Have him load up Adam and Eve in the back of one of our transport trucks and park it near the southern entrance to the park. Somewhere near Columbus Circle. Leave the back unlocked. I'll pick them up soon." Renfield nodded eagerly, eyeing the Nephilim. Until now, I'd just told Hugo to get it done. No one had known exactly what I intended with the Nephilim, thinking I just needed their permission to use Central Park. But the Nephilim were no longer a secret.

"They began to work much faster after I introduced them to Adam and Eve, one at a time, alluding to the fact that many more Nephilim roam the world, and that I wasn't at liberty to divulge how many you were currently working with, or how many you had already turned."

I chuckled, shaking my head at his tactics. The Nephilim folded their arms proudly.

"Have Aristos finalize the naval fleet plan," I told Renfield, "and verify that the distraction at Williamsburg Bridge is ready. And tell him to keep us informed about the authorities." Renfield nodded easily. "Valentine is in charge of communications on Liberty Island. Whoever is running things on the ground at each location will check in with one of them so that they can pass along information to the other battle fronts."

"They are already prepared, Master Ambrogio. All will be well." Then Renfield was guiding the Nephilim out the door. He paused to glance back. "Dr. Stein has called repeatedly. It sounded urgent." He exited the room without waiting for my response, and I heard him asking the Nephilim if they had ever tasted an avocado before. I chuckled, shaking my head.

Soon enough, I was alone with my devils—Natalie and Victoria.

I decided that I liked the name for Natalie and Victoria. "My devils," I murmured out loud. As I turned to face them, I felt a sharp pang of discomfort in my groin and hissed instinctively. Then I grew still, quickly concealing my reaction and forcing my face to relax as I realized what the pain was.

The pain of being brought to the brink of sexual tension—repeatedly—and not attaining release. But suddenly learning that I'd had an audience had doused my lust like a bucket of water over a fire.

My body chose not to accept this excuse, giving me another sharp pain.

My devils were grinning at my obvious ache, smiling sweetly.

"A wolf's gotta mark her territory," she said, not bothering to hide her focus on my pants.

Victoria chuckled, lifting the sheet over her lap. "Sorry, not sorry."

I sighed, shaking my head. "I'm going to go shower. You remember where you need to be tonight?"

"I don't," Natalie said. "We should probably have a meeting. In the shower. Now. Because I'm feeling *dirty...*" her eyes slowly shifted to Victoria and then me, "and I like to multi-task."

Victoria seemed to consider her suggestion, her skin suddenly pebbling as her lips parted. Then she sighed, shaking her head. "Soon enough, Natalie. Soon enough. We really do have a lot of work to do tonight. Everything is riding on this. We can...multi-task later," she said with a coy smile.

Natalie pouted theatrically, folding her arms beneath her breasts. "Adulting sucks."

I sighed regretfully, painfully making my way towards the bathroom as I wondered if I'd really tried hard enough with those glass manacles.

"The only one who has reason to complain is going to go take an ice-cold shower," I called out, making sure they could hear me.

"That's just because Renfield mentioned Dr. Stein," Natalie fired back. "She has that effect on men." I heard the pair of them hooting with laughter as I turned on the shower with a growl.

Calling them devils, I decided, was remarkably appropriate.

AFTER SHOWERING UP—INDIVIDUALLY—I changed into sturdy boots, a pair of comfortable jeans, and a thin sweater. Then I headed out to make last-minute arrangements with Hugo, Aristos, and Valentine while the girls took turns showering. Victoria had started leaving spare clothes in my closet last week, and we also had a dozen or so blood slaves of all shapes and sizes living in the catacombs if Victoria didn't have anything to fit Natalie's slightly smaller frame.

Knowing the dangers of involving myself in a woman's dressing room—even as an innocent bystander—I would have left my chambers even if there had been nothing to check on.

I was sitting in the chair, sipping a warm bloodee when they came out of my chambers. Natalie had found jeans and a black jacket to wear over a white t-shirt with the words, 'Save a heart, bang a fang,' on the front.

Victoria had also chosen jeans and a jacket. She wore the same shirt as Natalie, but in black. I arched an eyebrow at them.

Natalie shrugged. "Hugo had a whole box of them."

Victoria nodded her agreement. "He's making merchandise for the supernatural tourists. This one seemed...appropriate," she added in a suggestive tone and flashing me a wink.

I downed the rest of my bloodee and climbed to my feet. "I called Dr. Stein back. She's waiting for us at the Statue of Liberty. The storm won't be here for another hour or so, and I want to take one last look at her setup."

I didn't bring up that I was going to be leaving them behind at Liberty Island. They knew it already, and hadn't been very pleased, even though they understood my reasoning.

But I still chose not to mention it again.

31

I entered the lobby of the Statue of Liberty, grimacing with frustration. On the way here, the skies had been full of dark, ominous clouds, but no rain. The skies grumbled and groaned with deep rolling thunder, but no lightning. The very air seemed to hum with electricity and each breath felt like I was swallowing cool steam.

But no actual lightning.

Natalie was skipping beside Gabriel—who had driven our boat to the island—chatting excitedly, looking like a talkative granddaughter telling her infinitely patient grandfather a story.

Gabriel was a startlingly handsome old man with medium-length, wavy white hair, bright green eyes, and a clean-shaven face. But he had the body of a twenty-something athlete, like he should be on the billboards I had seen advertising underwear in Times Square.

He had been a soldier when he was younger, fit from training. That hadn't been the case a few weeks ago, back when I had initially met him underground. He'd been the first man to accept my offer of becoming a vampire.

Victoria was speaking with Renfield—who had left the museum with us—to go over their own plans and tasks to make sure nothing had been forgotten or overlooked. We would all be busy tonight, and not all of us working in the same place. That was key. To keep our enemies guessing on what we were up to.

My main task here was to speak with Dr. Stein before heading back to Central Park.

I slowed my stride as the elevator door opened and Stevie exited. He froze, his face slowly morphing into an annoyed scowl as he saw me. I sighed, realizing I would finally have to talk with him. I needed him focused tonight, and this petty dominance issue was beginning to get under my skin. Fucking werewolves and their asinine power struggles.

The Alpha of the Crescent—in charge of the five sub-alphas of the boroughs of New York City—shifted his attention away from me, catching the sound of Natalie's voice as she spoke with Gabriel.

Stevie froze, his hand idly drifting to his chest to touch his beard. I realized that his hand had begun to shake and that he looked noticeably pale. I frowned, shooting my attention back to Natalie, only to find that her back was to Stevie and that she was casting a puzzled look at Gabriel.

Because Gabriel had a similar look on his face. Natalie finally glanced back, saw Stevie and grimaced.

"You..." Stevie said from across the lobby, his voice quivering with emotion, but I couldn't tell if it was anger or sadness or joy—or all three. I simply recognized that the potential for lethal violence had just dramatically increased.

Natalie sighed in resignation, opening her mouth to answer her old alpha. "Listen, Stevie—"

Gabriel, my lead underground vampire, cut her off, gently shoving her to the side as he slowly approached Stevie, pointing a finger and letting out a sharp gasp. "Frederick?" he whispered, his voice catching on the name. "You haven't aged a day!"

I watched anxiously, wondering what this was about. Hadn't they met before? Everyone had been working closely together to get everything ready for tonight. Gabriel had been tasked with delivering all the vampire corpses from their graves to the Museum of Natural History for inspection and labeling—giving each viable body a chain necklace with their names stamped into metal tags—before transporting them to the Statue of Liberty for the approval of Dr. Stein and Nero.

Stevie had been working at both the museum and Liberty Island, so it was somewhat baffling that the two had never actually *seen* each other. I knew they had at least spoken over the phone and were aware of each other's first names.

Stevie slowly shook his head at Gabriel. "Frederick was my father," he rasped. Then he blushed furiously. "I'm sorry. We've never met, but...my father chose my middle name to be Gabriel...in honor of *you*." He whispered, tears actually falling down his cheeks. My eyes widened at the raw emotion between the two dangerous men. "He spoke about you every day. I had no idea that the Gabriel I've been working with was *you*," he said, shaking his head.

Gabriel's smile had faltered, and he was blinking rapidly at the sudden onslaught. "Oh, my god. You're Frederick's boy?" he rasped, shaking his head. Then his smile slowly returned, and he began to laugh—the sound echoing off the walls. "That rat bastard finally did it!" he hooted, pumping a fist in the air. "He finally proposed to Angela, didn't he? She's your mother!"

Stevie gasped, his face contorting in joyous pain as he nodded vehemently. "She is."

Gabriel laughed, closing the distance to grab Stevie by the shoulders, inspecting him up and down with firm slaps of approval over his shoulders, jostling the much broader werewolf. "I can't tell you how many times I told him to stop being a coward and propose to the only woman in the world who would put up with him!" he chuckled, shaking his head. "You look just like him, my boy." Then his features changed to mock disapproval. "Although it seems he never taught you that self-respect starts with a clean shave," he growled teasingly.

Stevie let out a cracked, emotional laugh, nodding jerkily. "He said the same thing," he stammered.

Gabriel grinned, squeezing and jostling Stevie some more. "How is the old dog?"

Stevie blinked, looking abruptly crestfallen. "He...died."

Gabriel's head sunk down to his chest, his shoulders slumping. "I'm...so sorry, my boy." Then he deftly wrapped his arms around

Stevie, enveloping the alpha of New York City into a bear hug. Stevie stared over Gabriel's shoulders, wide-eyed, and frozen. His face slowly contorted into a rictus of pain, and like a melting glacier, his shoulders relaxed, and he hung his head over Gabriel's shoulder.

And then he began to cry.

Grown men crying—really crying—was both a beautiful and terrible thing to behold. I began to turn away as Stevie let out a strange whine, like a frightened little boy who'd just been reunited with his father after getting lost in a busy crowd.

Renfield stared at the men intensely, his face a portrait of pain. His blood-shot eyes stared unblinkingly, even as tears fell down his cheeks. His jaw trembled and I saw his hands clenched into fists, shaking violently as he squeezed even tighter. Victoria finally seemed to notice Renfield's reaction and she immediately blanched, overcome by his severe heartache. I peeled my eyes away, knowing exactly what Renfield was thinking of.

His own daughter, Kassandra. How he would have given anything to embrace his daughter one last time rather than watching her grow old from afar. But Dracula had taken that from him.

And tonight, we were taking the first steps to avenge that crime. My own pain at seeing Renfield in agony only served to fuel my resolve, and I felt Victoria and Natalie's blood sloshing and bubbling up within me, begging for release. I took a shuddering breath, calming myself.

Then I looked back at Stevie. He was now staring at me from over Gabriel's shoulder, and I couldn't tell if he wanted to murder me or not. It was a very thin line. He shakily dislodged himself, gripping Gabriel by the shoulders. "I need to make an introduction," he told the older vampire as he guided Gabriel towards me.

Gabriel frowned, wiping at his face. He shot me an apologetic frown. "I...uh, already know Master Ambrogio. He gave me a new life through our bond. Without it, I would be a broken shell of a man."

Stevie flinched as if struck, the word *bond* striking close to his own personal disagreement with me over Natalie. "But Sorin does not know *you*," Stevie said, almost aggressively to make up for his flinch.

I waited, uncertain what this was about. Stevie stared me in the eyes, stopping two paces before me as he enveloped the older, smaller vampire with one beefy arm around the shoulder. "This is Captain Gabriel Shelby," he said. "He saved my father's life at the end of the Vietnam War. I was born ten months after my father returned home. I wouldn't be here if it weren't for Captain Shelby."

Gabriel lowered his head, obviously uncomfortable. "You are too kind, son. I'm sure Frederick had some small part to play in your birth," he added wryly, attempting to shift the attention away from himself. I chuckled in an effort to help.

Gabriel had told me about the war in general terms; I'd wanted to learn about the war from firsthand knowledge rather than reading about it in a book—like I was forced to do with most other historical events in order to catch up on my five-hundred-year slumber. The war had cost Gabriel his vision and a broken back, leaving him crippled and blinded for life.

Until vampirism had healed him of both, of course.

Gabriel sighed. "I went underground to avoid people. I couldn't see them, but I could feel them staring at me, pitying me. I hated it. Like now," he added in a softer voice.

"Gabriel," I said sternly, knowing he needed me to save him. He looked up, wincing at my tone. "No one is pitying you. I'm actually wondering why you haven't finished the tasks I gave you. Perhaps you lost your work ethic along with your eyes in the war. Leaving your messes in the trunk of my car for me to deal with, and now you're standing around as worthless as a lump on a log, blubbering like a snot-nosed runt." I folded my arms, scowling in disapproval.

Stevie's eyes widened in outrage. Natalie and Victoria let out indignant squawks behind me.

But Gabriel...

Gabriel burst out laughing. Stevie stared at him, dumbfounded.

Gabriel finally managed to somewhat regain his composure, his eyes crinkling at the corners as he beamed up at me. "Right you are, sir. Totally worthless."

"Get out of here and do something useful, soldier." I extended my hand and he grinned, grasping mine firmly.

"Yes sir," he said, still chuckling. He cast one last look at Stevie and a sad but happy smile split his cheeks. "When this is all finished, I'd like to visit him. If you don't mind."

Stevie nodded, still looking confused but pleased at the idea. "We'll go together."

Gabriel smiled, slapping the werewolf's shoulder again. Then he turned away, shaking his head and laughing. "snot-nosed runt," he chuckled, slapping his thigh.

We silently watched him leave before Stevie slowly turned to look at me with a puzzled frown. "I don't understand."

I smiled. "He's a soldier. The good ones hate attention—at least in public. That's why he chose to live underground in the first place. To avoid the looks and the people. Men like him just want to work hard and watch the effects from afar. They do it because they must, not because they want the praise. I've found that one of the best things you can do for them is give them another task. The harder, the better. Gabriel struck me as that kind of man. It's why I put him in charge of the fledglings. He's a wolf. He'll never be a domesticated dog to sit at the fire."

Stevie nodded thoughtfully, brushing his beard idly with his fingers and thumb. "I...didn't mean to embarrass him. I just wanted him to know he was my father's hero. Mine, too."

I stepped forward, squeezing his shoulder. "And that meant the world to him. Your words just hit him a little too close to the heart. You did nothing wrong, Stevie. Trust me."

I wasn't entirely sure how to explain it without telling him that he had handled it wrong. Because he had and he hadn't. People needed to hear heroic stories so they knew what was possible with the power of dedication. The hero just needed the next challenge.

"Gabriel was the first man I spoke to underground," I said, shifting the subject. "He couldn't even see me, but he heard me. I asked if he needed anything and he said that he just wanted a friend..." I said fondly. "I tried giving him money, but he shook his head. He asked if my money could buy him a new back so he could fix the leaky pipe over his bed. That damned pipe was what really irked him, even though he was blind, crippled, and in constant pain. I offered him drugs to help with the pain, but he shot that down too. He wanted to know why I was trying so hard to be nice to a nobody." I let out a breath. "I told him I was looking for a friend who I hadn't met yet. He got a real kick out of that," I said with a grin, recalling his laughter.

Victoria and Natalie were standing on either side of Renfield, wrapping their arms around his shoulders, and smiling sadly at my story.

Stevie chuckled. "That sounds like the same Gabriel my father described," he finally murmured. "A goddamned angel living in Hell and still remembering how to laugh. And to fix a pipe, apparently." He briefly met my eyes. "Thank you for giving him a new challenge, Sorin."

I waved off his comment, shaking my head. "He did all the hard work. I just offered him drugs or a new life."

Stevie sighed. "Well, despite what you did for Gabriel, I'm still kind of miffed about Nat—"

Natalie stepped forward, cutting him off as she placed her hands on her hips. "Then you and I can go talk about that outside, Stevie, because I am sick and tired of your pouting. The only thing Sorin did was save my life. He didn't try to do anything more. I swear it. Victoria wasn't even near us and she got roped into this bond. But if he hadn't acted, I'd be *dead* right now!" she snarled, not seeming to realize that she was actually shouting. "Rather than meddling in our personal lives like a nosy stepmother, perhaps you should go back to being the alpha of New York City! Just because you're no longer *my* alpha doesn't mean I think any less of you. What you're doing right *now* is what makes me think less of you."

He stared at her for a long, silent moment. Finally, he gave her a stiff, resigned nod. "I...know. I've got possession issues. You were one of my best, Natalie."

"The operative word being *were*, past tense," she said sternly. "And I wasn't *one of* your best, I was *the* best. But Benjamin was a close second, and you still have him. Show Benjamin how a real alpha handles difficult situations. Your pack is watching how you deal with this."

He nodded angrily. "A fact which concerns me greatly. That they will see me losing control."

"Or," Natalie said, holding up a finger. "They could see you passing along a bride. Much like a father adores his daughter but must one day give her up no matter how much he loves her. Stop being my nosy step-mother, and be my *father*, Stevie. You already are in my eyes." Her eyes were misting slightly, and I averted my gaze so as not to embarrass her. I hadn't known she felt that way about Stevie...

From the look on Victoria's face, she hadn't known either.

Stevie cocked his head, smiling as he considered her words. "That... just might work," he said thoughtfully. He seemed to notice her shirt for the first time and grunted in disapproval.

I was suddenly glad she had worn it.

"Is that what this is?" he asked with a slight frown. "A marriage?"

My heart dropped out of my chest like a lead weight. "NO!" I practically shouted.

Victoria and Natalie had been shaking their heads as well, but they froze at my vehement shout, slowly turning to look at me as if with one mind, furrowing their eyebrows in displeasure.

"I just don't want to jump into anything," I said quickly, trying to backpedal. "There is a lot to consider in this new bond. A lot to think about—"

"I advise silence, Master Ambrogio," Renfield murmured softly, risking his life for me.

"Quiet, Renfield!" they spun, hissing at him. He bobbed his head, lowering his eyes.

Stevie was casting me a smug grin. "I see this is not what I thought."

"It is what we *tell* him it is," Victoria snapped. "Majority rules. We didn't have a say in joining this bond, so he doesn't get a say in how it functions."

Natalie nodded, lifting a palm. Victoria slapped it without even looking.

Stevie burst out laughing. "Maybe I should have gone easier on you, Sorin. For someone who always seems to know what you're doing, you grossly miscalculated on this one."

"I didn't know it was even happening," I muttered. Then I found myself smiling. "But...I probably would have done it anyway," I admitted.

My devils shot me moderately satisfied looks. "Better," Victoria murmured.

Natalie turned back to Stevie. "So, the pack hunts tonight, and I request to hunt with the pack—if you will accept a lone wolf."

Stevie's eyes widened, shooting towards me.

"Don't look at *him*!" Natalie commanded, slapping his chest with a backhanded swipe that made him grunt.

Victoria piped up. "I'd like to join, too. As long as you're staying here, of course."

Stevie gave a slow, resolute nod. "I am now. I'll tell Benjamin to stay at the park."

My devils nodded primly, as if they'd expected nothing less than the utter emasculation of every male in the vicinity.

I waited a few moments to make sure it was safe to speak. "How many wolves do we have in total?"

Stevie cast a wary look at my devils before answering. "I called everyone. All five boroughs hunt tonight. We have close to three hundred wolves—two hundred at Central Park because there is more ground to cover, and they can search faster than your vampires. The other hundred are here on Liberty Island, guarding the dock."

I nodded. "Good. If these vampires don't wake up friendly, and Nero can't shut them all down with the journal, we might have our own war right here."

Which was another reason I had agreed with Dr. Stein's choice for her laboratory—the new vampires wouldn't be able to escape as easily if we lost control of them.

"The witches are still out there, too, waiting to attack at any sign of weakness. I can feel it," I said. "And we have no idea how many vampires Dracula has managed to sneak into the city. Gabriel caught two more last night."

"We should also keep an eye out for ex-wives," Victoria said in a cool tone, a dangerous gleam flashing in her eyes. Thankfully, her ire didn't seem directed at me. "They like to cause trouble."

I nodded to her. Stevie shot me a curious look, but I didn't elaborate. "Or them. There is no way for us to hide what we're doing once we begin. Expect human and supernatural interference. Tomorrow morning, the world will be unable to deny that monsters exist."

He nodded grimly, letting out a breath.

"We'll update him on the plan," Natalie said.

Victoria nodded, grinning wickedly. "You've got a date with Dr. Stein."

Then the two of them were tugging Stevie along by the arm, leaving me and Renfield alone to face the mad doctor.

"I have a few more details to wrap up, Master Ambrogio," Renfield said apologetically.

At least he bowed before abandoning me.

32

I stood inside the Crown of the Statue of Liberty, gazing out through the wall of twenty-five windows to marvel at the view from two-hundred-sixty feet above the frothing black water. From my vantage, I could see the tablet held in the statue's left hand, but the torch in her right hand was too high for me to see.

An open door to my right revealed a service ladder leading up to the torch itself, but it was reserved only for maintenance crews.

The climb from the pedestal to the crown had been arduous, but it was the only way up here, and the stunning view was definitely worth it. I could see Brooklyn and lower Manhattan, as well as the Verrazano Bridge—at least according to Nero.

To me, it was just pretty lights.

Looking down, I could see the open grass lawns of the island. Werewolves and vampires patrolled the perimeter in groups of four, looking like overkill for such a small island. Depending on how things went, they might not be enough.

I leaned away from the window, turning back to the others.

Dr. Stein and Nero had already been working up here, but Nosh and Isabella had joined me when I passed through the tenth floor, eager to finally see what all the hubbub was about far above the pedestal. Mr. Hyde and Mr. Poole had shot me a questioning look when they realized their charges were planning to ascend. Not wanting to risk Hyde falling down the steep spiral stairs and obliterating everything below him, I'd given him a discreet, reassuring nod. I could watch over Nosh and Isabella for a short while.

Hyde had looked relieved, but Poole had looked crestfallen, absently caressing the butt of the massive gun strapped to his back. I recalled Dr. Stein's comments about his shooting accuracy and found myself wondering where he would set up.

The climb up the spiral stairs—over one-hundred-fifty steps—had been tiresome, but seeing the sickly-sweet grins on Nosh and Isabella's faces as they experienced a romantic first together...

Well, I would have climbed it twice to be a silent witness to that. I'd even given them a head start so as not to intrude. Nosh had paused at the suggestion, staring at me for a long, silent moment. Then he had nodded with a grateful, but somehow saddened smile.

As if he'd felt sorry for the lonely old vampire. It did make me wish I'd thought of bringing Victoria and Natalie up here for a private visit. That would have been nice.

Because we might just destroy it with what Dr. Stein had planned with her Phoenix Project.

"So, this is it?" I asked Dr. Stein. "Project Phoenix?" I added with a doubtful frown. A row of metal towers that were each the same height and width as me hummed loudly against the interior wall, warming the air. I didn't envy the poor bastards tasked with lugging equipment up here. The tops of the towers flashed with dozens of blinking lights, while the lower halves had masses of cables plugged into them. The cables led back towards the pedestal, hanging through the empty air rather than trailing down the spiral stairs—both for convenience and the fact that using the stairs would have increased the amount of cable needed to reach the pedestal and the sleeping army of vampires far below.

Another cable, as wide as my leg, was connected to the back of one of the metal towers, leading through the maintenance door and then up the statue's arm to the torch high above. Some type of plastic ties had been used to fasten the unwieldy cable to the ladder rungs.

On a very basic level, I knew what was going on here, but my understanding faded rapidly after the first word:

Lightning.

Between that word and the final result of bringing my already necromantically-raised vampires to actual life was just a void of black, depthless nothingness. Which...was oddly fitting, given the topic.

Nero cleared his throat to speak in a low, officious drone. "In the beginning, God-Stein said, '*Let there be lightning.*' And it was so."

The god in question paused from her study of a thick book on the nearby table to shoot him a stern look, but I sensed the merriment dancing in Dr. Frankie Stein's eyes.

"Lightning is going to fix Deganawida's problem from the journal? Prevent my army from becoming raging, mindless beasts?" I asked dubiously.

One thing I had learned in my many centuries of tyranny and conquest was that if I wanted something done, but didn't know how to do it, I needed to find someone much smarter than me who could. Then, rather than asking them questions that only proved to establish my ignorance, it was wisest to cast polite doubt over their plan.

And then to watch them momentarily sputter incoherently before they began walking me through every step of their process, trying to prove to me how right they were.

From that point on, my job was to simply nod on occasion, but to keep that same concerned, pensive look on my face, as if wondering if I should find a more intelligent person to solve my—

"Shut up, Sorin," Dr. Stein said dismissively. "The cavemen you competed with umpteen centuries ago didn't know about reverse psychology. Today, seven-year-old girls use it on their daddies before they even know what they're doing. By the time they hit thirteen, they are goddamned Machiavellian. You're out of your league."

I stared at her, struggling to process her words. My tried-and-true plan...

"Just to be clear," Nosh said, sounding highly amused, "are you calling Sorin a caveman or a thirteen-year-old girl?" he managed to ask before he burst out laughing.

Nero coughed suspiciously, bending behind one of the towers to act like he was doing something useful when everyone could tell he was just as clueless as me. His part had already been done—raising the vampires in the first place with Deganawida's necromancy.

Dr. Stein bumped me aside with her hip and a snort, for good measure. "Maybe the seven-year-old," she muttered, waddling over to Nero to swat him across the back of the head and then banish him from her vicinity with a shooing gesture. "You don't know anything about this, Sorin, so just stand over there and look pretty."

I blinked, feeling like the world didn't make sense anymore. That had been my thing. It worked every time.

"There. Just like that," she said, pointing in my general direction. "But farther away."

Nosh was biting his fist and Isabella was pretending to look out the window to mask her flushed cheeks.

I scowled as Dr. Stein shuffled past me again—bumping me back a step on her way by—to check some other metal box on the table with lights and buttons and dials and—

She was right. I didn't know a thing about any of this.

Since I now looked like a fool anyway, I went with my contingency plan—asking asinine questions until my target broke down and answered me in terms I could understand. "Beyond lightning, elaborate one more time. For Nosh, because he's too busy adoring Isabella to process difficult explanations."

Isabella made an aww sound, kissing him on the cheek.

I folded my arms, smirking at him smugly. He turned away from Isabella to look at me, cupping a hand to the side of his mouth. "I studied this kind of stuff in school, Sorin," he whispered loud enough for everyone to hear.

I muttered defeatedly. "Fine! But I'm going to start swinging a club and banging rocks together until someone explains it in terms slightly more evolved than grunting and hand gestures."

Nero sighed. "Gather round, children." We did, standing before the windows. "Necromancy is the magical art of reanimating a dead body, bringing it back to life so that it can function—at least physically— much the same as we do. Unless they're missing a limb or something that makes them less than ideal candidates. We found many of those that we had to put back."

Isabella shuddered. Being a white witch, I wasn't sure if she found this fascinating or horrifying. In a way, it was healing. But in another way, it was the worst kind of abuse—disturbing the peace of the dead. "Where did you find your...subjects?" she asked.

"Deganawida's journal listed just over one hundred vampires he had killed in his day. It also showed where he had buried them," Nosh answered in a gentle tone, picking up on her unease.

Nero nodded. "That. Luckily, they were all within a few hours from here, and buried in groups. Gabriel and I sought them out, bringing them back to the Museum of Natural History where I could use Deganawida's spell to reanimate them. Then we brought them here."

Isabella blanched. "They're already reanimated? We've been *sleeping* here!"

Nosh looked suddenly uneasy as well. "If they're so dangerous, why the hell would you do that?" he demanded.

"We immediately sedated them. That's what all the IV drips and crates are on the lower levels. The vampires are all hooked up to minimal blood sources to keep them alive, and sedatives to keep them unconscious."

"How many did you recover?" Nosh asked.

"We are down to seventy-seven," Dr. Stein said absently, fiddling with one of the dials on the tower and then jotting something down on a pad of paper. "We recovered ninety-two, but fifteen of them were not viable upon further inspection, so we incinerated them."

I watched her eyeing Nosh sidelong when no one else was looking. She was absolutely terrified of him, even though her pulse remained steady and she didn't show any visible concern.

"The problem with Deganawida's necromancy spell," Nero continued since it was his area of expertise, "is that the *body* of the person comes back to life, but not the *brain*. Their instincts and animal minds are alive and well, but not the cognitive capabilities of a human. They can obey commands, and that's pretty much it."

"Except with vampires, it's worse," I said, recalling Deganawida's notes. "The bloodlust takes over everything, making controlling them an impossibility."

Nero nodded. "Exactly. After speaking with Dr. Stein about this, I learned she'd made a personal study of the brain and electrotherapy. Since I am also the equivalent of a caveman in this regard, I'll make it simple. She believes she can restart the brain, much like you can jump start a heart on occasion. Like CPR." He noticed my frown and smiled. "Like when someone drowns, but you can force the water out of their lungs while doing compressions on the heart to bring them back." Nero pointed a finger out the window towards the torch. "Lightning strikes the lightning rod on the torch, the electricity is fed through these cables, and then redistributed to the bodies in the floors below. You probably noticed the hundreds of cables lying all over the place." He clapped his hands, rubbing them together excitedly. "Vampire army. Old, experienced, warrior vampires. We hope."

The room grew silent.

Nosh cocked his head. "You said *viable* a couple times. I assume they need both a heart and a brain for this to work, right?" Nero smiled at his intended line of deduction, waving a hand.

"Deganawida only listed vampires that he had beheaded, not those he staked through the heart." He paused for a moment. "Because he sewed the heads back on before burying them."

Isabella gagged.

I glanced out the window, peering up at the sky. I blinked. "The clouds are entirely gone. All of them."

Dr. Stein rushed over, staring up at the sky. Her face paled and she whipped out her phone. After a minute of growing tension, she frowned. "That's impossible. A storm can't simply disappear out of nowhere between one minute and the next."

I glanced up at the sky again. "Well, nature doesn't concur," I said with a frustrated growl. "Did we just do all this work for *nothing*?" I demanded. If so, I couldn't do anything about it. I would just have to focus on my other plan and hope for the best.

Nosh cleared his throat, turning away from the window with a pensive frown. "You just need lightning, right? Plugging them into the outlets on the walls isn't enough power, I assume?"

Dr. Stein recoiled, offended by his relegation of her science to plugging a wire into a wall.

"Just trying to understand, Dr. Stein," he reassured her, looking skittish.

She nodded brusquely. "No engine or power source I have tested has quite the same effect as the wild, erratic qualities of lightning," she said longingly. "Something about its unpredictable nature made it more successful than the other power sources I tried. It is wild at heart, and we are trying to bring some of that spontaneity back to a living corpse. Perhaps it is a little bit of Lady Luck fiddling with the genetic dice of existence." I didn't know any Lady Luck, but I knew about Hermes, and doubted he would have bet on our odds. He might also be one of the Olympians desiring to kill me. "It's why I chose the Statue of Liberty. They call her Lady Liberty, which was about as close to Lady Luck as I could get. And we're liberating bodies. Giving these poor souls a second chance—another hand at the card table of life."

Everyone was staring at her, surprised by her very unscientific explanation, and then to see a nostalgic smile on her face.

She noticed and abruptly snapped out of it, glaring at the men in the room. "My daddy used to gamble. Lost everything on a bad roll of the dice." She glared out the window, silently cursing the entire world —past and present—with two beady eyes. "Looks like I followed in his footsteps like a blind fool."

Nosh cleared his throat. "Hello? Shaman, here. I can get you lightning," he said with an anticipatory grin. "I know a rain dance that works wonders," he muttered. "Every time. I spent a few years in the Southwest."

33

I eyed him discreetly, wondering if he had conned these Native Americans in the Southwest as well—adopting a new body to make them think he was part of their tribe—because the way I recalled it, tribes didn't often share with other unrelated tribes. They usually just tried to kill one another. Nosh shot me a stern glance when no one was looking.

I didn't really care as long as it gave us a storm. "What do you need?" I asked, recalling some of the traditional dances I'd seen Deganawida's tribe perform. It typically involved sacred feathers, turquoise, and other precious or symbolic items.

Nosh grunted. "Surprisingly enough, I think I have it all in a duffel bag downstairs. I sent that mustached alcoholic over to my place to get Isabella and me a change of clothes—" Isabella elbowed him so swiftly it may as well have been a scalpel between the ribs. He gasped for air, unable to do more than wheeze.

Isabella winced. "Sorry. I felt a shiver. Left my jacket downstairs."

She was wearing a jacket, but I wasn't dumb enough to point that out. Especially when she obviously didn't want anyone knowing she had stored clothes at Nosh's home.

Nosh managed to regain his breath, narrowing his eyes at Isabella.

"I had him grab my bag of ceremonial gear. With the witches hunting me, I didn't want to risk them stealing it. Dangerous stuff inside."

"How long would it take to get a storm?" I asked, glancing up at the sky. The clouds had returned, but they seemed to be fighting each other in a strange, unnatural way. Like...they were being manipulated.

Was I imagining things? Being paranoid? Or had the Olympians come out to play like Selene had warned me? Were they messing with the weather? How much did they know about my plan?

What else had she warned me about that I had overlooked? My name—although I didn't see how that answer would help me fight the Olympians tonight.

"It's not really a science, Sorin," Nosh said, unaware of my internal panic. "It's taken anywhere from a few days to an hour," he said, shrugging. "But the odds improve if I have others dancing with me."

Dr. Stein was frowning up at the sky quizzically, muttering under her breath. She didn't look convinced by Nosh's suggestion.

"My parents owned a casino, Dr. Stein. Maybe we can count that as an extra bit of luck?"

Dr. Stein went still, slowly turning to face the shaman. She glanced back up at the sky. "Something is strange about those clouds, but I can't put my finger on it. Perhaps a little more luck is precisely what we need. Can't hurt, anyway."

I frowned over at Nosh. "Others dancing with you?" I asked. "We're fresh out of other shamans to help, and none of us know the dance."

Nosh studied me with a sincere smile. "It's not about the knowing, it's about the needing—the spiritual desire for rain. The drums and my words carry my request up into the sky, but the more dancers I have, the louder and more insistent my request will be. The magic will be stronger. I just need people who really want it to storm—deep in their hearts." He paused. "You need the lightning very badly, don't you, Sorin?" he asked, shooting me a meaningful look. "Maybe you know a girl or two who might want to help me out? I've got one right here," he said, pointing at Isabella.

Her eyes widened in alarm. "Oh, I couldn't possibly—"

Nosh placed a finger over her lips and kissed her on the forehead.

"You'll do wonderful, Izzy. Just cut loose and let your hair back. I don't need any skill, just raw passion. You have that in spades."

She blushed profusely, still looking uncertain, but pleased by his compliment. "I'm not sure, but if you get a few others to join, at least I won't be the only one making a fool of myself."

I smiled, nodding. "Worth a shot," I said, thinking of Natalie and Victoria. This was the universe paying them back for the cold shower I'd been forced to take. I just knew it.

Dr. Stein was still staring up at the clouds uneasily. "Not normal," she murmured under her breath, sounding troubled. "Not normal at *all.*"

I ignored the icy shiver that traveled down my spine as thoughts of the Olympians came to mind as the obvious answer. "You guys get started as soon as you can. Do not wait for me. I have a quick errand to run and I'll be back."

"Don't worry," Stein muttered, "our world will somehow continue to rotate without you for an hour or so. But once the light show starts, you better get your ass back here in case we have a problem. I need someone to stand over there looking pretty while I change the world. And our new horde of vampires will need to see their father. I'm not sure how they'll react if he's late for dinner."

I nodded in understanding. We were in uncharted territory. Nero knew how to kill all the vampires if necessary, but if that was our only option, then there was almost no point in even attempting this insanity. All our work would have been for nothing.

Nero shot Dr. Stein a silent look and she nodded imperceptibly. Then he was following us out, leaving Dr. Stein alone in the Crown of the Statue of Liberty, staring out at the world in which she was about to birth seventy-seven vampires.

I was more concerned with how I was going to talk Victoria and Natalie into a rain dance.

I caught up to Nosh on the stairs, leaning in to whisper into his ear. "Be careful. The moment you start doing shaman stuff, the witches might sense it. And there might be other, more powerful, foes to worry about."

He nodded, not seeming concerned by my warning of other foes as he whispered back to me. "Do you think they bought the rain dance thing?"

I missed a step, almost tripping on top of him. "What?" I hissed, soft enough so that Isabella didn't overhear.

He grinned. "I've never been to the Southwest and a rain dance won't get us rain in the timeframe you have. There is magic in the air tonight, Sorin. Even with an authentic rain dance, it wouldn't break through the magic I sense up there. I intend to throw a whole helluva lot of magic back at it and see if I can make the skies explode. Find out who these more powerful foes are."

I grabbed him by the shoulder, pulling him back. Nero shot us a concerned look, but I waved him on past, giving us a moment of privacy. I stared at Nosh, leaning in close. "You better know what the hell you are doing, Nosh."

He nodded. "I do, Sorin. I've been doing this for a while, you know. Few hundred years, to be precise," he said softly, gauging my reaction.

I arched an eyebrow. "You know, there are better times to mention things like that. Like when we spoke earlier."

"We weren't talking about a shaman or fake rain dances back then," he said dryly, not mentioning the obvious topic—that he was also a skinwalker.

"What kind of power do you sense up there? Can you explain it?" I asked curiously. "Is it familiar to you? Witches maybe?" I asked, almost hoping for a yes. It would be better than the Olympians.

I think.

He shook his head. "No. I've never felt anything like it. It's almost not even accurate to say magic. But it's powerful enough that I think I can figuratively throw a match at it and watch it explode."

"Then why not just tell everyone that?"

He gave me a flat look. "Tell everyone that some unseen force is preventing the storm and that I want to pick a fight with said unseen force because it is so powerful? Or maybe I should let them think that I am so powerful that I can single-handedly make it look like Armageddon up there? That won't make me any new friends, and Dr. Stein is already terrified of me. No one will want to come near me. This way I can blame it on the rain dance—an inanimate ritual."

I sighed irritably. He wasn't right, but he wasn't wrong.

"And we get to see the girls dance and laugh. Which I think we could all sorely use right now," he added with a genuine smile. "You probably shouldn't miss it, so hurry up with whatever you're doing."

Then he was jogging down the stairs ahead of me.

After an indeterminable period of time spent descending the spiral staircase, I found Nero waiting for me at the base. I stared at him with a wary frown, having trouble meeting his eyes rather than staring at the crucifix branded into his forehead. He'd taken to letting his hair cover his forehead, but up close it was hard to ignore.

"Walk with me," he said without preamble, guiding me towards a small office. He opened the door and then shut it once we were inside. I stared at him, waiting. He hadn't turned the lights on. "You need to take me with you to Central Park."

"Why?" I asked, wondering if this had something to do with Dr. Stein's silent nod upstairs.

"Because you'll need to get back quickly. I can do that."

I threw my hands into the air. "I can get anyone to drive. You're needed here!"

He shook his head firmly. "I've learned a thing or two while you were sleeping, Sorin. I can make portals between places—as long as I set up a totem in my destination." He grabbed a replica of the Statue of Liberty off the nearby desk, pressed it to his lips and then murmured a word. Then he set it back down on the desk with a satisfied nod. "Now I can bring us back here to this office in *seconds* as opposed to driving through the rain and traffic, and then getting in a boat. Imagine how much could go wrong during that trip—especially when things have already kicked off. And then imagine how much you might miss in that span of time..." he trailed off meaningfully.

I gaped at him in disbelief. "And you're just *now* telling me this?" I demanded.

"We weren't exactly on the right terms for you to entertain my requests. I was trying to earn your trust, not bribe you. Me telling you about some amazing magic that required you to remove my collar? You would have laughed in my face, trusting me even less than you already did, and then who knows how long it would take you to—"

"Did you just say remove your collar?" I asked very slowly, eyeing the collar he still wore around his throat.

Nero's confidence crumpled and he let out a sigh. "See?" he said dejectedly, turning his back on me to reach for the door handle with his remaining hand. "I understand. I'll make sure a boat is ready—"

I touched the back of his collar, interrupting him. The device snapped off, falling to the floor with a metallic clang. He gasped in disbelief, spinning to face me.

"We still have to drive there, though, right?" I asked, smiling at the joy on his face.

His joy faltered minutely. "I wasn't permitted to leave the Museum as the Necromancer. Dracula wanted me to be a nameless, faceless, collared menace. So, yes. We need to drive." He paused, a ghost of an old, familiar smile splitting his cheeks—the smile of my old friend, not the smile of my recent prisoner. He was taking a gamble, gauging how much damage had been repaired with my gesture of trust. "And you're on indefinite probation from driving. You have to be at least sixteen years old, and I have it on good authority that you are merely a seven-year-old girl."

He grinned, dashing out the door as I crouched to scoop up the collar with a growl.

He laughed all the way to the elevator. So did I, chasing him with the collar and cursing his birth mother's existence with flavorful expletives not spoken for hundreds of years.

Just like old times.

It felt...nice.

Nosh and Isabella watched us with the strangest looks on their faces, making me laugh harder.

"Tell my devils—Natalie and Victoria—that I command them to take part in your rain dance!" I bellowed at Nosh, even knowing they would punish me for it.

The experience might be fun.

But I wasn't brave enough to tell them to their faces. Especially when they might later learn the rain dance was just for show.

34

Nero drove, drumming his fingers on the steering wheel. "It's exciting, Sorin! That's all I'm saying. You just took two Nephilim souls for crying out loud. Who *does* that?"

"The Devil," I replied dryly, leaning forward to stare up at the sky. Clouds hovered over the city, but they were constantly shifting as if blown about by wind—yet there was no wind. "You'll see the Nephilim soon enough."

"You're beginning to look like the man you used to be, before America," Nero said cautiously.

I nodded distractedly, glaring up at the clouds, and wondering which Olympian was causing it. "I remembered the words of my father —that there's no point improving on perfection."

Nero was silent for a few moments. "You didn't know your father," he said slowly.

I shrugged. "I'm sure he was thinking it deep in his heart when he abandoned me." Nero's answering silence told me that he had finally caught on to the fact that my earlier humor had dissipated, replaced by stress. "Sorry, Nero, but right now I need to think," I said tiredly.

"Of course. Sorry."

Despite my obvious stress, part of me felt like shouting and dancing at the task ahead. It was the waiting that always soured my mood.

I had no way of knowing for certain if my assessments about turning the Nephilim and affecting the castle were accurate, but I truly believed them. Otherwise I wouldn't have told them so, knowing full well that a lie would permanently tarnish our relationship. If my theory about them infecting the castle was right, and I was able to summon my castle to New York City with the coffin dirt Nero had originally recovered, then there was a very strong chance that it would instantly throw the castle into war—both factions of vampires believing that it was their home. Not just in their minds, but in their hearts.

Because the bond was a very powerful magic.

The castle had been originally bonded to me, and my vampires were bonded to me, forming a continuous link between all of us.

Dracula's faction was the same. In my absence, the castle had bonded to him—whether willingly or unwillingly, I had no way of knowing. He could have altered the castle so much that it no longer bonded with me at all.

Which was why my coffin dirt was crucial. It repaired and solidified the bond between me and the castle. No matter what Dracula had done, the fortress would have to respond—even if it no longer wanted to. In a way, the obsidian palace was a living entity, not just a pile of stone and marble. I was its maker. Its father.

Back when the castle was mine, it was a constant source of magic, empowering my existing vampires and then growing as I added yet more vampires to my horde. We had a symbiotic relationship.

And I was about to confuse the living hell out of it. There was every chance that my act would split the structure in two, right down the center, the castle forced to obey both masters—Dracula and Sorin.

Which was another reason I'd been turning more and more vampires in recent weeks—in preparation of me bringing my castle back. The castle would need my vampires as much as they would need the castle. Especially if I broke it. The stronger I was, the more likely my side of the castle would be larger and more powerful.

In that regard, I had so far turned close to two hundred vampires, keeping them largely apart from one another in the beginning, letting

Gabriel and a handful of others he trusted oversee their changes. To make sure they handled it without turning into mindless monsters.

I'd only suffered six vampires that required immediate execution, which was rather impressive. To give a man the power of a god and then hope that he didn't instantly abuse that power the moment he killed his first victim...that wasn't an easy thing to predict.

On a more positive note, the city's crime rate had dropped dramatically due to my expanding army. Two hundred vampires meant two hundred victims to finalize their transition to full vampire—and I'd only let them choose their first kill from known criminals. The type of men who walked out of jail hours after they were arrested.

We became the new system of justice in New York City—making it preferable for criminals to remain locked up rather than be released back onto the streets where my hungry vampires awaited them.

Even though it hadn't been openly known they were being consumed by vampires, the criminals knew deep in their hearts that a new king silently ruled the streets—and that he had zero tolerance for hardened criminals.

Even if no one ever saw him or his soldiers, they all knew he was there.

The Devil now walked the streets of New York City, and he was making it a safer place.

And now I was about to shatter that safety by bringing Dracula and his ilk here.

I sighed tiredly, hoping my passion wasn't overruling my reason. That my hunger for vengeance wouldn't result in more harm than necessary. There would be innocent casualties that I would have to carry on my shoulders—but I was sure that number would be smaller than what Dracula desired.

Nero glanced over at me, made uncomfortable by my grim silence.

Just then, a muted but thunderous explosion boomed in the distance, causing Nero to swerve and cry out. "What the *fuck* was that?" he demanded, frantically checking his mirrors for the source of the sound.

Must be nice, mirrors.

"Williamsburg Bridge," I said. "Forgot to tell you."

He slowly turned to stare at me with a horrified look on his face. "You just blew up the Williamsburg Bridge?" he croaked. "*Why?*"

I gestured vaguely. "Not the bridge. Just a large boat near the bridge. I had Aristos put a bunch of the dead criminals that my newest vampires consumed on the boat. They're wearing life jackets, so they float," I explained with a sinister grin.

Nero looked appalled; his hand was even trembling on the steering wheel. "How many is a bunch?"

"Fifty. The police will be very busy tonight saving the dead bodies. Then they are going to have a very strange couple of days when they begin to discover that the dead bodies are all the missing persons—criminals—they've been searching for over the past few weeks. And then they have to puzzle out how they all managed to take a ride on the same unlucky boat at the same time." I chuckled darkly. "The Mayor will look like a fool—enough of one to lose his reelection campaign in a few months. It wouldn't have had to happen this way if he had just approved the fifty-thousand-dollar grant for my new charity, Kassandra's Tears."

Nero slowly turned to stare at me, shaking his head in disbelief. "What the *hell* are you talking about?" he sputtered. "What fucking grant? You've got millions stashed away. Who cares about fifty-thousand-dollars?" he demanded, his eyes dancing wildly.

I turned to him, narrowing my eyes. "Orphans, Nero. What kind of monster says no to orphans?" I grunted, folding my arms. "I gave him fifty headaches for rejecting fifty-thousand-dollars. At least I can rest peacefully knowing that he'll never forget the number *fifty* again. That's enough for me. Fucking monster," I repeated, shaking my head. "Anyway, that was just an extra benefit to my plan. Short answer—I needed the police busy." I hadn't told anyone about my intent to ridicule the mayor with the boat explosion. Other than Renfield, anyway. He'd wholeheartedly agreed, of course. He'd come up with the lifejacket suggestion.

"Remind me never to accidentally spill your coffee or anything, you fucking sociopath. You might take it out on the random stranger who sold me my shoes!"

I shrugged. "I'd consider it. If I thought it would teach you not to spill my coffee." I thought about it. "And if the random stranger deserved it," I added.

He muttered under his breath, shaking his head.

The sound of emergency service sirens soon filled the air and I smiled. "And it worked," I said, nodding. "Now the boat police will be too busy to bother with anything strange happening on Liberty Island."

"The boat police," he said flatly.

"Whatever they're called."

We drove in silence for a few moments. "And what if they still come to Liberty Island?" he asked with hesitant curiosity.

I chuckled. "I have a plan."

He cursed, slapping his stump on the steering wheel. "Of course you do. I don't want to hear it. I'm still processing the first one. I won't even ask." Nero lost his appetite for conversation after that.

35

I sighed, glancing back up at the clouds as I thought about Nosh's comment that someone or something was holding back the storm. And then there was Dr. Stein's apprehension over the unnatural weather. Was it an Olympian or something else? The clouds did indeed look agitated. I wondered how long this mysterious storm whisperer could hold it steady—and what consequences there would be for them preventing nature from taking its course.

Because there were consequences to magic. Balance. Stopping the storm here tonight could cause a cataclysmic storm two-hundred miles away—whether inland or out in the ocean was a flip of a coin.

My thoughts drifted back to the sinister encounter with Selene, wondering how much I could trust her, if at all. Since I entertained every possibility, I had seriously considered that it hadn't been Selene at all, but some other god disguised as her.

Or maybe a skinwalker, even.

Dismissing those improbable but not impossible theories, and instead accepting what I had seen at face value, was even more unsettling.

Selene had seriously injured Natalie and had intended to harm Victoria—all for show, or so she said. But that wound over Natalie's chest had been more than a show. If I hadn't been present, her healing abilities wouldn't have been enough to save her. But I had been present, and Selene had known that. And she knew me, inside and out. How I thought, how I reacted...

And then there was her drastic personality shift back to the woman I had known. And her secret message. From the face that haunted me in my dreams, the face I saw when I stared up at the moon—not the semi-familiar Olympian version of Selene. I had seen the raw pain in her eyes. It had been genuine. Or an incredibly crafty illusion. Some Olympians could do that.

And she had called me Ambrogio, my old name. The only name I had used back then.

Ambrosia—the root word for Ambrogio—roughly translated to *nectar of the gods*.

Sorin meant *sun*.

But the gods had cursed me. Their nectar, so to speak, had been a poison.

I realized I was growling, and that Nero was leaning away from me, his face pale.

I took a calming breath and made a decision. Rather than wait for another of the Olympian bastards to curse me, I would take the fight directly to them. They would never expect it because no one was bold enough to pick a fight with them—and especially not when they were already dealing with Dracula and the Cauldron.

Except Sorin Ambrogio was that bold. Or that clever. Or that stupid. Only time would tell.

I was already on my way to take care of Dracula.

Which left the witches of the Cauldron. Rather than seeing me as an ally for kicking out Dracula's forces, they saw me as a weaker threat to eradicate. And now they also wanted to kill me for my association with Nosh and his tomahawks. And for killing a few of them.

And then killing their kittens, of course.

Particularly the one hit by the big fucking truck. That one probably boiled their potions.

I discreetly patted my pocket, feeling the arrowhead within—one of Nosh's magical tomahawks. The skinwalker blades. A secret weapon if I needed it. My mind continued to boil like a witch's cauldron, evaluating the pieces on the board and how best I might manipulate them.

Despite the very real dangers involved in my current undertakings, I hadn't felt more alive since my days back in Europe. I was back in the game, the intrigue, the plots, and the scheming. That had always been more of a rush than blood ever was—the challenge of coming out ahead and leaving everyone else in my dust, scratching their heads as they tried to figure out what had just happened.

It had led me to conquering most of Europe. Surely, one city wouldn't be as difficult.

Nero slowed as we approached a make-shift blockade of shopping carts, tents, and even a few parked cars. A veritable mob of homeless men and women stared at us with deadly glares in an attempt to enthrall us. "Keep your head down, Nero. Just to be safe." He had already done so, even though it was highly unlikely any of them would have stood even the slightest of chances at success against the warlock —especially now that he had his collar off.

I stuck my head out the window, letting them see who it was. They gasped in surprise, letting out a chorus of cheers. "Master Ambrogio! Sorry, sir!"

I waved a hand, dismissing their apology. "You're doing exactly as I ordered. Any trouble?" I asked, eyeing the shoddy blockade. If police saw that, they would absolutely investigate. Which was why my vampires were enthralling anyone who approached.

A young slip of a girl stepped out from the crowd, shaking her head. She wore dirty jeans and an oversized coat with a jagged tear down one sleeve. Despite her muddy face, her fiery red hair and vibrant green eyes almost took my breath away. Cleaned up, she would look stunning and elegant. I hadn't met her before, but she wouldn't have stepped forward to speak if she hadn't been chosen as Captain of this area, and she wouldn't have been chosen as Captain if Gabriel hadn't personally vouched for her.

"Few tried, but we turned them away without a problem," she said with a strong accent that I couldn't place—which wasn't surprising, given that I had no frame of reference for most accents. "Just like you asked, we've been giving the homeless humans we round up from the park a hundred bucks to fill in any gaps on the other streets leading to the park. Gabriel asked me to keep an eye out for anyone who might qualify for a more permanent position," she said with a meaningful look. "I've got twenty names so far. The Captains are running a little contest," she admitted with a guilty smile.

I laughed. "That's great."

"We heard the explosion a few minutes ago. Was that the boat near the Williamsburg Bridge?"

Nero grumbled unhappily. I nodded. "By the time we're ready to move, local authorities should all be rushing to the scene or already investigating."

She nodded. "I've seen a few cop cars racing that way."

Indeed, I could hear more sirens in the near distance, all heading *away* from Central Park.

"I haven't heard of any breaches, but we've got enthrallers at every point of entry." She plucked out a cell phone with a grin and then pointed at a few bicycles leaning against the blockade. "Any problems and they can call for backup, then we can ride over and plug in the gaps. Or send one of the werewolves to scare the living hell out of the humans and watch them soil themselves. Depends on their attitude, really."

I chuckled, nodding. "Good. Just remember that we are doing this to keep them safe. The real threat will happen once I do my part." I glanced ahead at the park further down the road. "You won't be able to miss it."

She nodded, licking her lips eagerly at thoughts of the castle to come. "Yes, sir. Lord Hugo told us the plan." She curtsied awkwardly. "Thank you, Master Ambrogio. You might not realize it, but you've already changed hundreds of lives."

I smiled gratefully. "Together, we will change even more. What's your name?"

"Susanna, Master Ambrogio."

I smiled. "Well, Susanna. Tonight's success depends on you holding this line. From both directions."

She nodded and the others cheered raucously. "We will, Master

Ambrogio. You can count on us. After all, you're giving the homeless a home," she said, pointing towards Central Park.

I smiled. "Indeed. Thank you, Susanna."

She snapped a command to a few men, and they rolled aside part of the blockade to let us pass.

Nero continued on down 7th Avenue until we reached Central Park South, the street walling in the southernmost tip of Central Park. I saw a white van parked on the sidewalk directly in front of us, just like Hugo had told me. I pointed it out to Nero.

"Park next to it," I said, pointing at the van. It wasn't like anyone was going to stop us—not with the entire area vacated. It was eerily haunting to see no cars driving on the streets. Nero seemed to feel the same way, his shoulders hitching up anxiously as he parked. We got out of the car and approached the back of the van. I stopped at the rear, glancing over at Nero and checking our surroundings. I spotted dozens of men and women wearing black clothes and holding umbrellas in their hands. Each wore a red band around their right arm, signifying they were one of Stevie's werewolves or my vampires.

In the event that a war soon erupted in Central Park, at least we would know our allies from our foes.

I saw no one else in the park.

I spotted more crowds of homeless vampires on the nearby side streets that funneled into Central Park, all of them preventing anyone from coming closer. They also wore red on their right arms—whether it was red string, a red glove, or a red strip of tape. I wasn't sure how long they could maintain their blockades, but I hoped it would be a while. "You ready to see the Nephilim?" I asked Nero with an excited smile.

He nodded, licking his lips.

36

I opened the doors and stepped back. "Come on out, Adam and Eve. The coast is clear."

From within the box truck, I saw the familiar flickering root system of shifting ruby light that decorated the Nephilim. Nero stared in awe. Two pairs of crimson flames danced as the Nephilim unfolded from where they had been seated on the floor. The truck creaked and groaned as they moved, apparently still weighing a significant amount despite being the same size as us.

Nero gasped, backing up a few steps as he stared at Adam and Eve. "They're naked, Sorin."

I sighed, shaking my head.

The Nephilim ignored Nero as they peered out into the street, sweeping their fiery gazes across the massive buildings and skyscrapers surrounding us with glowing lights everywhere, and the abandoned city streets.

They hopped out, cracking the concrete where they landed. "It's both beautiful and terrible," Adam said in a low rumble, still eyeing the buildings. "Their miraculous achievements lack a sense of soul. The lights try to replace the emptiness within."

Eve nodded sadly before slowly turning towards the park itself. She froze, sucking in a sharp breath. "It's beautiful," she breathed, smiling brightly. "So many trees and hills. And they destroyed something like this for something like that," she said, heartbroken as she frowned back at the buildings.

I nodded uneasily, realizing that I was about to further destroy her vision of beauty. I was here to destroy the last hint of nature in New York City. The most expansive anyway.

"The one-handed warlock is Nero, in case you missed him," I said, since they had blatantly ignored him.

They mumbled something vaguely polite, but they didn't turn to look at him. They stood side-by-side, staring out at the park. Nero frowned, his excitement to meet the Nephilim dashed.

"This is what we will destroy, Eve," Adam said, sounding resigned to the sacrifice but also saddened by it.

"To trap Dracula," Eve reminded him, reaching out to squeeze his hand reassuringly.

Adam nodded, seeming invigorated by Eve's touch. After a few moments of contemplative silence, he glanced over his shoulder at me. "Where are we doing this?"

I motioned for them to follow me as I walked towards the nearby entrance. I stared over the short stone wall and into the park, spotting a pair of werewolves loping beneath the tree cover, their noses high in the air as they scented for any humans they may have missed. They spotted us and skidded to an abrupt halt, tucking their ears back as they stared at the two Nephilim behind me with sudden wariness. I waved a hand at them and they relaxed—slightly—before resuming their search. I tried not to wince at the heavy thuds of the Nephilim walking behind me.

"Wherever we spill my coffin dirt will end up being the front gate, so I want to put some distance between that spot and the street," I said, glancing over my shoulder. "I also want to preserve at least some of the park." Eve smiled warmly, dipping her chin at me.

As confident as I was in my decision to do this, I was cognizant of the fact that history was about to be made. From this point forward, humans would no longer be able to deny that monsters existed.

The only justification was that I knew the humans had already been prey to Dracula's sinister touch—they just hadn't known about it since he worked from the shadows, hiding his vampires behind legitimate businesses while they fed, slaughtering innocent people. I glanced up at the apartment buildings and skyscrapers around me, wondering if some small child was staring out the window, smiling at all the trees, excited to play in the park tomorrow.

The only ones playing in the park tomorrow would be monsters. Indefinitely. Until I could oust Dracula for good. Then I would find a new place to take the castle. Somewhere hidden from mankind. Or...maybe not.

We turned to enter the park proper, passing an abandoned hot dog stand on the corner. I frowned to myself, hoping that the owner managed to get it back soon, even though I knew he probably wouldn't.

Because as soon as my castle arrived, this entire area would repel most life. Humans would subconsciously not want to live here. Not that anyone would voluntarily choose to live here anyway—not after a castle appeared out of nowhere overnight.

It was more than that.

The castle exuded magic that urged everyone away—at least from setting up a permanent home nearby. People could accidentally wander too close and feel the exact opposite sensation—that they desperately wanted to go inside and explore. That was the castle attracting food for the Master.

But anyone living too close to the castle would instantly feel the urge to move, abandoning their worldly possessions without even thinking about it. There had been close to a dozen farms around my castle overseas, all abandoned, and all fully-stocked with linens, furniture, dinnerware, and even chests of meager treasures that had been left behind when the owners fled.

I glanced up sadly, staring at the apartment buildings and hotels, imagining that small child again. Not only would he not see the park tomorrow, his parents would probably flee the neighborhood in search of a new home. Property values near the park were about to plummet, costing millions of dollars of losses.

It was an unavoidable consequence. Because there was another requirement to moving the castle. It had to be an area where I had an already semi-established home. I couldn't just arbitrarily pick an empty field somewhere far away from the city—not without living in that field for a few weeks. I had to genuinely *exist* in a place—meeting associates, sleeping, eating, laughing, loving, and crying—if I wanted to permanently move the castle there.

Which meant New York City was my only option.

All the surrounding buildings would be empty husks within days. Unless my plan with the Nephilim actually broke the castle—either destroying it for good or turning it from naturally evil to something naturally good—or possibly neutral.

Nero set a hand on my shoulder, startling me. "You okay?" he asked, following my gaze up towards the sky. I realized I had stopped walking and was staring at the storming sky forming in the far distance towards Liberty Island. A slow smile crept over my cheeks, wondering if it was Nosh's doing. I didn't notice any lightning, but it was a stark improvement from earlier. The clouds above Central Park were thin and wispy, and seemed to be shifting towards the distant storm as if they were iron being drawn by a lodestone.

Even though it was far away, the clouds clearly looked like a slowly rotating ring of dark gray smoke. It definitely didn't look natural.

I turned to Nero, a smile stretching over my face. "I think it's working," I said, pointing.

The Nephilim loomed over my shoulder, staring out at the distant storm. "You're going there?" Adam asked warily.

I turned to look at him, nodding. "Yes. After we finish up here. As long as everything goes smoothly." I resumed my walk, scanning the park for an ideal location.

The trees loomed overhead, forming a tunnel of foliage that would typically mute the usual sounds of the city—not that noise was an issue tonight. The air grew sweeter and fresher as we walked, and I heard the Nephilim taking deeper, contented breaths.

I spotted more than a dozen werewolves—both in human form and full-on werewolf form—patrolling the inner sections of the park, deep enough in to avoid being spotted from the buildings looming all around us. Not that it truly mattered anymore. I hoped they had gotten everyone out.

I motioned one of them over as we crossed a short bridge with a sign that read *Dipway Arch*. The wolf loped up to us, matching my pace as he stared up at me. I had no idea if I had met him before.

"Any trouble? Witches or vampires?" I asked.

The wolf shook his head.

"Is the park mostly clear?" I asked.

The wolf hesitated before nodding.

I sighed. "That will have to be good enough. I want you to let the rest of the pack know to clear out. In five minutes, all hell is going to break loose and anything within the park will likely be destroyed or trapped inside the castle."

The wolf tucked his tail between his legs, letting out a faint whine before nodding.

"Once the castle appears, I will need all the wolves to run up and down the perimeter of Central Park, searching for openings in the castle walls to make sure Dracula's vampires don't pour out and flank us. I'm not sure how much—if at all—the castle has changed since I saw it last. Have Benjamin call Hugo if he has any questions. I told him my plan."

The wolf nodded.

"Changed?" Nero asked. "Could the castle have grown larger?"

I glanced at him, considering the full scope of his question. "I don't think so, but I can't be entirely certain." I turned back to the wolf. "Be ready to expand the perimeter if the castle breaks out of the park's walls. Set up some kind of alert so the others know."

The wolf nodded. He walked beside me in silence for a few more seconds as if making sure I had no other commands. Then he peeled away, leaving me to the business at hand.

A few seconds later, he let out a long, hair-raising howl that made my teeth hum. Matching howls echoed his in the distance—other wolves receiving and then relaying the message in an attempt to cover all eight-hundred-forty acres of Central Park.

I pointed past a nearby playground. "There." No matter how ridiculous it was, I refused to destroy the playground by bringing up the castle right here—even knowing that no child would ever use it again. I could pretend that the playgrounds further into the park didn't exist, but actively watching one destroyed right before my very eyes? No way.

I wasn't a heartless monster like the Mayor of New York City.

37

I glanced over my shoulder at Adam and Eve. They had been silent for some time. I smiled to find them holding hands. They stared back at me with hard, determined looks on their marble faces—their crimson eyes flickering with resolute steadfastness. I nodded my approval, sensing that strange trinity connecting us.

Our purpose was one purpose—mine.

Our bond was entirely different from the bond I shared with Natalie and Victoria. Thankfully.

Our bond was also unique from the connection between me and my other vampires, although I couldn't point my finger at the exact difference. It felt deeper, more like our souls had bonded rather than our blood—even though I had no soul in which to bond. Mine was with Hades in the Underworld.

"Why don't you two stretch your legs?" I asked with a smile, wanting to shift my thoughts away from any Olympians. "The bigger the better."

In response, they flashed me eager grins, cracking their necks from side-to-side as if to loosen up. Then they began to grow. I turned my attention back to the front, smiling as I listened to the crack and groan of marble behind me.

Nero gasped. "Holy shit, Sorin! Are you seeing this?"

"Keep walking and stop staring," I hissed, shushing him. "You're embarrassing me in front of my giant vampires."

Nero grunted. "Tell me you didn't give each of the fucking giant vampires a pair of giant fucking blood scythes, you giant fucking psychopath!" he snapped, on the verge of panic. "Those blades are bigger than *us*!"

I frowned. Blood scythes?

I glanced back and immediately sucked in a breath to see that they had taken me at my word. They were *much* larger than before—at least twenty feet tall—and they each had a pair of red crystal scythes across their backs. The ruby striations across their bodies had lessened somewhat, as if it had been condensed to form their new weapons.

For obvious reasons, I noticed Eve first, because her colossal, perfect breasts would have made even her God cry with rapture.

In fact, if He had started His Creation process with this version of Eve and made Light second, He probably would have abandoned any later projects, forgetting all about humans and their spinning rock of water.

I still wasn't entirely sure what to think about that contradiction in my life—that God had obviously created the Nephilim, or they wouldn't be here, yet I knew for a fact that the Olympians were also very real.

Had one created the other? Did they both exist independently? Did it really matter?

Or were Eve's giant breasts causing me to suffer a spiritual crisis?

Yes. Yes, they were.

I managed to peel my eyes away, saving my mind from further calamity. The arced blades of her red crystal scythes fanned out over each shoulder, resembling demonic crimson wings. The handles crossed at her back so that the ends of the shafts extended out below her narrow waist within easy reach in the event she wanted to chop a building in half—or two at the same time, one with each hand.

On that note, Eve calmly unsheathed one of her blades, grinning down at it in surprise. She glanced at a nearby tree and shot me a curious look. I nodded silently, unable to speak, wondering if she thought I had given them to her.

Nero had been right. The blades themselves had to be as long as I was tall.

As if it weighed no more than a feather, she swung her scythe at a massive tree beside the road, slicing completely through the five-foot-thick trunk as if it were a strand of hair. The tree crashed to the ground, charred where it had been kissed by her scythe. She spun it around her wrist with a whooshing sound that hurled a blast of air my way. Then she calmly slipped it into place over her back in some invisible sheathe.

"Tick-tock! I've heard of a grandfather clock, but never a Godfather Cock!" Nero hooted, pointing at the pendulum-like appendage swinging between Adam's legs. Eve's eyes were burning brighter as she stared at the same thing, looking as if she'd been hypnotized by it. "Good lord, man! Slap a bush over it at least. There's a playground right there!" he shouted, pointing.

Adam frowned. "I celebrate the body I was given. What about Eve?" he grumbled.

Eve snapped out of her daze with a start, blinking a few times and shaking her head.

Nero glanced back to appraise Eve with the appropriate considerations. "Eve is delightful. Don't change a thing, doll."

She beamed back at him, nodding her head. "I like this little magician. He's funny."

"Warlock," Nero corrected with a sudden frown.

"Is there a difference?" Adam asked, scratching at his chin curiously.

"Magicians do *tricks*. I do real magic." He was glaring openly at the both of them now.

"A child's first laugh is magic. Can you do that?" Eve asked with a hopeful smile. I coughed into my fist, trying not to laugh as I motioned for them to follow me off the sidewalk and into the grass.

"Can you make your hand grow back?" Adam asked in an awed tone.

"Never mind," Nero muttered, following behind me. "You'll see soon enough."

I clapped my hands, drawing their attention as I came to a halt ahead of the playground. "This will do," I said, nodding firmly.

I reached into my pocket and pulled out the silk pouch of coffin dirt I'd taken from my chambers in the museum. There was a gentle breeze in the air, and I watched the pouch sway freely back and forth as I held it up for everyone to see. I wasn't entirely sure how this was going to work out. If it was just me, I would have sprinkled some of the dirt on the ground and then dribbled a circle of my blood around it.

But it wasn't just me.

I wanted the Nephilim directly involved in my summoning, incorporating them into the very walls. I didn't want to rely solely on our shared bond.

I carefully untied the silk pouch and knelt down on both knees. "Kneel beside me, Adam and Eve," I said. They did, making the very ground shake. I glanced up, realizing their heads were still a good fifteen feet above the ground. "Okay, kneel all the way down or sit beside me." They did, making me feel like I was stuck between two cliffs.

Nero was grinning, rolling his eyes. "Smooth. Maybe you should have waited to make them bigger until after the ritual."

I shot him a scowl. "I already considered that. Then I considered how quickly I would like them to be battle ready if things don't go our way."

His smile faded. "Yeah. Good point."

I turned to the two Nephilim vampires, hefting the bag. "This is my coffin dirt. I'm going to sprinkle some and then cut my hand. I'll let my blood drip down *around* the dirt—not touching it—to make a circle. When I'm finished, Adam will do the same, making a circle around my blood—*without* letting any of it touch my blood or the coffin dirt," I emphasized, meeting his eyes until he nodded. "Then Eve will make a circle around Adam's blood—again, not touching our rings of blood or the coffin dirt. Got it?" They nodded soberly, shifting on their rears on either side of me. "Then I will let my blood pour into the dirt itself and call up the castle."

Everyone was silent, comprehending the gravity of the situation.

Nero snorted. "That's it? There isn't a spell or anything?" he asked, sounding disappointed.

I shook my head. "No. That's it."

"You're going to move an entire fucking castle halfway across the world with some dirt and some blood, and you don't even have to say anything?" Nero demanded, looking flustered.

I shrugged. "Yes."

The Nephilim casted dubious looks at me out of the corners of their eyes. "It does sound rather...simple, Master Ambrogio," Adam said.

"Perhaps the funny magician has a point," Eve added.

Nero scowled murderously. "Warlock."

I narrowed my eyes at the Nephilim. "Ignore the funny magician. My magic is *inside* me. Magicians have to take additional steps because they are borrowing the magic from the world around them." Nero cocked his head, his anger fading as he pondered my words. "In this, I *am* the magic. Don't listen to the magician."

"Warlock," Nero protested weakly.

The Nephilim nodded soberly, taking my word as testament.

Nero narrowed his eyes at me and finally waved a hand. "Whatever."

I took a deep breath and then reached into the pouch to sink my fingers into my coffin dirt. It was unnaturally hot and damp, and it moved and shifted of its own accord, pressing against my fingers like a cat rubbing against its owner's shins when it was hungry. My fingers began to tingle, and I shivered nostalgically. I scooped up a hot handful. Then I pulled my hand out for everyone to see the faint green glow emanating from within the steaming, pitch black soil. Nero watched from the side, licking his lips as he stared intently past Eve's—

I shot him a dirty look and he blushed, shifting his attention from her bared breasts to the very important and complicated vampire magic. "Here we go," I murmured, holding my hand a foot above the grass.

I dropped the dirt and it hit the ground like a full swing from a blacksmith's hammer, sinking an inch into the grass with a puff of green vapor. The gentle breeze instantly ceased.

The grass around it began to wither and decay, blackening as it slowly spread. The Nephilim gasped, but I ignored them. I quickly extended my claws and sliced into my palm, holding my palm up so they could see how I did it.

Then I clenched my hand into a fist—careful to keep my blood from touching the coffin dirt—and dribbled a thick bloody ring around it, making sure not to leave any gaps. "Ambrogio," I said in a cool tone, not consciously choosing to do so. The coffin dirt let out a dull thump and sunk another inch into the earth. A pool of green fog appeared within the shallow grave.

I felt the magic in my blood begin to sing, humming like a struck tuning fork. I shuddered with anticipation, recognizing the faint hum. It was my home.

Adam unsheathed his claws—great, massive daggers as big as my head—and sliced his palm. My eyes widened to see white and crimson blood pool into his hand. He carefully clenched a fist to dribble a complete circle around mine. "Ambrogio," he said in a rumbling tone, choosing to duplicate my actions rather than my verbal instructions. Then he lifted his other hand beneath the wounded one so as to catch any errant drips before they tarnished either the rings or the dirt.

My coffin dirt let out another thump, making the very ground quake before it sunk deeper into the earth. The green fog dropped with it, instantly crackling and hissing like a fire as it flared brighter. I stared, transfixed, as another tone joined the singing within my blood, a duet.

Eve repeated the process without error, her eyes flaring brightly. "Ambrogio," she hissed, also cupping her hand once finished so as to protect the final design.

The coffin dirt blazed with a roar of green flame and the ground actually jolted as the coffin dirt sunk even lower, deepening the fresh grave.

A third, higher-pitched hum joined the singing sensation in my blood, and it seemed to dance within my very bones, making the back of my tongue tingle.

Our concentric rings of blood steamed in the dead grass, flaring with crimson and white light.

I licked my lips, unable to wipe the smile from my face as I extended my bleeding fist over the open grave of green fog and fire. "AMBROGIO!" I yelled at the top of my lungs, clenching my fist tight enough for my blood to pour into the fresh grave one final time.

38

I hadn't intended to say anything this time, and I definitely hadn't anticipated Adam and Eve to join in at the exact same time—as if compelled to do so.

Our three voices visibly blasted out ahead of us in a braided vortex, pulverizing a row of trees and sending them flying deeper into the park, the wood decaying and rotting even as it flew through the air.

A banging sound boomed out from within the grave—like a great beast was pounding at the ground below us, begging to be freed. This had never happened before, but it felt...

Right.

I sensed a shrill scream from deep within the earth, separate from the desperate banging sound—something fighting *against* my call. I snarled furiously.

Dracula had heard me knocking on his door and was fighting back.

"AMBROGIO!" the three of us snarled in unbidden unison, loud enough to strain our vocal chords. This time, the braided vortex of power born from our combined shouts made the very air ripple and distort in a retaliatory shriek. I shoved both of my claws deep into the fresh grave, my arms sinking all the way to my elbows, until I latched onto an ice-cold bar of familiar, ancient metal.

It had been forged long ago, and rather than quenching it in oil and water as the blacksmith had requested...

I had quenched it in my own cursed blood.

The metal sang in my hands, vibrating wildly as the banging and opposing screaming sounds grew louder, battling for dominance. I shifted in order to set my feet flat on the ground, hunched over the fresh grave. Green fog now poured out from within the grave, spilling and pooling all around us like a boat's hull filling up with sloshing water as it began to sink into the deepest, blackest depths of the merciless ocean.

I squatted low, still gripping that bloody bar of metal as wind screamed and howled all around me, whipping my hair back and forth. I clenched the bar tighter, battling against an unseen force that was struggling to pull it back down—Dracula fighting to keep that which was not his.

"CASTLE AMBROGIO IS MINE!" the three of us screamed as I drew deep on my blood reserves—infused with Victoria and Natalie's potent power. I exploded upwards, straightening my legs as I let out a beastly roar, my skin steaming until I felt like I was sweating blood.

A great chiming sound shattered the peace of Central Park and the ground erupted before me. I held the top of my Castle Gate a few feet above the grave, my entire body shaking as my muscles screamed in defiance of Dracula's will. Hot tears streamed down my face and I laughed. Nero shouted something that I couldn't comprehend as I glanced left and right with a victorious roar. The tops of the Castle Walls had torn up from the earth, stretching at least one hundred yards in either direction.

White and green fog poured up from the torn earth and familiar haunted howls welcomed me back, crying out to their master, begging for my return.

My body shook as I stared down at the metal in my hands. The black metal was tinged with a red stain, almost seeming to glow as it drank the blood from my wounded palm.

I strained a few more inches, desperately needing to see the name welded into the gate—the name of the castle's true owner. Its maker. I cackled as it finally came into view, screaming up from the torn earth with more green and white fog.

Except someone had hammered a wooden slat over it, attempting to cover up the name.

I snarled, risking a free hand to slice through it with two powerful strikes. I almost lost my grip in the process, but Adam and Eve suddenly stepped up beside me, supporting my efforts and holding the castle gate in place. The metal throbbed with a sudden white sheen, responding to the additional blood that had helped bring the castle back to her true master.

Then the Nephilim began tugging the gate higher, much more easily than I had.

I finally released my hold on the gate rather than being hoisted high up into the air as the Nephilim continued to heave with all their blessed and cursed might, grunting and snarling like wild beasts.

I fell to my knees, crying tears of joy as my gate rose before me, no longer desecrated by the wooden slat covering the owner's name.

The red and black metal of the gate had been forged into one word —a piece of the very gate itself and literally impossible to remove— which was why Dracula had only been able to cover it up.

AMBROGIO.

The Nephilim roared as they worked in tandem, alternating so as to keep raising the gate and surrounding wall higher and higher until it loomed even taller than their own height. The fog was now up to my waist and had shifted to a solid white color, so thick that I couldn't even see my own feet. I quickly crouched down to search for my sack of coffin dirt before I lost it. I hurriedly tied it closed and shoved it back into my pocket and then watched the results of my Nephilim's work.

With the sound of a struck bell, the walls and gate thudded into place, no longer moving.

I heard a man scream from the very depths of his soul and I gripped the metal bars, peering through to stare beyond the protective wall we had just lifted. Dracula was screaming—but he wasn't able to stop this. I felt him finally surrender with a furious scream.

"Mine, boy. Mine," I snarled under my breath.

Central Park exploded as spires of obsidian and ivory tore through the earth like sewing needles through fabric, rising up into the night sky so quickly that the very air screamed and roared as trees and dirt beyond the wall simply fell into a newly-formed, unnatural abyss. A lone bridge of alternating black and white stones stretched across the abyss from the gate to the front of the instantaneous castle that defied reality. It loomed overhead, dwarfing the surrounding buildings, easily as wide as Central Park, although I couldn't tell how far back it stretched.

The full moon shone brightly overhead, broken up by the towers of black and white stabbing up at the skies like a fistful of daggers. The dreaded castle loomed over us, seeming to growl in warning at the neighboring buildings.

I wondered if the moon's presence was an omen.

And whether it was a good or a bad one.

Because it reminded me of Selene and her bizarre appearance in my chambers. Her even more bizarre warning. I wondered again if she had been trying to warn me about tonight. Everything had gone perfectly here, but we had another battle to fight. A battle possibly already taking place on Liberty Island. I took a calming breath, knowing I had to be certain about the castle before I left.

Whatever I had just done with the Nephilim had definitely worked, because my castle had always been black obsidian. Those intermittent white ivory spires and towers and keeps and balustrades were all thanks to the Nephilim.

I shook my head, openly weeping as a missing part of me clicked into place—my castle.

Castle Ambrogio.

I glanced over at a strange sound to find Adam and Eve sobbing with wondrous smiles, clutching their chests.

Werewolves howled in the distance, but everything outside the walls was a blanket of thick fog that was slowly rising up to my chest.

"I can feel her," Eve whispered. "She sings to see you again, Master Ambrogio. She sings to *me*, too, welcoming me and hugging my very soul," she whispered, squeezing at her breast.

Adam nodded shakily. "She loves me and welcomes me into her

bosom. She's been tormented in your absence, Master Ambrogio. She cries at her salvation."

I nodded, wiping at my nose as I set my bloody palm on the gate. The castle purred like a cat—both in my heart and in the fog-strewn landscape of what had once been Central Park.

"Sorin! You're about to lose your warlock!" I spun to see Nero hopping up and down to keep his head out of the fog. Adam chuckled and calmly walked over, hoisting Nero up onto his shoulders like a child astride his father's back.

Eve carefully scooped me up and put me on her shoulders. I was careful not to fall back onto her crimson scythes—which seemed to be quivering with energy.

Nero cheered, pumping a fist in the air. "You crazy sumbitches! I *told* you words were best! But your stupid vampire magic is awesome!"

I grinned over at him. "I told you!"

"What's next?" Nero asked, staring over the wall at the sprawling estate of my castle with a look of both awe and concern on his face. "Where are all the assholes?"

I smiled, having already sensed the truth. "They are trapped!" I laughed, grinning at Adam as I planted a fat kiss on Eve's hair. "They can't even touch the *doors*!" Because I could feel hundreds of hands within my castle, all clawing at the doors to no avail, screaming and wailing in terror and pain as their skin burned upon contact.

I even felt Dracula seated upon my throne, panting with impotent rage as he chanted my name over and over again in a breathless snarl. Unbelievably, I saw a metal waste bin beside him that was overflowing with postcards—the ones Renfield had been sending him for the past few weeks. I grinned from ear-to-ear.

Adam turned to stare at me, smiling proudly. "That is us, isn't it?" Adam asked.

I nodded. "It is all three of us, but it wouldn't have been possible without you two. I can tell you that much."

Nero was staring at me incredulously. "You mean Dracula and all his vampires really are trapped inside? You weren't exaggerating?"

I shook my head, hardly able to believe it myself. "Our blood gave the castle enough power to lock the doors and windows, poisoning both sides of the exterior walls." I let out a stunned sigh. "That...is unbelievable," I breathed.

There was still much to learn about the castle and what I should do next, but I knew beyond a shadow of a doubt that those within would not be able to leave—not even to throw themselves out a window. Every exterior surface was the equivalent of holy silver. Lethal to Dracula and his vampires.

And equally as lethal and invulnerable to any external force if Dracula's local vampires tried to break them out. I glanced behind us, wary of a police army gathering.

I saw crowds of vampires and werewolves filling the streets leading to Central Park, staring wondrously to see us looming over the fog. Everything from the walls to the surrounding buildings was an ocean of solid white fog. I lifted my arms and screamed, pumping my fist at the crowds of monsters.

My vampires and werewolves cheered and howled in reply, but they didn't approach. They were wary of the fog.

I turned to Nero. "We have more work to do tonight. The castle is safe for now."

Adam and Eve spoke up. "We will stand guard at the gate. Just in case."

I nodded, glancing down at the ground. The fog was clear around her and Adam's feet. "Set me down, please, Eve." She crouched, obeying my request. I took a few steps and the fog rolled away from me, making me grin. I glanced up at Nero. "You try."

Adam set him down and Nero hesitated. "I don't know, Sorin. It feels...aggressive. It doesn't want anyone close to your castle—not even me, and I'm your friend."

I nodded, understanding why the werewolves and vampires had retreated to the outer streets. "Try walking like I did."

Nero let out a nervous breath and then stepped forward. The fog swamped over him and he began to shout for help. I jogged over to him, the fog rolling away from me. Nero stood there with wide eyes, relieved to see me. "I couldn't see or hear anything! It was like I fell underwater. I couldn't even use my magic!"

I arched an eyebrow, stunned. "Wow. That's actually a relief to hear.

No one is coming close to the castle without me or the Nephilim." I grinned broadly. Then I turned to Eve. "I need you to go talk to the vampires and werewolves over there. Give them the good news. Have one of them call Hugo so he can spread the word. Tell them to help get the humans out of the surrounding buildings without causing a stampede. Every single person inside is suddenly going to want to leave, and we can't have them trampling each other. Nero and I have another job tonight—"

A sudden flash of light on the horizon drew my eye and I sucked in a breath. Lightning on the horizon. Nosh had finally succeeded in breaking through the magic around Liberty Island.

Eve nodded. "I will speak to the little ones. Adam will stand guard until I return."

"What if something changes with the castle?" Adam asked me. "What if Dracula finds a way to break out? How do we contact you?"

I smiled. "You should feel it the moment he tries. You should even be able to see him—in a way—inside the castle. I saw him seated on my throne, cursing my name. Once you get a feel for your bond with the castle, you should be able to communicate with her. And she will communicate with you. We will all know if something is wrong. Even from a distance."

They nodded uncertainly, but then the castle suddenly purred reassuringly.

Their frowns shifted to awe. "Yes. I see what you mean," Eve breathed.

I turned to Nero. "Open your magic doorway. Do you need some complicated ingredients, a song, and an assortment of other random things or can you do it as easily as we just did?" I teased with a smug grin.

He narrowed his eyes at me. "Show off."

Then he grabbed my hand without warning and the world simply winked out of existence.

39

Betsween one moment and the next, we were standing back in the office on Liberty Island where Nero had left his totem. I gagged, clutching at my stomach.

"Weakling," Nero sneered pompously. "That's *real* magic—"

I backhanded his chest, adamantly shaking my head as I forced myself to hold my breath. "Not your magic," I snapped. "*That* magic!" I pointed through the office's window at the thick haze of shifting purple smoke in the main area. Even in the privacy of the closed office, the smoke's putrid stench of rot and decay seemed to have permeated the very walls, making it impossible for me to breathe without gagging.

The area beyond had been a war zone, and only the roiling purple smoke remained.

The walls and supporting pedestals were covered in gouges from claws, bullet holes, scorch marks, and bloody smears. The floor was strewn with rubble, spent bullet casings, and alarmingly familiar broken glass vials—the source of the purple smoke.

And dozens of bodies. Both friend and foe, vampire, werewolf, and—

"Witches," Nero snarled murderously.

Muted sounds reached my ears through the exterior wall of the building, coming from outside—lightning cracked, thunder growled, werewolves howled, men and women screamed, and gunfire chattered. The fight raged on across the lawns of Liberty Island, where Nosh had most likely performed his fake rain dance with Natalie, Victoria, and Isabella. Which, based on the lighting dancing across the sky, had been successful.

Once the storm began, Nosh and the girls had probably rushed inside to battle the witch invaders and defend Dr. Stein. It would be faster and more efficient for me to go up to the Crown—allowing me to assess the statue's interior threats, check on Dr. Stein, and get a clear view of the battle raging outside from the wall of windows.

A louder crack of lightning struck nearby, close enough to make me jump in fear of the roof crashing down over my head. Thankfully, it didn't. That bolt of lightning had to have struck the statue—close enough for it to initiate Project Phoenix.

But it hadn't. I'd felt no vampires suddenly come to life.

In addition to the obvious battle, something was wrong. Very, very wrong.

I suddenly remembered that I could check for my precious devils through our bond. I reached out, frantically feeling for Natalie and Victoria, my heart racing wildly in my chest. I almost let out a cry of relief to feel them, but I bit it down.

Because the bond didn't tell me what kind of danger they faced.

Just that they were close. And they were absolutely terrified.

"NO!" I shouted, exploding into a cloud of crimson mist. I spread my form across the ceiling and bled through the wall towards the main area of the pedestal's top floor, braving the potential dangers of the purple smoke. Luckily, the smoke didn't reach the ceiling, and where it did, it reared away from my mist as if repelled. And I could no longer smell the nauseating stench, which was a relief. I had to find my devils. They needed me. I hugged the ceiling, knowing it was my best—and fastest—option to locate them and get a clear view of the situation without alerting the witches of my presence. Hardly anyone ever looked up. I could move about unseen, and without the fear of running headlong into a trap.

I began to hunt; committed to saving my lovers from harm at any cost.

And equally committed to drinking so much blood that the enemy corpses I left behind would resemble nothing more than dehydrated husks.

The purple smoke avoided me as if repelled. I scanned the dozens of mutilated, charred, dismembered, and shredded bodies as I moved, recognizing many faces and counting over twenty brutally slaughtered witches. Some of the familiar faces no longer had bodies attached.

I pressed on, bottling my rage and using it for fuel to fight down my panic over Natalie and Victoria. Near the base of the spiral staircase that led up to the Crown—and hopefully, Dr. Stein—I finally came upon my first sign of life. Three gray-haired witches stood with their backs to me, staring down at three prisoners kneeling before them. But the angle of the three witches' bodies blocked me from identifying the faces of the prisoners. A fourth, much younger witch, stood farther from the staircase than the others, holding a glass vial over her head in a threatening manner. She was facing me and didn't seem to notice—or care—that her nose was bleeding freely, dripping down her lips and chin, staining her white shirt. She alternated her attention—and aim— between the main area and the kneeling prisoners.

Although she hadn't looked up at the ceiling, her almost manic wariness prevented me from advancing or acting. Instead, I sunk the majority of my mist into the ceiling, and shifted laterally to discern who had been caught.

My heart thundered wildly as I stared in horror at Natalie, Victoria, and Isabella. Their attention was fixed on the three old witches standing between us. I somehow refrained from attacking the witches' backs in one explosive shower of blood, knowing that the younger witch would toss her vial the instant I moved. Also, my instincts were screaming a warning at me.

That the situation wasn't as simple as it seemed. It was the hardest thing I'd ever had to do, but I trusted my instincts. They had never led me astray before.

Natalie and Victoria were both gagged with filthy strips of cloth wound around their heads, and I watched as one of the old witches approached Isabella, humming to herself as she plucked out a deadly glass vial from a jacket pocket. Isabella stared back at her with calm fury.

"Oh, how I love the Sisters of Mercy. Their screams are just so rewarding," the witch croaked.

It took everything in my power to remain hidden within the ceiling, only emerging enough to observe the crisis below.

The witch knelt down to pinch Isabella's jaw, forcing her mouth wide so she could slide a large vial into her mouth. Then she wound a long strip of cloth over Isabella's head, tying a knot in the back, and preventing the white witch from spitting out the vial.

I stared in horror, suddenly realizing what was going on—why they were all gagged. If the hostages bit down, the vial would break. And the vial had seemed big enough that even the slightest pressure would be enough to do the deed, forcing the hostages to frantically keep their mouths wide open.

What hellish potion was within? Something explosive? Poisonous? Acidic?

I carefully began to drift closer, sliding through the ceiling unimpeded, wondering how quickly I could kill all four threats, and if it would be fast enough for them not to somehow magically trigger the potions lodged inside the hostages' mouths. Could they do that?

I had no idea.

"Good evening, children," a different, broader and shorter witch said, sounding like a loving grandmother. "My name is Beatrice. Please stand." Natalie and Victoria's eyes danced with impotent fury, and the three of them stood, moving carefully so as not to jostle the vials. Beatrice clapped delightedly. "Excellent. Now, bite down for me if you're uncertain about your current predicament," she said sweetly.

Thankfully, each of the women had been paying close enough attention to Beatrice's words, rather than instantly obeying out of fear.

Beatrice harrumphed, sounding disappointed. "No? Well, if you had, I suppose this conversation would have ended rather abruptly, what with all of us blown to smoldering globs of unidentifiable body parts. Before you do anything clever, rest assured that I can snap my fingers and blow us all to hell as well. So, we have that going for us."

I snarled silently. The witches could kill them at any point with a simple gesture.

A thunderous crack from high above the staircase interrupted Beatrice, and the youngest witch's head simply exploded. She dropped her vial as she simply folded to her knees, where it exploded in a vertical column of blazing purple fire. It winked out within seconds, leaving behind a perfect circle of charred stone, and absolutely no evidence of a body.

"We've got all day, bitches!" Poole's familiar voice shouted down, his words echoing within the hollow tower. Remembering the gun that I'd seen him carrying earlier, I felt a rush of hope. He was shooting at them!

The surviving witches cursed angrily, but they didn't move, apparently knowing the stairs protected their position. The second witch snorted indelicately at their dead ally. "Idiot child."

And that was all she had to say about that.

"Tell that beast of a man and his associate with the gun to stand down," the third witch snarled, leaning close to tug sharply on Natalie's earlobe, willing to risk an explosion if it sated her appetite for petty cruelty. "We only came for the shaman. We know he fled up the stairs, too cowardly to face his fate. So, I will say it one more time. Tell those foolish men to stand down and we shall let you live."

Natalie glared back at her with an almost divine hatred. The witches were obviously lacking in common sense, not seeming to realize that their prisoners couldn't talk, even if they wanted to.

Beatrice waddled up to Victoria, sensing that Natalie wasn't going to help her associate. She spun a short, wicked dagger in her palm, and then she abruptly buried it to the hilt into Victoria's inner thigh, leaning in close with a loud sniffing sound as if she was attempting to inhale her victim's agony. Victoria screamed through her gag, her eyes shooting wide open as blood instantly gushed down her leg. She was unable to even clamp her mouth closed against the pain.

40

I stared in horror, knowing I didn't dare move unless I could get them all in one heartbeat. But Victoria's wound was deep. I could scent it in the air. If she didn't get help in the next few minutes, she would bleed out.

"Remember," Beatrice murmured into Victoria's ear, still clutching the hilt of the dagger buried into the vampire hunter's thigh, "one wrong move and we *all* die. I'm willing to sacrifice myself for my grand mistress. Can you say the same?" Beatrice gave a slight upwards tug on the dagger, chuckling at Victoria's instant scream. Victoria shuddered, her foot slipping in the pool of blood forming at her feet. Beatrice continued in that same sweet voice. "No? Then be a dear and give up the shaman. You can keep worshipping your pathetic vampire master, whatever his name is," she muttered, obviously not knowing my name and not seeming to care.

Which was strange. My name wasn't a secret, and I'd killed some of them. And their kittens.

Beatrice finally grunted, tugging the dagger free with an annoyed sigh. "Have it your way." Victoria staggered, tears streaming down her face, even as she blinked sleepily, struggling to remain upright—in so much pain that her body was attempting to simply pass out. Beatrice cleared her throat and then shouted up towards Poole. "We're coming up the stairs to take what is ours. You'll have to shoot through these women to stop us!"

And then Beatrice shoved Victoria towards the stairs, almost knocking the vampire hunter down as she again slipped in her own blood. Beatrice gripped her by the waist of her pants, saving her at the last moment. Then she forced Victoria up the steps, ducking behind her for cover. My heart raced as I stared at her bloody footprints, snarling silently. *Turn around, turn around, turn around...*

Isabella went next, trembling with fear as her witch guided her after Beatrice—a few steps back so that Isabella couldn't attack Beatrice from behind.

I waited, my entire form quivering with anticipation. If I waited too long, I would risk Beatrice rounding the corner on the second rotation, able to see my attack coming. But Victoria moved slowly, dragging her wounded leg to leave an alarming trail of dark blood in her wake.

Which prevented me from moving too *early*. The timing had to be perfect.

The last witch finally turned Natalie around, and shoved her ahead.

I saw the whites of Victoria's eyes rounding the stair above as I zipped towards the lowermost witch, materializing just in time to decapitate her with such precise violence that she made no sound— just a spray of blood.

I silently lowered the body and then spun Natalie around to face me. I ignored her shocked look as I kissed her forehead while slicing off her gag. Then I held a finger to my lips and pointed at the witch ahead. She carefully extracted the vial from her mouth as I shifted back to mist beside her.

The werewolf stalked her prey with the Devil over her shoulder.

I waited anxiously, ready to burst forward for the final witch, Beatrice, the moment Natalie had the second witch out of commission. Natalie moved like the wind, exploding forward to repeat the same attack I'd used on her captor, but I didn't stay to watch, already zipping up the stairs. Beatrice suddenly paused just ahead, swiveling her neck to look back over her shoulder.

I materialized before her and decapitated the witch in the same fashion as the others. She spun at the force of my blow, her grip on Victoria's waistband jerking the dazed vampire hunter off balance and causing her to twist and slip in her own blood, which was proving to be almost as treacherous as the witches. I dove forward, catching her in my arms at the last second, stunned that she hadn't clamped her jaw closed in the process.

She watched me, looking delirious and sleepy as I gently sat her down on the stairs. I carefully sliced off the gag and slipped the fingers of my clean hand into her mouth, scooping out the vial with extreme caution. I flung it over the side of the stairs and shuddered in relief as it exploded down below. "We're safe!" I shouted, sensing Natalie and Isabella stealthily creeping up behind me.

But Victoria was still in danger.

I used my hands to quickly spread her legs wide because the gaping wound on her inner thigh was too high up for me to reach with her hips in the way. I slid my grip to the backs of her knees and lifted them up over her ribs, bending her body double. Then I sunk my fangs into her wound as quickly and gently as I could. Licking her wound would only close it up. She needed something more.

She needed her blood replenished. Clean, pure, blood. And I only knew one way to get it into her fast enough to save her life.

I didn't drink a drop from her body.

Instead, I thought of five simple words—a prayer. I kept them on the tip of my tongue, fueling them with my blood reserves until I felt my lips tingling.

Then I sent out my five words—my prayer—to the only one who could save her.

Castle Ambrogio.

She's mine! Please save her! I begged Castle Ambrogio.

In my mind, the words rang out, screaming through the ether to the bond I'd just reestablished with Castle Ambrogio. I felt her purr warmly, and I felt the Nephilim grow concerned, unaware of what they were suddenly feeling, but knowing that it was me and that I was in distress.

But Castle Ambrogio understood me and was eager to assist her long-lost master. She knew how much losing Selene had hurt me long ago. How the cruel, petty Olympians had ultimately won, keeping us apart. She knew I couldn't bear to lose another love.

Especially with my cursed offspring trapped within her walls—Dracula, who had done everything in his power to overthrow his figurative father despite all I'd done for him.

Having me back, finally, no longer fearing that I was dead, Castle Ambrogio now understood the true scope of that betrayal and how she had been an accomplice to my pain, harboring my enemies, even if she had been unaware.

With a mother's love, she embraced me—her touch a silent apology for her previously unknown role in my suffering.

I felt her essence swell within me, the essence and memory of every drop of blood ever spilled within my castle. Through me—my fangs buried within Victoria's thigh—the castle assessed Victoria's blood like a connoisseur sampling a vintage wine...

And she suddenly knew *exactly* what type of blood my immortal devil needed.

Through memory and magic, and the awareness of every drop of blood ever spilled within her walls, my castle brewed the perfect amalgam of power for Victoria Helsing, bringing it to life with a concussive crack of lightning that seemed to strike simultaneously at Central Park and the Statue of Liberty.

And Castle Ambrogio sent that newly-birthed power through my fangs, directly into Victoria's body. The exact opposite of what I normally did when biting her.

Victoria gasped, latching both hands onto the back of my head and squeezing tightly as the metaphysical amalgam of blood flowed through my fangs and into her, somehow replenishing Victoria with the spirit of blood rather than the real thing.

In a way, it was infinitely more powerful. Victoria cried out with an echoing scream as pure energy raced into her bloodstream, infusing her with a small taste of the almost depthless power of Castle Ambrogio.

All too soon, the transfer of energy faded, and I felt Castle

Ambrogio drift away in satisfaction. Victoria panted loudly and I extracted my fangs. I still held her knees spread and tucked back to the sides of her ribs, bending her body double so that I still had the best access to heal the actual wound with a lick. As my tongue trailed across her flesh, I looked up into her eyes to make sure she was okay.

She stared back at me with a profound look of awe on her face.

"Now *that* is my kind of hero," Natalie chuckled, eyeing our positions—me kneeling between Victoria's legs with my head buried deep. "Saving and sexing in equal measure."

I released Victoria's legs and rose to my feet, casting Natalie a grin. "All in a day's work."

Victoria slowly rose, propping herself up with her hands as she shook her head from the bewildering experience. "What...was that?" she whispered. "I feel *amazing.*"

I smiled. "That was my castle saying hello. I'll take you there soon, but first I need to check on Dr. Stein and Nosh." Because I could still hear the sounds of pitched battle outside the statue.

And a fear had come to the forefront of my mind while I was connected to Castle Ambrogio. Or maybe an understanding. And it began to make a lot more sense now that my concern for Victoria had evaporated. It was almost as if my castle was trying to warn me of something I hadn't considered.

Victoria nodded, sensing the desperate need in my eyes. "Okay, Sorin."

I wrapped her up in a tight hug, caressing the back of her head. Then I pulled back and kissed her on the mouth, inhaling her startled gasp.

I pulled away, grinning at her stunned expression. Then I spun to face Natalie, who looked equally confused, even though she was smiling. I stepped closer, cupping her cheeks in both hands. Then I leaned forward and kissed her on the lips, relishing her instant shudder.

Then I pulled away just as abruptly. "Now I can see to Dr. Stein."

"Talk about high and dry," Natalie whispered, breathlessly.

"You better find Nosh and immediately send him down here," Isabella muttered, folding her arms. "Because if I don't get a kiss like that in the next hour, I'm throwing him off the top of the statue."

I bowed, grinning at the frustrated look on her face. "As you wish."

I wasted no time, shifting into a cloud of mist and racing through the air to the top of the stairs. It was time to wake up my children.

41

Hyde and Poole were standing guard at the top of the stairs, blocking the entrance to the Crown. I stilled myself to hover a pace away from them, hoping to show them that I wasn't a threat. They cried out, and Poole swung a pistol my way, firing rapidly. The bullets tore through the mist without harm. He continued shooting anyway, just to be thorough. I shifted my attention to the room beyond, ignoring his efforts, but also to let him see that I obviously wasn't hostile. Him running out of bullets would also give me time to actually explain myself in a few moments.

Through the windows, I saw lightning stab down at the earth in explosive strikes, seemingly intent on destroying everything *but* the Statue of Liberty.

Thunder roared in a constant peal that made my vaporous form vibrate and ripple.

I spotted movement in the room beyond, so I zipped right past Hyde and Poole, ignoring their furious shouts. I coalesced back into my normal form and lifted my hands above my head as I spotted Dr. Stein seated on the floor beside one of the towers, looking a little wild around the eyes. "It's me, Sorin."

Hyde and Poole stopped shooting abruptly, or they had finally run out of bullets, letting me know that I was no longer in immediate danger of friendly fire.

I knelt down before Dr. Stein and gripped her hands. "What happened?" Because with this much lightning, my vampires should have been brought to life a hundred times over.

Dr. Stein stared at me with a haunted look on her face. "Not normal," she rasped. "That lightning is alive," she whispered, her voice barely a croak.

Her words made my skin crawl, especially since they seemed to support my own budding theory—the fear that had come unbidden to my mind while I had been connected with my castle and Victoria.

"Rest, Frankie," I murmured, squeezing her hands again. "We still need your brain. Don't get lazy on me."

Her eyes flashed with brief, indignant rage before she saw my smile. She nodded, too tired to waste her energy on arguing or reprimanding —which proved how exhausted she was. She set her hand on a lever protruding from the machine. A blinking red light seemed connected to the lever. "When it turns green...I'm ready," she said determinedly.

A sharp crack of lightning seemed to strike the actual Statue, and my heart skipped a beat in a decidedly strange manner. I glanced at the red light by Dr. Stein's lever, waiting for it to turn green. It didn't, and I frowned.

The thunder and lightning abruptly stopped between one moment and the next. I slowly turned my head to look out the window at a black sky.

"That...isn't possible," Poole said nervously.

"Lot of that going around," Hyde murmured. "In the wise words of Mr. Miyagi, bolt on, bolt off, Poole-san."

I had no idea what Hyde was talking about, but Poole's blank stare made me feel better about not catching the reference. I continued to stare out the window, my pulse quickening as I silently went over my newest theory in my head, connecting dots and crossing others out. Selene had tried to warn me about the Olympians interfering in my plans. As I stared out at the eerily dark sky, my theory unbroken after my analysis, a name I had previously dismissed kept striking me like...

Well, bolts of lightning.

Zeus.

I'd initially dismissed his involvement, unable to wield the necessary hubris required to truly believe that the King of the Olympians might actually care enough about me to want to kill me. Not when I already had Apollo, Artemis, and Hades giving it their best efforts.

But...Zeus was their direct superior, so perhaps he'd had enough of their excuses, no longer willing to tolerate their constant failures staining the family reputation. And Selene had warned that my enemies would do anything to stop me tonight, even turning some mysterious *him* against me. Had she been trying to warn me about Zeus?

No wonder she hadn't used names.

And the lightning had disappeared so *quickly*. Nature didn't work that fast. Dr. Stein had even pointed it out. It was almost as if a certain god of lightning had simply decided to stop throwing bolts down upon us. And it had been turning off and on all night.

A banging crash made me jump to my feet with a hiss, baring my fangs and unsheathing my claws, as I spun towards the open side door that led up to the torch. I froze, blinking in surprise to find Nosh sprawled out across a pile of cable, groaning in pain. A smoking, ceremonial head dress sat beside him, the feathers mostly burned away. "Ow."

Hyde and Poole muttered dark curses, but kept their distance as I rushed over, gripping the shaman's shoulders. "Nosh!" I said, jostling him. "What happened?"

"S-Sorin?" he mumbled woozily.

"Yes, Nosh. I'm right here."

His eyes threatened to roll back into his head, but he jerked his chin defiantly, scowling in stubborn refusal of his body's demands. "Should have...d-done a real rain dance..." he stammered drunkenly. "He...packs a...m-mean punch," he murmured.

My skin pebbled at his words. "What happened, Nosh?" I whispered.

But I knew what had happened. Nosh had stepped into a fight that he hadn't been equipped to handle. Zeus had come to finish me off, but then Nosh had thrown some magic back in his face, figuratively punching Zeus in the jaw. And with me nowhere in sight, Zeus had decided to swing back. At Nosh.

The shaman was silent for a few precious seconds. I stared down at him, watching as a lone tear spilled out from his right eye, rolling down his cheek and splashing onto my hand. "S-sorry...for lying," he mumbled, his lips quivering as another tear spilled onto my hand. He glanced up at me, his focus clarifying for just a moment. "I was scared to tell you...Dad."

His head slowly went limp and his eyes finally rolled back into his skull. His chest rose and fell, letting me know he was still alive.

I stared down, utterly still, unable to even breathe.

Dad...

My eyes suddenly burned, and my jaw trembled unsteadily—just like Nosh's had done. I felt a howling scream rising from the darkest depths of my mind—snarling and biting and clawing as it tore to the forefront of my mind, begging to be let free. *Sorry for lying.*

Dad...

A tear fell from my cheek. My blood reserves suddenly sloshed and boiled, frothing and foaming within me. *I was scared to tell you, Dad.*

Dad...

The encounter between Nosh and Zeus had been even more significant than I had first thought. Nosh hadn't just been stepping in to help me raise my army of vampires. He'd been trying to help his dad heal an army of brothers and sisters.

He'd been trying to help his dad...by picking a fight with his dad's enemy.

I was entirely sure that my soul was locked away in the Underworld.

But the thought of Nosh picking a fight with a god to stand up for his dad...yeah.

I might not have my soul, but something even more powerful, and infinitely more sadistic rose up inside me, begging to taste some godly blood—my inner demon. Zeus had hurt my *son.*

I felt Hyde kneel beside me, hulking over me. "He's alive," he breathed, sounding relieved. I didn't move. Hyde reached out to scoop Nosh up—

I hit Hyde directly in the chest with my palm, feeling his bones crunch upon impact. Hyde slammed into the wall, denting the metal with an alarming creaking sound and rattling the maintenance ladder. He clutched at his chest with a gasp of pain, staring at me wide-eyed.

I calmly settled my palm on Nosh's chest, feeling the rise and fall of his breath. "Mine."

Hyde slowly nodded, lifting his hands in a calming gesture as he extracted himself from the dented wall. "Okay, Sorin. Okay," he said, not taking a step closer.

I turned to stare at the maintenance ladder, my gaze slowly rising.

Hyde noticed my attention, and slowly pointed at the cable. "It came unhooked topside and fell. I was about to lug it back up and reconnect it when Nosh ran past us, climbing up the ladder and shouting about witches coming for Dr. Stein."

Poole was studying me warily. "Do you know why he would go up there alone, Sorin?"

I climbed to my feet. Both men jumped back a step, keeping their distance. I met Poole's eyes, and he winced. "He went up there for the same reason I'm going up there."

Hyde frowned. "What reason is that?"

"To pick a fight." The two men shared uneasy looks. I glanced down at Nosh. "Look after him, Poole. And make sure Stein pulls that fucking lever. Hyde and I will be back shortly." Poole nodded, licking his lips nervously.

"Excuse me?" Hyde demanded. "I don't need to fight anyone. In fact, I'm more of a lover—"

He wilted under my sudden glare. "Pick up the cable and follow me. Now."

I walked to the ladder and began to climb, needing the monotonous rhythm to keep from destroying everything in sight. I heard Hyde gathering up the cable, murmuring to Poole as he carefully moved Nosh to the other room with Dr. Stein.

Then I felt Hyde's massive bulk climbing up behind me. "What if the lightning comes back?"

I paused, glancing down at him. "I'm counting on it, Hyde. I have a family to raise, after all."

I continued to climb, going over my memory of Selene's warning, wondering how I wanted to approach this. The Olympians had cursed me long ago, but those curses seemed to be fading somewhat. I had touched silver without being burned. I could withstand sunlight for longer periods than ever before.

What had changed? And what did it mean? Was that why they were hunting me? Because they feared the answers? Was that why Zeus had finally stepped in, taking advantage of my plan tonight to end me once and for all?

The obvious change was that I had woken up after a centuries-long slumber. That had to have sent the Olympians into a blind panic—to suddenly learn that they had failed yet again. I still had no answer as to why my name or existence inspired such lethal levels of jealousy.

But Selene's warning had been accurate on too many accounts for me to doubt the rest of her message. So, I continued running it through my mind as I climbed, searching for answers.

Regardless of any big picture reasons, I had one of my own that would keep me focused.

This god had almost killed Nosh...my son. And I had a very strong opinion about that.

42

I stood on the circular platform of the torch, gripping the railing as I stared out at the roiling black clouds, ignoring the torrential rain soaking me to the bone. The golden flame loomed behind me, rising up from the center of the platform, but I'd only taken a cursory glance at it and the detailed design of the short wall enclosing the platform.

The current storm raging around me was not conducive to adoring artisanship, and my current murderous mood was not conducive to feckless reverie.

It had taken Hyde less than thirty seconds—and just as many cursing complaints—to hook the cable back up to a simple metal box with a tall metal lightning rod that stretched as high as the flame. He'd wasted no time in ducking back into the shelter of the statue's arm, closing the hatch as best he could with the cable in the way, and promising to support the cable's weight from within so that it didn't fall again.

Although I didn't believe it had fallen. I believed Zeus had made it fall in an attempt to lure me up here. Except Nosh had responded in my stead, rushing up here to fight above his weight class.

But now his father was here to set the record straight.

"Fight me, coward," I snarled, not bothering to shout. He could hear me. I could feel him watching me even now. Because I'd repeated the same thing over and over for the past few minutes.

All while I drew deep on the power of every curse inflicted upon me. Then I drew deep on every morsel of resulting power I'd accumulated since my curses: Castle Ambrogio, my Nephilim, my vampires, and most importantly...

My devils, Natalie and Victoria. Their blood sang within me, screaming for release.

I could occasionally hear the sounds of battle far below, but there was nothing I could do about it from here, and the wind and sheets of rain made it almost impossible to clearly see details anyway.

"Fight me, coward!" I said, louder this time, clenching the metal railing tighter.

Selene had tried to warn me that the Olympians were coming. That they'd failed to kill me too many times in my life, and that they wouldn't make the same mistake again.

I held out my arms, baring my breast. And then I called upon my cloak of shadow and blood. It whipped and cracked in the wind, and the distant clouds immediately flared with the first signs of lightning returning. I grinned, flashing my teeth. I knew he had been watching.

"Zeus! I hear you have a message for me. A message that your worthless brethren could not deliver themselves. The overcompensating Apollo couldn't do it. The sun god who is terrified of his own shadow and any man who dares to take a toy that doesn't belong to him. Artemis also failed to deliver the message, resorting to poisoning my heart and taking the woman I loved when her arrows missed their mark. Hades tried trickery and deceit, capitalizing on my desperation to hold the woman I loved in my arms, and bargaining my soul for a shadow of a dream."

The wind screamed, pulling at my cloak, and the crackle of lightning grew brighter.

"What is so dangerous about a humble adventurer looking for love? I'm genuinely curious."

A deep, noncorporeal voice replied, seeming to come from everywhere. "I know nothing about you, vampire. Just that you have mocked my Olympians for the last time. That you took gifts from the gods and perverted them for your own selfish gains. They thought the stain of your monstrous existence ended long ago, yet here you stand again. I have come to finish what they couldn't."

I stared out at the skies, considering his words. It was as I'd thought. He wasn't part of the conspiracy Selene had mentioned. He hadn't even known who I was. He was simply here as the final representative of Mount Olympus—to do whatever it took to maintain honor for his fellow gods.

But Selene had warned me of something else.

Remember your name and who hurt you, because they know your plans this night and will do anything to stop you, even turning him against you.

And it looked like she had been right. The *him* was Zeus, and he had indeed been turned against me. But...rather than attempting to clear up his view of the situation, I could use it to my advantage.

"Well, here I am!" I roared, stretching my arms wide. "Give me your best shot!" And I immediately tapped into the gifts Artemis had given me, slowing time to a crawl, knowing that even I wasn't faster than lightning.

Zeus obliged, and I watched it all in slow motion.

A bolt of lightning blossomed to life in the blackest of clouds before me, crackling almost horizontally through the air—an entirely unnatural trajectory—towards my heart.

Even with time slowed, the jagged bolt moved alarmingly fast. But it gave me the opportunity to see it slowly enough to momentarily witness a bizarre phenomenon.

The lightning bolt was not a continuous, hundred-yard, arc of electric force.

It was actually a rather small glass dagger shaped like a jagged *S*. It was simply moving so fast that it rapidly displaced the energy around it, creating an electric reaction from the empty void of space between his hand and his target, birthing a long tendril of...lightning.

Zeus, the God of Lightning, was throwing a glass stick at me.

I shifted to crimson mist, even as I processed the sight before me. Zeus' glass blade—and the trailing bolt of lightning—ripped through me without harm to crack into Dr. Stein's metal pole behind me.

Because I had very purposely chosen my placement before challenging the Father of Olympus.

I watched the lightning grasp the metal pole, flickering up and down its length almost too quickly for me to observe, even with time slowed. I felt a deep humming in the air and then utter silence as the skies grew dark again. Zeus' task was completed, and he was leaving.

A moment later, I felt a pinprick of fire and ice poke the center of my mist. Then another.

Then more. By the dozens.

My vampire army came to life and I gasped, my form quivering as Dr. Stein's experiment flourished, creating life from nothing—and all thanks to Zeus' ignorance. And since Nero and Dr. Stein were exceedingly thoughtful, they'd made sure to include a dose of my blood within each blood bag that had been sustaining them over the last few weeks.

Permitting me the chance to command them now, even though we hadn't fully bonded yet.

Kill the black witches. Kill any vampires not bonded to me. Everyone else on the island is a friend. Father will embrace you soon.

The hunting screams of dozens and dozens of vampires sang their first song on Liberty Island, a celebration of their liberation. I liked to think of it as robbing Hades of a prize long thought safe. Seventy-seven souls had just been stolen from the God of the Underworld.

But I still had work to do. I coalesced, standing atop the platform again. "I was not finished speaking to you, Zeus!" I shouted.

I felt a stunned stir to the air. Then, rather than the clouds speaking to me, a man suddenly appeared on the platform, clutching a trio of glass daggers in his fist. He stared at me incredulously. The wind whipped his long white hair, shoving at his snowy white beard, but he stared at me unblinking, his eyes crackling with golden light. He wore only sandals and a war skirt of white leather strips that hung to just above his knees, each strip tipped in gold at the end.

"No one could have survived that. Not even a Titan," Zeus breathed.

"I am not a Titan," I muttered. "I am a highly-motivated, pissed-off orphan."

The god stared at me in silence, obviously at a loss for words. "What is your name?"

I remembered that he hadn't known my name. His fellow Olympians hadn't told him before setting him on the warpath to kill me. "Sorin Ambrogio."

I wasn't sure what I had expected, but I hadn't expected him to stumble back a step, his free hand slapping his chest as he gasped. "Impossible," he breathed. "Hera killed you."

I blinked, ignoring the icy shiver that crawled up the back of my neck. Selena had mentioned the Olympians trying to kill me as a young orphan. "Your wife?" I asked, very carefully. "Why would she do such a thing? How do you know me?" I demanded, suddenly panicking. What the hell was this?

He stared at me with a haunted expression, seeming to take me in from head-to-toe. Then his eyes grew distant, lost in a memory. "I saw it with my own eyes!" he whispered, as if arguing with himself. "I checked the house and found her and the baby, both dead in the chair that I made for them," he whispered. "Hera claimed credit, warning me of the cost of my infidelities."

Another icy shiver rolled up my arm as I stared at Zeus, knowing full-well his legendary penchant for sowing his seed. "No," I said, shaking my head in denial.

Olympians were schemers and tricksters. This was just another cruel ploy—

"I called her my ambrosia, my nectar of the gods. She must have named you after that silly pillow name. I think I actually loved her. Your mother," he said with a saddened smile. "She fled before I was able to see you, fearful of Hera's wrath. But she didn't run far enough. I came too late to save her."

I was shaking my head. "No. You saw your son dead. A name is just a name—"

"I can show you her face," he said, almost eagerly. "Would you remember that?"

I froze, staring at him, suddenly feeling panicked. "I...no. I wouldn't. I don't remember what she looked like," I whispered.

Zeus suddenly scowled, glancing over his shoulder. "I must leave.

No one can see us together. No one must know of this, my son. All of Olympus would come down upon you—my son. Hera would destroy the world if she knew. We will talk soon—"

And he was suddenly gone in a peal of thunder that scorched the metal.

I stared at the empty space where he had been standing, unable to move.

My father was Zeus. And Nosh was my son.

Which meant Zeus had almost killed his grandson tonight.

I heard the hatch open behind me and I spun, extending my claws. Hyde was staring at me with wide eyes, his mouth hanging open. "I knew we were going to be good friends, but that was before I learned you were a fucking *demigod*! Now, we are *best* friends."

I couldn't make my mouth work, so I just stared at him. I took a step and immediately crumpled, my legs simply giving out. I rolled over onto my back, taking a deep breath as the rain splashed over my face. Then I closed my eyes. "No one can know about this, Hyde."

"Of course."

"Make sure everyone is okay for me. I'm just going to lay here for a few minutes. I'll be down later."

"Okay, Sorin." I heard the hatch open and close, but I didn't open my eyes. I just needed some time to myself to try and wrap my head around the night's events.

43

I walked the exhibits of the Museum of Natural History, holding hands with Victoria and Natalie, smiling absently. It had been two days since my night atop the Statue of Liberty, and they had been busy but cathartic. No one had come into the museum for work since the night the castle appeared, given our proximity to Central Park. I doubted they would be returning any time soon. We had the entire museum to ourselves.

Natalie pointed excitedly at various exhibits, chattering endlessly, as we walked, occasionally pulling me along with her—and by extension, pulling Victoria along as well. We had found our way to the Ancient Greece exhibit, so I had grown quiet. Until I had confirmation, I wasn't about to tell anyone of my supposed Olympian blood. Not even Natalie and Victoria. Not even Nosh.

But right now, I was simply staring at the couple walking ahead of us. Nosh and Isabella walked as if they were the last two people in the world, smiling and whispering like thieves.

Several times Nosh had glanced back at me with a hesitant smile. I'd returned it with a warm one, still trying to process his delirious statement, and wondering if it was possible that he was really my son.

Deep in my heart, I felt it was the truth. But I had no way of verifying it. Not with his skinwalker blood. The only true way to verify it was to sit down and talk.

And...neither of us were ready for that yet.

So, we walked through the museum. Two passing ships in the night, occasionally flashing our lanterns at the other in greeting as we weathered the storms around us—sometimes drifting apart, sometimes coming alarmingly close to wrecking each other.

Renfield and Gabriel had managed to round up all the new vampires on Liberty Island with minimal effort. They had annihilated the surviving witches without mercy, but had found no invading vampires, thankfully.

Dr. Stein had run what seemed like fifty different tests on the new vampires before allowing them to return to the museum where they could be watched over by Hugo, Aristos, and Valentine. Hugo was even making them study the *Reborn Vampire Handbook*, which covered the rules of my Kiss and reviewed everything they may have missed while dead.

He even had tests planned, requiring passing marks before they were permitted to advance to the next courses of their choosing— including technical courses like the Subtle Art of Exsanguination—or internships at any of our numerous business ventures. Hugo had also scheduled field trips upstairs to the museum, now that it was abandoned. Since the vampires hadn't been very talkative, Aristos and Valentine were planning a social mixer for them tomorrow night, with over one hundred blood slaves required to attend.

I'd paid close attention to the news, eager to hear that the mayor was indeed in hot water over the bodies found floating near the Williamsburg bridge. Like sharks sensing blood in the water, a mob of political hit-pieces had already begun to circulate, accusing him of many more suspicious activities. I had no idea if they were warranted or not.

Strangely enough, we'd so far managed to keep the obvious news of Castle Ambrogio out of the press. I knew it wouldn't last, but Hugo had greased enough palms so that he could control the narrative. Sooner or later, the humans would learn the truth, no matter what story was told in the news. With a cell phone in every pocket and the internet only a thumb-swipe away—for those fortunate souls allowed to have smart phones, anyway—it was only a matter of time.

Nero and Stevie had set up a time for me to perform the favor I had indirectly promised the alpha for stealing Natalie from his pack. I had no idea what it entailed, but I had grown suspicious after Nero's involvement. He had promised me that it would be both terrifying and fulfilling—and he had looked scared as hell saying it.

Wanting to reduce the amount of stress in my life, I had let it be. I would find out soon enough. I had Castle Ambrogio to occupy the majority of my thoughts. The Nephilim stood guard at the Castle Gate without rest. I'd visited them earlier tonight just to make sure they weren't lonely, but upon finding them giggling and rolling around in the bushes—destroying everything in their wake—I'd left with a satisfied grin.

Adam and Eve had finally discovered what their bodies were designed for, learning how much pleasure could be derived from a guilt-free heart and a genuine smile. I was confident they had learned other pleasures as well, judging by some of the sounds I'd heard.

Victoria had recovered from her near-death experience, and I'd twice found her sitting on the steps of the museum, staring out at Castle Ambrogio with a sad smile on her face. Victoria was now able to communicate with my castle, as was Natalie, by extension. Hyde had told no one of my meeting with Zeus. Just that I had helped him fix Dr. Stein's lightning rod. I had no idea whether that bit of news regarding my paternity was true or not either, but it did answer a lot of questions I'd accumulated over the years.

Natalie suddenly spun to face me, grinning wickedly. "I thought they would never leave!"

I arched an eyebrow, frowning. "What?"

She pointed ahead of us to where Nosh and Isabella had been walking moments ago. "They called it a night," she grinned.

"And we finally have some privacy," Victoria purred.

Natalie studied me up and down. "One reason I got into this was because of the sex, and so far, that has been sorely lacking. In fact, I've been knifed by a crazy ex, almost killed by witches, and I even starred in a truly beautiful rain dance ritual—that you missed," she said with a stern glare. I kept my face composed, not daring to tell her that the ritual had been fraudulent. "And I learn about your son—who is older than me..."

"And a kiss," Victoria said, touching her lips with a dreamy smile.

I nodded, not entirely sure how to respond. "It was a very stressful couple of days."

"The samples have been incredible," Victoria pointed out, biting her lip as she eyed me up and down.

Natalie pursed her lips analytically. "Until I get the real thing, I can't be so sure."

I rolled my eyes, finally giving in. I turned to Victoria. "How fast can you run?" I asked, grinning.

In response, she suddenly bolted away, laughing as she sprinted down the halls of ancient artifacts with the swiftness of Artemis, the Goddess of the Hunt.

I shot Natalie a hungry look. "Winner takes all."

Natalie bolted after Victoria, laughing delightedly.

I noticed that the nearby wall displayed a brief story about Zeus and Hera. I stared at it for a moment, pursing my lips.

Then I turned away, locking in on the laughter echoing from up ahead.

There was no way in hell I was going to let Natalie win.

The Devil of New York City returns in DEVIL'S BLOOD.

Turn the page to read a sample from Shayne's other worldwide bestselling novels in **The TempleVerse**—*The Nate Temple Series.*
He worked really hard on them. Some are marginally decent—easily a solid 4 out of 10.

TRY: OBSIDIAN SON (NATE TEMPLE #1)

There was no room for emotion in a hate crime. I had to be cold. Heartless. This was just another victim. Nothing more. No face, no name.

Frosted blades of grass crunched under my feet, sounding to my ears alone like the symbolic glass that one would shatter under a napkin at a Jewish wedding. The noise would have threatened to give away my stealthy advance as I stalked through the moonlit field, but I was no novice and had planned accordingly. Being a wizard, I was able to muffle all sensory evidence with a fine cloud of magic—no sounds, and no smells. Nifty. But if I made the spell much stronger, the anomaly would be too obvious to my prey.

I knew the consequences for my dark deed tonight. If caught, jail time or possibly even a gruesome, painful death. But if I succeeded, the look of fear and surprise in my victim's eyes before his world collapsed around him, was well worth the risk. I simply couldn't help myself; I had to take him down.

I knew the cops had been keeping tabs on my car, but I was confident that they hadn't followed me. I hadn't seen a tail on my way here, but seeing as how they frowned on this kind of thing I had taken a circuitous route just in case. I was safe. I hoped.

Then my phone chirped at me as I received a text.

I practically jumped out of my skin, hissing instinctively. "Motherf —" I cut off abruptly, remembering the whole stealth aspect of my mission. I was off to a stellar start. I had forgotten to silence the damned phone. *Stupid, stupid, stupid!*

My heart threatened to explode inside my chest with such thunderous violence that I briefly envisioned a mystifying Rorschach bloodblot that would have made coroners and psychologists drool.

My body remained tense as I swept my gaze over the field, sure that I had been made. My breathing finally began to slow, my pulse returning to normal, as I noticed no changes in my surroundings. Hopefully, my magic had silenced the sound and my resulting outburst. I glanced down at the phone to scan the text and then typed back a quick and angry response before I switched the cursed phone to vibrate.

Now, where were we...

I continued on, the lining of my coat constricting my breathing. Or maybe it was because I was leaning forward in anticipation. *Breathe*, I chided myself. *He doesn't know you're here.* All this risk for a book. It had better be worth it.

I'm taller than most, and not abnormally handsome, but I knew how to play the genetic cards I had been dealt. I had shaggy, dirty blonde hair, and my frame was thick with well-earned muscle, yet still lean. I had once been told that my eyes were like twin emeralds pitted against the golden-brown tufts of my hair—a face like a jewelry box. Of course, that was two bottles of wine into a date, so I could have been a little foggy on her quote. Still, I liked to imagine that was how everyone saw me.

But tonight, all that was masked by magic.

I grinned broadly as the outline of the hairy hulk finally came into view. He was blessedly alone—no nearby sentries to give me away. That was always a risk when performing this ancient rite-of-passage. I tried to keep the grin on my face from dissolving into a maniacal cackle.

My skin danced with energy, both natural and unnatural, as I manipulated the threads of magic floating all around me. My victim stood just ahead, oblivious of the world of hurt that I was about to unleash. Even with his millennia of experience, he didn't stand a chance. I had done this so many times that the routine of it was my only enemy. I lost count of how many times I had been told not to do it again; those who knew declared it *cruel, evil, and sadistic.* But what fun wasn't? Regardless, that wasn't enough to stop me from doing it again. And again. Call it an addiction if you will, but it was too much of a rush to ignore.

The pungent smell of manure filled the air, latching onto my nostril hairs. I took another step, trying to calm my racing pulse. A glint of gold reflected in the silver moonlight, but the victim remained motionless, hopefully unaware or all was lost. I wouldn't make it out alive if he knew I was here. Timing was everything.

I carefully took the last two steps, a lifetime between each, watching the legendary monster's ears, anxious and terrified that I would catch even so much as a twitch in my direction. Seeing nothing, a fierce grin split my unshaven cheeks. My spell had worked! I raised my palms an inch away from their target, firmly planted my feet, and squared my shoulders. I took one silent, calming breath, and then heaved forward with every ounce of physical strength I could muster. As well as a teensy-weensy boost of magic. Enough to goose him good.

"*MOOO!!!*" The sound tore through the cool October night like an unstoppable freight train. *Thud-splat!* The beast collapsed sideways into the frosty grass; straight into a steaming patty of cow shit, cow dung, or, if you really want to church it up, a Meadow Muffin. But to me, shit is, and always will be, shit.

Cow tipping. It doesn't get any better than that in Missouri.

Especially when you're tipping the *Minotaur*. Capital M.

Razor-blade hooves tore at the frozen earth as the beast struggled to stand, grunts of rage vibrating the air. I raised my arms triumphantly. "Boo-yah! Temple I, Minotaur o!" I crowed. Then I very bravely prepared to protect myself. Some people just couldn't take a joke. *Cruel, evil,* and *sadistic* cow tipping may be, but by hell, it was a *rush*. The legendary beast turned his gaze on me after gaining his feet, eyes ablaze as he unfolded to his full height on two tree-trunk-thick legs, hooves magically transforming into heavily-booted feet. The thick, gold ring dangling from his snotty snout quivered as the Minotaur panted, and his dense, corded muscle contracted over his human-like chest. As I stared up into those brown eyes, I actually felt sorry...for, well, myself.

"I have killed greater men than you for less offense," he growled.

I swear to God his voice sounded like an angry James Earl Jones. Like Mufasa talking to Scar.

"You have shit on your shoulder, Asterion." I ignited a roiling ball of fire in my palm in order to see his eyes more clearly. By no means was it a defensive gesture on my part. It was just dark. But under the weight of his glare, even I couldn't buy my reassuring lie. I hoped using a form of his ancient name would give me brownie points. Or maybe just not-worthy-of-killing points.

The beast grunted, eyes tightening, and I sensed the barest hesitation. "Nate Temple...your name would look splendid on my already long list of slain idiots." Asterion took a threatening step forward, and I thrust out my palm in warning, my roiling flame blue now.

"You lost fair and square, Asterion. Yield or perish." The beast's shoulders sagged slightly. Then he finally nodded to himself in resignation, appraising me with the scrutiny of a worthy adversary. "Your time comes, Temple, but I will grant you this. You've got a pair of stones on you to rival Hercules."

I pointedly risked a glance down towards the myth's own crown jewels. "Well, I sure won't need a wheelbarrow any time soon, but I'm sure I'll manage."

The Minotaur blinked once, and then bellowed out a deep, contagious, snorting laughter. Realizing I wasn't about to become a murder statistic, I couldn't help but join in. It felt good. It had been a while since I had allowed myself to experience genuine laughter.

In the harsh moonlight, his bulk was even more intimidating as he towered head and shoulders above me. This was the beast that had fed upon human sacrifices for countless years while imprisoned in Daedalus' Labyrinth in Greece. And all of that protein had not gone to waste, forming a heavily woven musculature over the beast's body that made even Mr. Olympia look puny.

From the neck up he was entirely bull, but the rest of his body more resembled a thickly-furred man. But, as shown moments ago, he could adapt his form to his environment, never appearing fully human, but able to make his entire form appear as a bull when necessary. For instance, how he had looked just before I tipped him. Maybe he had been scouting the field for heifers before I had so efficiently killed the mood.

His bull face was also covered in thick, coarse hair—even sporting a long, wavy beard of sorts, and his eyes were the deepest brown I had ever seen. Cow shit brown. His snout jutted out, emphasizing the gold ring dangling from his glistening nostrils, catching a glint in the luminous glow of the moon. The metal was at least an inch thick, and etched with runes of a language long forgotten. Thick, aged ivory horns sprouted from each temple, long enough to skewer a wizard with little effort. He was nude except for a beaded necklace and a pair of worn leather boots that were big enough to stomp a size twenty-five imprint in my face if he felt so inclined.

I hoped our blossoming friendship wouldn't end that way. I really did.

Get your copy of OBSIDIAN SON online today!

MAKE A DIFFERENCE

Reviews are the most powerful tools in my arsenal when it comes to getting attention for my books. Much as I'd like to, I don't have the financial muscle of a New York publisher.

But I do have something much more powerful and effective than that, and it's something that those publishers would kill to get their hands on.

A committed and loyal bunch of readers.

Honest reviews of my books help bring them to the attention of other readers.

If you've enjoyed this book, I would be very grateful if you could spend just five minutes leaving a review (it can be as short as you like) on my book's Amazon page.

Thank you very much in advance.

ACKNOWLEDGMENTS

I couldn't do this without my readers—those wayward souls who crave adventure, encouragement, tears, laughter, danger, and confidence. You are all enablers to my madness.

And I love you for it. I'll keep wording, you keep reading. I'll do my goodest.

Also, take a gander at that kick ass cover! I know a wizard, obviously. Check her out here:

Cover Design By Jennifer Munswami - J.M Rising Horse Creations

ABOUT SHAYNE SILVERS

Shayne is a man of mystery and power, whose power is exceeded only by his mystery...

He currently writes the Amazon Bestselling **Nate Temple** Series, which features a foul-mouthed wizard from St. Louis. He rides a blood-thirsty unicorn, drinks with Achilles, and is pals with the Four Horsemen.

He also writes the Amazon Bestselling **Feathers and Fire** Series—a second series in the TempleVerse. The story follows a rookie spell-slinger named Callie Penrose who works for the Vatican in Kansas City. Her problem? Hell seems to know more about her past than she does.

He coauthors **The Phantom Queen Diaries**—a third series set in The TempleVerse—with Cameron O'Connell. The story follows Quinn MacKenna, a mouthy black magic arms dealer in Boston. All she wants? A round-trip ticket to the Fae realm...and maybe a drink on the house.

Shayne holds two high-ranking black belts, and can be found writing in a coffee shop, cackling madly into his computer screen while pounding shots of espresso. He's hard at work on the newest books in the TempleVerse—You can find updates on new releases or chronological reading order on the next page, his website, or any of his social media accounts. **Follow him online for all sorts of groovy goodies, giveaways, and new release updates:**

Get Down with Shayne Online
www.shaynesilvers.com
info@shaynesilvers.com

f   facebook.com/shaynesilversfanpage

a   amazon.com/author/shaynesilvers

BB bookbub.com/profile/shayne-silvers

O   instagram.com/shaynesilversofficial

    twitter.com/shaynesilvers

g   goodreads.com/ShayneSilvers

BOOKS BY SHAYNE SILVERS

CHRONOLOGY: All stories in the TempleVerse are shown in chronological order on the following page

SHADE OF DEVIL SERIES

(Not part of the TempleVerse)

DEVIL'S DREAM

DEVIL'S CRY

DEVIL'S BLOOD

NATE TEMPLE SERIES

(Main series in the TempleVerse)

FAIRY TALE - FREE prequel novella #0 for my subscribers

OBSIDIAN SON

BLOOD DEBTS

GRIMM

SILVER TONGUE

BEAST MASTER

BEERLYMPIAN (Novella #5.5 in the 'LAST CALL' anthology)

TINY GODS

DADDY DUTY (Novella #6.5)

WILD SIDE

WAR HAMMER

NINE SOULS

HORSEMAN

LEGEND

KNIGHTMARE

ASCENSION

FEATHERS AND FIRE SERIES

(Also set in the TempleVerse)

UNCHAINED

RAGE

WHISPERS

ANGEL'S ROAR

MOTHERLUCKER (Novella #4.5 in the 'LAST CALL' anthology)

SINNER

BLACK SHEEP

GODLESS

PHANTOM QUEEN DIARIES

(Also set in the TempleVerse)

COLLINS (Prequel novella #0 in the 'LAST CALL' anthology)

WHISKEY GINGER

COSMOPOLITAN

OLD FASHIONED

MOTHERLUCKER (Novella #3.5 in the 'LAST CALL' anthology)

DARK AND STORMY

MOSCOW MULE

WITCHES BREW

SALTY DOG

SEA BREEZE

HURRICANE

CHRONOLOGICAL ORDER: TEMPLE VERSE

FAIRY TALE (TEMPLE PREQUEL)

OBSIDIAN SON (TEMPLE 1)

BLOOD DEBTS (TEMPLE 2)

GRIMM (TEMPLE 3)

SILVER TONGUE (TEMPLE 4)

BEAST MASTER (TEMPLE 5)

BEERLYMPIAN (TEMPLE 5.5)

TINY GODS (TEMPLE 6)

DADDY DUTY (TEMPLE NOVELLA 6.5)

UNCHAINED (FEATHERS... 1)

RAGE (FEATHERS... 2)

WILD SIDE (TEMPLE 7)

WAR HAMMER (TEMPLE 8)

WHISPERS (FEATHERS... 3)

COLLINS (PHANTOM 0)

WHISKEY GINGER (PHANTOM... 1)

NINE SOULS (TEMPLE 9)

COSMOPOLITAN (PHANTOM... 2)

ANGEL'S ROAR (FEATHERS... 4)

MOTHERLUCKER (FEATHERS 4.5, PHANTOM 3.5)

OLD FASHIONED (PHANTOM...3)

HORSEMAN (TEMPLE 10)

DARK AND STORMY (PHANTOM... 4)

MOSCOW MULE (PHANTOM...5)

SINNER (FEATHERS...5)

WITCHES BREW (PHANTOM...6)

LEGEND (TEMPLE...11)

SALTY DOG (PHANTOM...7)

BLACK SHEEP (FEATHERS...6)

GODLESS (FEATHERS...7)

KNIGHTMARE (TEMPLE 12)

ASCENSION (TEMPLE 13)

SEA BREEZE (PHANTOM...8)

HURRICANE (PHANTOM...9)

Made in the USA
Coppell, TX
24 October 2020

40233565R00173